W9-CEK-230

HOSE MONKEY

TONY SPINOSA

BLEAK HOUSE BOOKS

MADISON | WISCONSIN

Published by Bleak House Books,
an imprint of Big Earth Publishing
923 Williamson St.
Madison, WI 53703

ISBN: 1-932557-18-0

Library of Congress Cataloging-in-Publication Data

Spinosa, Tony, 1956-
Hose monkey / Tony Spinosa.
p. cm.
ISBN 1-932557-18-0
1. Ex-police officers--Fiction. 2. Long Island (N.Y.)--Fiction. I. Title.
PS3553.O47445H68 2006
813'.54--dc22
2006023447

For Mimsie and Denise and Grace Bruen
And
In Memory of
Dorothy "Ma" Gloria

Acknowledgements
I would like to thank Robert Gloria, all the guys at Bell
Oil, Inc., the gang at General Discount and Richard Helms for
his lecture on the effects of head trauma. I am also indebted
to Mitchell L. Schare, Ph.D., Ellen Schare for being my first
reader, and Rosanne Coleman, OTR, for her expertise on Down
Syndrome and mental retardation.

Sometimes, I feel like an old cemetery, laden with coffins.
– Ken Bruen *The Killing of the Tinkers*

HOSE MONKEY

Monday Morning
Presidents' Day
February 16th, 2004

SODA CAN

J oe Serpe just assumed there was no more, that things had moved well beyond loss and grief, beyond worsening. He was only about an hour from learning there's always more and there's always worse.

He felt like the leftovers from autopsy class. Mulligan, the last thing he had left to show for fifteen years of marriage, was pawing the empty Absolut bottle, pawing at it then pouncing on it. But it wasn't the cat or the scraping of the bottle as it rolled over the gritty linoleum floor that had slapped Joe out of his stupor. That honor went to the phone.

"Fuck!" He propped himself up on one elbow. Trying to sit would have ripped him in two. Still, it would have been easy enough to reach over and slide the volume switch to zero on the answering machine. He didn't move. Instead he counted the rings, his lips moving silently, the numbers resonating in the fog. Two ... Three ... Four ... The voice that filled the room was not his own.

This is Vinny. I'm out swallowing smoke or stout. If it's a one-alarmer, leave your name and number and a message. If it's a two-alarmer, call 911. If it's gone to three alarms and you're still in your house making this call, bend over and kiss your ass goodbye, cause you're screwed. Have a nice day.

Joe had written those words for his brother to say. Scripts helped Vinny with his stuttering. It's how he dealt with emergencies on the job, how he had passed the entrance test. Joe's heart raced every time he heard his little brother's voice. It was all that was left of him. Sure, there were pictures—hundred of pictures—and Vinny's uniform shirts that still hung in his closet like offerings in a lightless shrine. There was his badge and his crushed helmet and the flag that had draped his coffin and the stories from the newspapers. But those were things, artifacts, fossils, as dry and meaningless to Joe as a squirrel skull dug up in the backyard. No, the message tape was alive. It was more a reflection of Vinny's life than any object or eulogy.

September 11th, 2001 had robbed a lot of people of a lot of things, but Joe Serpe could not and would not be convinced that anyone had lost more than him. When you're already in a place where further down looks like up, any loss, never mind that of your baby brother, is magnified, amplified a thousand fold. Few people who knew Joe, even those cops who didn't speak to him anymore, would argue the point. It was Vinny who took him in after the divorce. Vinny who stood by him through all the departmental hearings. Vinny who stopped him from eating his gun.

Vincent Anthony Serpe was just one of three-hundred-forty-three New York City firemen killed that day. Some had died heroic deaths. Some not. From all accounts, Vinny's was neither particularly heroic nor inglorious. He was felled by debris as he ran for cover when the first tower collapsed. In fact, Joe Serpe had been told he was lucky. Vinny's body, at least, had been recovered intact. A lot of the men who had perished were pulverized. Their families would bury empty coffins.

Joe knew he was supposed to take comfort in a full coffin. He took none. He found the concept of closure the purist form of bullshit ever conceived by man. The way people talked about closure it was as if grief was as simple as going back to cross a forgotten "t". Whether his brother's coffin contained a broken torso or a sack full of rocks was of no consequence to Joe. Dead was fucking dead, body or no body. What mattered was that of the two creatures left on earth whom he loved and who loved him back, one was gone forever. Two and a half years of facing that reality hadn't lessened the ache of it. Neither, as it happened, had the vodka.

"Mr. Serpe, this is Captain Kelly," a booming voice poured out of the little speaker. "I was your brother's commander. We met at his funeral. It's Monday and I know I'm callin' real early, but I got alotta calls to make. I just wanted to let you know that Pete Hegarty's wife Pam's throwin' a second birthday party for the twins and … "

Joe half-listened to what Kelly had to say. The tone of the captain's voice intrigued him. Clearly, Kelly was annoyed by the continuing presence of Vinny's voice on the answering machine. Joe couldn't have cared less. He'd stopped caring about what other people thought of him a long time ago. He'd had to. It was a matter of survival. Given the last four years of his life, caring would have crushed him as surely as the hurtling concrete and steel had killed his brother.

Joe was shocked to find the phone in his hand. "Captain Kelly, this is Joe Serpe here."

If it had been almost anyone else from the department, he would have turned down the answering machine and gone back to his coma, but he remembered Kelly as being good to Vinny, welcoming him, mentoring him. Unlike the other hypocritical pricks at his brother's memorial, Kelly had cried real tears. The rest of them, as far as Joe was concerned, could all go to hell. These same men who carried his coffin and called him brother in death had taunted Vinny for his shyness, his stuttering, and called him fag, retard, and Va-Va-Vinny on September 10th. Death was too big a price to pay to finally get into the fraternity.

"Hello, Mr. Serpe, I was just callin'–"

"Yeah, I know. I heard."

"Pam Hegarty wanted me to … She thinks we need to be together."

"I can't make it."

"But, I haven't given you the date and–"

"Whenever it is, I can't make it." Joe was regretting having picked up. His head was pounding and he could feel the tears beginning to well up. He knew he had better speak his piece and get off. "Listen, Captain, I didn't get a chance to say this at the funeral, but I wanted to tell you that I really appreciated the way you treated my little brother. He told me how good you were to him."

"Your brother was a fireman's fireman," Kelly said.

The phone was back in its cradle.

Mulligan had given up trying to slay the bottle. He wanted real food, the smell of which induced a round of vomiting in Joe the likes of which he hadn't experienced in years.

"Fuckin' cat," he whispered, knowing he couldn't afford to alienate Mulligan. Mulligan was all he had left.

Joe threw on his stinky oil clothes from Saturday. After three years working oil, he had a week's worth of uniforms that he washed on Sundays. This past Sunday, he'd been a little too preoccupied researching the subtle differences between the flavors of Swedish and Polish vodka to care about the wash. Actually, his research had started late Saturday night. When he was first on the job, his wife used to say he smelled like a cop. That was crap. An oilman *really* smells like an oilman, especially in last week's clothes. Anyway, a fresh uniform didn't suit his mood. Nothing, not his breath nor even the snow that had fallen on and off since Saturday night, was fresh and clean. Things didn't stay fresh in Joe's world for very long.

The sun was just up when Joe squeezed into his Honda—Vinny's, really. They'd repo-ed Joe's car after the divorce—between the dumpster and a mound of exhaust black snow. He knew it was going to be a busy day. Winter Mondays always were, especially after it snowed. People got all psychotic about running out of heating oil when it snowed. It could be ten below and people didn't give a rat's ass, but if the weatherman mentioned snow, people went apeshit. Joe didn't mind busy. Busy was good. Busy meant more cash in his pocket. Busy meant no time to think. He was sick of thinking.

He was still a little unsteady when he got out of the car, the 7-Eleven coffee cup shaking in his hand. He glanced over to where the trucks were parked, making sure that Frank had started up the tugboat. That's what the drivers called Joe's old, green Mack. It's air horn had been broken for years and it sort of sounded like a fog horn. The big blue Mack was running. So was the red Mack, and the International cab-over, but not the tugboat.

"What the fuck?" Joe moaned, half-stumbling into the office.

Frank understood. "Sorry, Joe, the tugboat's off the road. The tank's got a pinhole leak and I'm taking her over to Suffolk Welding this morning. You're on the International today."

"I hate that truck. It's a bitch gettin' in and outta that thing."

"What can I tell you, Joe? You'll have the tugboat back tomorrow. Listen, in the meantime, there's like forty, fifty gallons a diesel left in the International's tank. You better pump it off before you go load, okay?"

"Whatever." Joe turned to leave. "Hey." He hesitated. "You hear anything about the kid?"

"Nah," Frank said. "It's too early. My guess is he's probably back at the home. You know him, how crazy he gets. He probably got all pissed off at something and freaked and couldn't handle it. In a way, it's good he didn't show on Saturday. I was thinking maybe of taking him off the trucks altogether and putting him back in the yard. Now I'm sure."

"He won't like that shit. And he's the best hose monkey we ever had, Frank."

"Yeah, well … "

By the time he got out to the truck, Joe had forgotten all about the kid. He had troubles enough of his own. He placed the nozzle into the hole atop an empty fifty-five gallon drum. He primed the pump and opened the nozzle trigger on the International, but instead of the expected gush of diesel, the thick, red hose barely stiffened. He heard a slow trickling echo inside the steel drum. Maybe Frank had been wrong about there being diesel left in the tank. It wouldn't be the first time. It's almost impossible to keep track of inventory when you pump a hundred thousand gallons of diesel and oil a month.

Joe closed the nozzle trigger, rechecked the meter, the primer handle and the tank valve, and tried it again. A thunderous clanging rose up from inside the three thousand gallon aluminum tank. Now the pump began straining so loudly he could barely hear the L.I.R.R. train pulling in at the Ronkonkoma Station. Joe had never heard anything like this. He thought he saw the big truck shudder and he immediately closed the pumping trigger. The truck quieted back down.

"What the fuck was that?" Frank screamed as he came racing out of the office. "Did you open the goddam valve?"

"C'mon, Frank, you know better than to ask me that."

"Yeah, well, you're lookin' a little fuckin' shaky this morning, buddy."

Joe thought about denying it, but knew he wasn't going to fool anybody, least of all Frank. "The valve's open. Look for yourself."

Frank did, put on a spare pair of rubberized orange gloves and opened the pumping trigger. Once again the clanging rose up, the pump straining fiercely.

"Fuck!"

"I'll get up top," Joe said, already climbing the ladder on the rear of the tank.

Once up, Joe thought he saw the problem. The top of the truck was still covered in snow and ice. The hatch vents were clogged. If those vents were sufficiently clogged, you could either create enough back pressure buildup to blow out the tank or a powerful vacuum capable of crushing the tank like a soda can. Joe Serpe got down on his hands and knees, brushed the snow away and chipped at the ice to clear the vents.

"Try it now," he called down to Frank.

It was no good. If anything the clanging was worse. Joe could feel the pump shaking the truck. Frank shut it down. Joe opened the hatch and had a look. Even in full summer sunlight, it was dark inside a tank. On a bleak February Monday, it was like looking into a black hole.

"Throw me up a flashlight," he yelled.

"Here she comes," Frank warned, tossing up a Maglite.

Joe grabbed it in midair, clicked it on and nestled on his knees in the snow at the side of the hatch. He aimed the beam through a hole in the rear tank baffle.

"Well … " Frank called up

He heard Frank, but couldn't answer. His lips moved, but there was no sound.

Frank was impatient. "What the fuck is it, Joe? Something caught in there?"

"Call 911," Joe thought he heard himself say.

"What?"

"Call the cops, Frank. Call 'em right now."

(Two Days Earlier)
Saturday Morning
Valentine's Day
February 14th, 2004

INVISIBILITY

Joe Serpe hopped from foot to foot on the concrete slab porch, watching his breath form clouds on the glass storm door. Early Saturday deliveries were a bitch. Everybody wanted their oil early, but no one was ever up in time to receive it. His knuckles were already raw from knocking and this was only his second stop. There were three doorbells. None of them worked. They never did in this town. Why is it, he wondered, did poor people always have so many doorbells and none of them worked? It was the same when he was on the job. Nothing works the way it's supposed to in poor neighborhoods. It sucked being poor. There was nothing profound in that thought, but there it was.

Sometimes, customers taped a money-fat envelope to the inside of the storm door, or under the front mat or in a bag attached to the oil fill pipe itself. Joe had already checked. There was no money. This one time, he'd been instructed that the money would be in the glove box of a car parked in the front yard. When he pulled up in the tugboat, there were eleven abandoned cars in the front yard. He went through five of them before finding the money. He laughed to himself thinking about that stop. He wasn't laughing now.

This shit drove him nuts. He knew someone was home. There were two cars in the driveway. One of them had a warm hood. Joe had checked that, too. Old cop habits die hard. And he thought he could hear a TV coming from inside the house. Though he'd only driven an oil truck for three years, he knew what was going on. Three years, that's what he'd been told. It takes three years as an oilman to see everything. There's a learning curve in all professions. Compared to the cops, the learning curve for an oilman was a piece of cake. For a street cop, the learning curve extends past retirement and into the grave. In oil, there's trucks and tanks and houses—one pretty much like the next. In police work … Well, it was just different.

Joe, the stubborn fuck that he was, banged hard on the door one last time, his fist print smudging the coating of fog his breath had left on the glass. He ran his fingers up and down the row of impotent bells and rapped his knuckles on the front window. His rapping was particularly urgent because now not only was he cold, but he had to pee something wicked. No answer. He knew the drill. These pricks had dialed every oil company in the *Pennysaver* and had already taken delivery from the first truck that showed. *Scummers*, that's what Frank called them. They were on the other side of the door holding their breaths until Joe gave up and drove on. It killed him to do it, but he had twenty other stops to do and an impatient bladder to deal with. He wrote a familiar message on the ticket:

NO ONE HOME/NO MONEY/NO OIL
CALL TO RESCHEDULE

He split the three part ticket, impaling the hard cardboard copy on a broken aluminum prong of the storm door and shoving the top white copy in the mailbox. Joe saved the middle yellow copy to show Frank that he'd tried to do the stop. Not that Frank gave a shit. Frank just threw the yellows out without looking. Joe only got paid for deliveries, not attempted deliveries. As a sort of final *fuck you* to the people in the house, he threw the carbon paper on the front steps. Just as he let the carbons go, the front door opened.

A skinny Hispanic man in a dirty t-shirt stepped unsteadily onto the stoop. His hair was a mess and the whites surrounding his dull brown eyes were shot with blood.

"*Lo siento, jefe,*" the man slurred his apologies. "Sleeping."

"You Mr. Diaz? You ordered fifty gallons, right?" Joe began the scripted dialogue, some version of which he repeated more than 120 times weekly.

"*Si,* feefty gallons."

"That'll be $102.45 cash when I'm done pumping. Okay?"

"*Mucho dinero, jefe.*"

"*Si,*" Joe agreed. "*Muy mucho.* You got it?"

"I got," Diaz answered, staring at his bare cold feet on the concrete porch.

"That the fill pipe there?" Joe pointed at a black pipe extending about a foot out of the front of the house just left of the stoop.

"The pipe, *si.*" Diaz turned and went back inside.

Joe went into action. He reached into the cab of his old Mack, took out a fresh ticket, wrote it up and slid it into the meter at the back of the truck. With a quick forward twist of the dial at the side of the meter, he locked the ticket in place and cleared the mechanism. He set the meter at fifty, opened the tank valve, slipped on his once-orange gloves and primed the pump. He lifted the nozzle from its holster, threw the hose over his left shoulder and marched it to the fill pipe. At the fill, he unscrewed its cover, screwed the nozzle in place and slid the pumping trigger open. Joe had repeated this routine so often, he found himself acting it out in his sleep. More than once he'd startled awake dreaming he'd dropped the hose.

Almost immediately upon sliding open the trigger, Joe heard music to an oilman's ears—a whistle. When oil goes into a tank, air is displaced and that air comes howling up through a vent pipe. Only two things ever come out of a vent pipe: air, if you do the delivery right, or, if you fuck up, oil. When the whistling stops, the tank is full. Keep pumping after the whistle stops and you've got oil gushing through the vent pipe. Air was good. Oil was bad. It was that straightforward. That was one of the things he liked about the oil business. It was all black or white, good or bad, air or oil. Early on as a cop, Joe had learned that a cop's universe was shades of gray.

There was little chance of a spill when they ordered fifty gallons. Standard tanks held between 250 and 275 gallons. Joe knew that only poor people or fools ordered only fifty gallons. In this weather, fifty gallons would last five, maybe six days. Then he'd be back. At fifty gallons, oil was almost two bucks a pop. Smart people or people with money ordered two-hundred gallons. It was forty cents cheaper per gallon that way.

"They're idiots," he had said to Frank during training. "Why order so little? You get hammered that way."

"They're not stupid, Joe, just poor," Frank explained. "Poor people gotta make choices most of us don't ever gotta make. Some weeks, it's oil or food."

Joe felt silly for opening his mouth. Frank was right. He remembered how it was on the cops, in the bad neighborhoods. There, it was drugs or food. It was Joe's experience that drugs were more powerful than food or oil or God.

The whistle stopped almost before it got in full swing. Joe's old Mack might be a rickety piece of shit with no radio, but it pumped like a motherfucker. New equipment was an anathema to Frank. Sometimes Joe thought his boss would buy used oil filters if he could. But he respected Frank. He owed Frank a lot. Frank had saved him. Frank gave him a job when no one would touch him with someone else's ten-foot pole. Joe Serpe had his faults. Disloyalty wasn't one of them. He knew plenty of cops who might disagree.

Now Joe went through the routine in reverse: unscrewing the nozzle, replacing the cap, pulling the nozzle back toward the tugboat, reeling in the hose, taking off his gloves, closing the tank valve, unlocking the ticket from the meter with a reverse twist of the dial. He wrote up the price, added the tax, totaled the ticket and marched up the front steps. He opened the storm door and knocked. The front door pushed back.

Joe saw the TV was on, tuned to a Spanish language channel. There was a baby standing on his tippy-toes in a playpen a foot or two in front of the TV. The baby stared at Joe with happy eyes. A woman dressed only in a nicotine-stained nightshirt lay unconscious on a blue vinyl couch, her arms and legs splayed carelessly at unnatural angles. Seated perpendicular to the couch in a ripped up recliner behind the playpen was the man who had been on the porch. He held a thin glass pipe in his hand. One end of the pipe was pressed to his mouth; he held a disposable lighter to the other. Diaz sucked hard on the pipe, white smoke shooting into his lungs.

Disgusted, Joe ripped the yellow receipt copy and screamed in his pidgin Spanish: "*Donde esta* the money?"

The man, smoke leaking out of the corners of his mouth, pointed the cheap lighter at an envelope at the foot of the door. Joe counted the money. Exact change. He slammed the door shut. He could hear the baby begin crying behind him. He did not look back.

Almost from the first day he'd taken the job with Frank, Joe had noticed his gift of invisibility. Even now, three years later, he had trouble believing the things people let him stand witness to. His stop at Casa Diaz wasn't the first time he'd been treated to a box seat at crackhead Nirvana. In Wyandanch, he'd had to wait for a guy to finish shooting up before getting paid, and Joe had had more pot smoke blown in his face than he cared to remember. He'd watched parents smack their kids around, men beat their dogs and a woman slaughtering chickens. Invisibility had its perks. Semi-clad women of all shapes, colors and sizes often came to the door to pay him, some so scantily dressed that he was convinced he must indeed be invisible.

It was to laugh, he thought, turning onto Sunrise Highway from Fifth Avenue. When he was working Narcotics, what he wouldn't have given for the gift he now enjoyed. He had always known God was a bit of a mindfucker. God seemed to make a point of proving that to Joe at every opportunity. What Joe couldn't figure out was why God got such a kick out of beating the same dead horse over and over again. Joe looked up. "I get it," he said. "I get it."

Fuck! His bladder was screaming at him. He had forgotten to piss. He pulled to the service road curb, got out, and walked around to the passenger side. He positioned himself so that passing traffic could not see him. Joe knew the Almighty too well to rely on his intermittent invisibility. As the burn ebbed slowly away, he tried not to think about the baby's happy eyes.

★ ★ ★

Cain could barely contain himself, watching the clock blink the red seconds away until he went down to breakfast. It wasn't breakfast that so excited him. Breakfast was all right here; better than in some of the homes he'd been in, worse than others. Sometimes they helped him pick out his clothes for the day, but not today, not on Saturdays. On Saturdays he wore the rugged Carhartt uniform Frank had bought for him.

He thought his dusty black Wolverine work boots were really cool even though the staff hated the way they smelled of oil. When he first got the boots, Cain tried polishing them up after each shift and washing off the soles to get the stink out. Now he just let them be. He had come to love that smell. And like Frank said, "You're a workin' man. There's no shame in smelling like one."

Frank was right. Frank was right about a lot of things. Frank was smart. Sometimes Cain thought that if he were normal, he'd want to be just like Frank. Frank treated him with respect. His parents never treated him with respect. They still talked at him like he was a baby. He was retarded, not stupid. He was a man now, not a baby.

Cain found himself getting agitated, thinking about his folks. That wasn't good. When he got like this, he got in trouble. But nothing could ruin his day. It was Saturday. He got to work on the truck with Frank. He had only a few more minutes before heading downstairs.

He slipped on his thick woolen socks. Then he slid his skinny chicken legs—that's what Frank called them—into his thermal long johns. Next came his favorite piece of clothing on earth, his kelly green Mayday Fuel Oil, Inc. t-shirt. Though Cain liked the logo of a white tanker truck encircled by a life preserver on the front of the shirt, it was the back of the cotton tee that he loved best. He held it up before him:

KING KONG
HOSE MONKEY

He was smarter than a lot of people he had met in the homes. He could read. Sometimes he didn't understand all the words, but he could say them. Once he'd shown the shirt to his parents. It made his father sad and his mom had gotten all angry about the hose monkey. He tried to explain that they weren't making fun of him, that 'hose monkey' was what oilmen called a guy who rode shotgun on the truck and pulled hoses. They called you that whether you were retarded or not. He never showed them the shirt again. Cain pulled on the shirt and admired himself in the mirror.

There was a knock on the door. The imposing figure of the home aide everyone called Mr. French filled the doorway. Cain didn't much like Mr. French. The feeling was more than mutual. Their disdain for one another was immediate, but had deepened recently after Cain made a joke at Mr. French's expense in front of a cute occupational therapist.

"Do all people from Haiti hate other people like you do?" Cain had asked.

It hadn't helped that the therapist had laughed at Cain's pun on hate and Haiti.

French had a reputation for getting rough with the residents. He hadn't hit Cain, not yet, anyway, but he was riding him pretty hard lately, pushing him, trying to get him in trouble. Cain had told Joe Serpe about Mr. French. Joe, one of Frank's drivers, had once been a cop, though he didn't like other people to know that. Joe had promised to come down and have a talk with the health aide if he got tough with Cain, and Cain had told Mr. French as much.

"Man, it stink in 'ere." Mr. French held his nose. "You 'ave two minutes to get to breakfast, 'ose monkey," he snickered. "'ose monkey, indeed. The monkey is much smarter, no?"

Cain could feel himself getting worked up. He didn't need the mirror to see his face was burning red.

French stuck out his chin at Cain. "Come on, boy, you would like to 'it me? Your cop friend won't be able to 'elp you, monkey boy."

The back of Cain's left hand slashed across the rich black skin of Mr. French's cheek.

* * *

Bob Healy rolled over in bed. Eyes still closed, he reached instinctively across the bed for Mary. He'd dreamed about her. They were at Plumb Beach, alone at the shoreline in the semi-darkness, lazy planes gliding overhead toward JFK. He cradled her freckled face in his sandpapery palms, her green eyes sparkling as they had when Bob saw her that first time at the CYO dance at St. Marks.

She sighed as she always sighed when he first slid inside her. Just the sound of her, that soft sigh, the very thought of it could drive him to distraction. Even now, after thirty years together, he got hard imagining Mary's sigh. He had been no saint, straying every few years only to be disappointed at the results, always returning to Mary's side. Sometimes he lay paralyzed in bed in the dark and silence, wondering if Mary knew of his dalliances. If she did, she never let on. He was lucky to have her.

His arm fell across vacant air. Mary was gone. The sheet was cold where his wife had once slept. The best part of Bob Healy's day had come and gone in the span of a few breaths. The time between semi-consciousness and the realization that Mary was dead were the only pain-free seconds of his life. It had been six months now since he and the kids had buried her, but he hadn't adjusted to the loss. He wondered if he ever would. Some weeks were better than others. Days would go by without a misstep and then he'd dream of her or smell her perfume on a woman passing him in the aisle at Waldbaums. For the first few months, he'd lied to himself that his transition would have gone more smoothly had the kids still lived at home, but nothing on God's green earth could smooth over the loss of Mary.

This morning, Mary's side of the bed was particularly cold. The whole bed, the covers, the pillows, too, were icy. Bob touched the tip of his nose.

"Christ!"

He stumbled over to the thermostat, trying to rub the sleep out of his eyes so that he might read the temperature. It was 58 degrees in the house. When was the last time he'd checked the oil? Bob Healy was truly lost without Mary. He couldn't balance a checkbook. He hadn't even written more than a handful of checks until six months ago. He hadn't ever shopped for food or socks or underwear, for that matter. Although checking the oil tank was his responsibility, it had been Mary who would make a notation on the calendar and remind her husband.

As he trundled down the old wooden stairs to the basement, Bob could feel a case of the 'maybes' coming on. It always happened this way when he'd go into a spin over Mary. First came the hurt and then the maybes. Maybe if he hadn't put in his papers. Maybe if he hadn't ruined so many other cops' careers. He always feared there'd be a price to pay for his years in Internal Affairs, for the cops who'd chosen suicide instead of facing disgrace and jail time, but he thought he'd be the one picking up the tab, not Mary. Of course he understood it was completely irrational for him to connect his work to Mary's pancreatic cancer. God, as cruel as Bob knew him to sometimes be, wouldn't have done this to Mary. Still …

The red float indicator on the tank gauge was flush with the top of the tank. Empty. Just to make sure, Bob rapped his knuckles against the black steel tank. It rang hollow like the rest of his life. Upstairs, he couldn't find the number of the oil company. Calling for deliveries was Mary's job. Not anymore. Disgusted with himself, frustrated at his ineptitude, he reached for the *Pennysaver*. He flipped to the pages where all the oil companies advertised.

"Eeny, meeny, miny, mo … " he recited, "my mother says to pick this one!"

Saturday, Late Afternoon
Valentine's Day
February 14th, 2004

M'AIDEZ

The faint ghost of the winter sun was hanging low over the western L.I.E. The smell of snow mixed in the air with that of diesel exhaust. Joe Serpe was done for the day. *Say Hallelujah! Say Amen!* All told, he'd done twenty-five stops, loaded twice and pumped 3,453 gallons. At ten bucks a stop and ten a load, that was a neat 270 bucks cash in his pocket. It was a lot more in Frank's pocket, of course, but Joe didn't sweat that the way the other drivers did. He could do the math. With prices the way they were, Frank was grossing between fifty and sixty bucks a stop. Multiply that times three trucks and it's a nice chunk of change.

Sometimes, Joe enjoyed listening to the other drivers grouse about how much profit Mayday Fuel Oil, Inc. took in on a winter Saturday. It was an October to April ritual, a weekly big boys bitch-fest at Lugo's Pub in Ronkonkoma. Joe would just smile, empathetically nodding his head every now and then to show he was still listening. Sure, Frank made good money, but he had taken the risks, bought the trucks, rented the yard and office, paid for advertising, etc. At Lugo's, Joe would drift off trying to calculate how many millions of dollars he and his partner Ralphy had logged into evidence over the years. The numbers were staggering. He didn't like thinking about Ralphy.

"Ah, shit!" he screamed at the cell phone buzzing and beeping in his pocket. He had been schooled by the other drivers on the art of the tactical lie, but had chosen to ignore their advice. Now he was going to pay the price for that decision. He had done enough lying as a cop. In the end, it was what had ruined him and Ralphy both.

"Listen," one of the Lugo's crowd had advised early on, "call in when you're headed toward your last stop and say you've already done it and that you're almost back at the yard. Otherwise, if an emergency call comes in, you're screwed."

True enough. In boxing, it's cool to be the last man standing. In the home heating oil business, the last man standing is fucked.

"Yeah, Ma," Joe picked up. The dispatcher was Frank's mom. Some drivers called her Mrs. Randazzo or Donna, but Joe, his own mother long dead, just called her Ma.

"Oh, Joe," she rasped in her two-pack-a-day voice, "I hate to do this to ya, but I misplaced a stop before and the guy just called back looking for his delivery."

"Can't wait till Monday, huh?" Joe asked, already knowing the answer. "It's beginning to snow out here."

"Sorry, Joe, he's out and he's a new customer."

Yeah, sure, Joe thought, they're always out. It was one of those convenient lies people told to make sure you'd come in a hurry, or, when things were really busy, to make sure you'd come at all.

"Okay, Ma, lemme pull over here and get a ticket."

"The name's Healy," Ma said when Joe gave her the go ahead. "H-E-A-L-Y. He's at 89 Boxwood Avenue in Kings Park, off 25A. It's a fill up at the two hundred gallon price. Cash. The fill's on the right side of the house up the driveway. You copy that, Joe?"

He copied all right. Not only was he stuck doing another stop, but it was way the hell up on the North Shore. That's why Ma had sounded so guilty. Delivering oil is dangerous enough in perfect weather, but in the snow, in the dark … Forget about it! If you think controlling a skid is fun in your family car, try it in a Mack truck sometime. He pulled away from the curb and began slowly backtracking his way over the L.I.E., through Hauppague and Smithtown, up Landing Avenue, down Rose Street and onto 25A.

Fifteen slippery minutes later he was in Kings Park. Kings Park was a cute little town whose name had nothing to do with royalty and everything to do with the now shuttered psychiatric hospital that bore the same name. The hospital was established as an offshoot of Kings County Hospital in Brooklyn, hence the Kings in Kings Park. The town had grown up around the extensive hospital grounds situated on an inlet of Long Island Sound.

Joe turned onto Boxwood, his eyes trying to focus on some address, any address, just to establish the odd numbered side of the street. That was no mean feat at night with the snow piling up on the ledge of the tugboat's side windows and mirrors. Old Macks are great trucks, but their heating and defrosting systems are for shit. About a quarter of the way up Boxwood, Joe caught a number on a mailbox. 43. Bingo!

89 Boxwood was a neat split ranch—gee, what a surprise on Long Island. Normally, he would have parked the truck, gone to the front door and confirmed the delivery. He was too tired, too pissed-off to do his normal routine. He popped the air brake, put the truck in neutral, flipped on the PTO and shifted into third gear. He set the meter, primed the pump, yanked the hose over his shoulder and walked up a stranger's driveway for the twenty-sixth time that day. It was days like this Joe most regretted complaining to Frank about the kid. Cain wasn't a kid, not really, but his being retarded made him seem like one. Christ, he was a good two inches taller than Joe and strong as an ox for someone so reedy thin. Country strong, Frank called him. Retard strong; Dixie, one of the other drivers, was less kind.

It wasn't that he didn't like Cain. He did. Joe was the one who gave him the nickname King Kong. It fit—Cain Cohen, King Kong. The perfect moniker for a hose monkey. Even now as Joe shlepped the hose, he smiled thinking about the kick the kid got out of the nickname. He was so proud of it. The thing was, Cain drove Joe a little nuts. When they stuck to subjects like sports, they were okay. In fact, it kind of reminded Joe of riding the streets with his first partner, but you could only talk so much sports and Saturdays could be very long days.

The kid was a little too preoccupied with that Japanese anime crap. And the kid could fool you. He sometimes seemed almost bright, but Joe had learned there was a limit to the kid's range. There was just some stuff that Cain couldn't get no matter how many times you explained it to him. That wouldn't have been bad if the kid wasn't so freaking curious. He asked a million questions and it was one of these questions that had finally gotten to Joe.

"Why is Frank's company called Mayday, Joe?"

"Cause Frank thought it was a good name that people would remember."

"Why? It sounds like a stupid name to me. What does May have to do with oil? It's hot in May and we don't deliver a lot of oil in May."

"Mayday's got nothing to do with the month of May, Kong."

"Then what's it mean?"

"It means 'help me.' Even though we spell it m-a-y-d-a-y, it comes from the French m'aidez, m-a-i-d-e-z, which means 'help me.'"

"But we don't speak French in America, Joe, so that's stupid."

After about a half-hour of going round and round, Joe had cut off the discussion. That night he went to Frank and asked for the kid to be taken off the tugboat. Two months had passed since then. Cain had gotten over his initial hurt, but Joe still felt shitty about it. He had come to the realization that the kid's questions were painful echoes from his own life. His son, Joey, now fourteen and living with his mother and stepfather in Daytona Beach, had always been a curious kid. Worse even were the echoes of Vinny in the kid's questions.

Joe hooked up the nozzle to the fill pipe. He was about to start for the front door, when he heard a storm door slam shut and footsteps coming his way.

"Fill up?" Joe shouted.

"Whatever she'll take," a man answered back, his footsteps growing louder as they grew nearer. "I shoulda checked the tank a week ago, but … There's alotta things I shoulda done."

Joe said nothing. He heard this lament or versions thereof several times a day. He slid the trigger open and got a strong vent whistle. The homeowner was standing right behind him now. Joe didn't bother looking up. He wasn't interested in making friends and influencing people. He just wanted to get done.

"I really appreciate your coming so late."

"No sweat," Joe lied through clenched teeth.

"This weather sucks, doesn't it?" the customer asked. "My wife used to love the snow. Me, I got no use for it."

"Oh God," Joe muttered to himself, "a fuckin' talker."

"Did you say something?"

"No, nothing. Yeah, this weather sure does suck."

"It must be rough for you, working in this shit. No?"

Suddenly, a chill rode the length of Joe Serpe's spine. There was something about this guy's voice, the way he phrased things that was eerily familiar. Frantically, he searched his memory, trying to recall the customer's name. The whistle weakened, the tank almost full. Joe did not take notice as he tried remembering Ma spelling the name out for him. What was the name? Now, the whistle died completely. Joe did not slap the trigger shut. There was a loud gurgling in the vent pipe, oil rising up fast. Healy! Christ almighty! Joe snapped back into the present, smacking the trigger closed. Only a few drops of oil sputtered out the vent pipe turning the virgin snow beneath the color of cherry ices. The customer seemed not to take notice.

"Okay," Joe said. "I'll write you up and meet you at the front door."

"Good. I'll get the cash."

Joe did not turn to look as Mr. Healy retreated. Instead, he looked at the fresh footprints as he carried the hose back to the tugboat. When he removed the ticket from the meter, Joe noticed his hands were shaking. No, he thought, it had to be a different Healy. There must be hundreds of Healys on Long Island. Joe filled in the totals, laughing at himself for being such an idiot. He felt like some broken-hearted teenager who runs into an old girlfriend. He walked up to the door, bill in hand, an embarrassed smile on his face. He knocked at the storm door.

"One second. Gimme a second," a bodyless voice answered the knock.

Shit! There was that chill again. It *was* the voice. *His* voice. Just as he could not calculate the millions he had confiscated over the years, Joe could not count the hours he'd listened to that voice accuse and cajole, prompt and prod, jab and parry. He was tempted to leave the receipt in the mailbox and run, scream for Healy to send in a check.

But Joe Serpe hadn't run from anything in his life and he wasn't about to start now. Instead he cupped his hands around his eyes and pressed his face up close to the storm door. He looked at the framed collage of family photos on the staircase wall.

"Motherfucker!" he hissed. "It's him."

It seemed to take about a week for Healy to get downstairs with the money. At first, there was no sign of recognition in Healy's faded gray eyes. The lack of recognition wasn't lost on Joe. Maybe his invisibility was shielding him. But in his heart, Joe knew God would never pass up such a rich opportunity to fuck with his life. Sure enough, just as Healy began forking over the cash, a light went on in his eyes. Bob Healy's pupils got small as pinheads. His mouth formed that wry, mischievous smile Joe had learned to despise.

"Fuck if it isn't Joe 'the Snake' Serpe."

* * *

Frank was finishing his entries into the computer when he noticed just how dark it was outside the office. He considered giving Joe a buzz to see how that last delivery was coming, but he decided against it. He didn't want to insult the man. Anyone who could do buy and bust operations in the worst of the worst neighborhoods in New York City could handle a little snow and darkness. Frank had already decided to throw Joe an extra twenty for doing the stop. That would bring Joe's pay for the day up to a nice round three hundred bucks. All in all it had been a nice payday for everyone. Besides, Frank had big troubles of his own, things he didn't even want to think about.

Frank checked the window again. The snow seemed to be slowing its pace. Yet Frank felt unusually ill at ease. It was certainly true that he didn't like having trucks out in the dark and that early in his tenure Joe had been a bit of a hot-rodder, but that wasn't it. Frank loved reclamation projects, Joe best among them. Everybody who'd ever worked for him had been a reclamation project of one sort or another. There was Fat Stan the Psycho Man who had managed to get off welfare and get his life back in order while earning his keep for Mayday. What a character, Frank laughed, remembering the day he found Stan thumbing a ride outside the grounds of Pilgrim State Psychiatric Hospital.

Then there was King Kong. The jury was still out on him. He hadn't shown up for work today. While it wasn't the first time, it wasn't exactly a chronic problem either. Even though the kid claimed to like working with Frank, he wondered if Cain wasn't still feeling the sting of being tossed off the tugboat by Joe. He liked the kid a whole lot, but Frank had always been a little shaky about his decision to move Kong from working around the yard to hose monkey.

The group home was just a little ways down Union Avenue. If something went wrong in the yard, Frank could have someone from the home there in five minutes. The truck was something else altogether. It wasn't the work itself. Christ, you could train a monkey to pull a hose to a fill and back. Hence the job title. No, it was the 'what ifs' that gave Frank pause. What if the driver got injured? What if the truck were robbed? What if there was a spill? An accident?

From the first, Frank understood there was potential for disaster written all over taking the kid on. The people at the home had made

Cain's history and limitations abundantly clear. The kid had always been polite and respectful around him and Joe, maybe a little less so with the other drivers. Then again, they'd been a little less respectful of him. That seemed a pretty normal response to Frank's way of thinking. Yet Frank knew Cain had a history of sometimes striking out in anger and for going AWOL. But the kid's goofy enthusiasm was contagious and King Kong did good work. After his latest no-show, however, maybe the time had come to admit defeat and put the kid back in the yard.

Then in the stillness of the snow and night, Frank heard the comforting low rumble of the tugboat turning onto Union. A moment later, headlights flashed through the office windows.

★ ★ ★

Frank's words rang in Cain's head: "When a man fucks up, he gotta take what's comin'. A real man steps up. He don't wait to get found out."

Cain knew he was wrong for not showing up today without telling Frank. It killed him to disappoint Frank. He liked Joe Serpe a lot, but he loved Frank. Frank treated him like he wished his own father could. Frank taught him things. Joe taught him things, too, like how Serpe meant snake in Italian, but the things Frank taught him were life things, man things. Frank treated him special. His parents, the people at the homes, they all treated him like a dead end street. He didn't have the right words for it the way Frank would. The people who worked with him at the homes, even the really nice ones, were sort of doing what they had to, but like in front of a brick wall, almost like he wasn't there. The thing about Frank was that he treated Cain like he could learn anything.

That's why he knew he had to come talk to Frank. It was what a man did. And Cain Cohen was a man in spite of his being M.R., slow, delayed, challenged, handicapped or any of those other stupid words that meant he was different. The problem was he'd hidden himself in a secret place where no one would be able to find him and now he was frozen stiff, starving and tired. At first, the chill made some of the hurt go away. Now it made it worse. Finally, he'd gotten the courage up to apologize to Frank for being bad, but just as he started crawling out of his secret place, he heard a truck pulling into the yard. He would have to wait a little while longer. For Frank, he would wait as long as it took.

* * *

Joe nosed in, swung around and backed up between the blue and red Macks. The constant *beep, beep, beep* of the reverse warning horn cut through him like fork tines scraping on an empty plate. There wasn't much clearance and it was dark and there was ice on his mirrors, but he didn't figure his night could get much worse. The tugboat slid in neatly between the trucks on either side. Joe remembered a time when he was afraid to even put the damned truck in reverse. Then there was the time he got cocky about his ability to squeeze through tight spaces and creased the side of the tugboat's tank. Frank was less than pleased about that.

He pulled out the yellow parking brake on the dash. A loud *pssst* filled the night as the air brakes spit out excess pressure, kicking up a spray of snow and dust. He turned off the ignition key and choked the engine silent. Gathering up his paperwork, cell phone and map, Joe jumped down off the metal grate for the last time that day.

"A face from the past," Frank teased. "I was gonna organize a fuckin' search party."

"Here." Joe threw down his paperwork, map and phone in front of Frank.

"Hey, I'm sorry about that last stop."

"Not as sorry as me."

"I'm throwing you an extra twenty," Frank said, figuring to lift Joe's spirits.

"Keep it."

"What the fuck's eatin' you?"

"You wanna know?"

"No, Joe, I asked cause I enjoy the sound of my own voice. Yeah, I wanna know."

"Healy," Joe barked, "the last stop in Kings Park."

"What about it?"

"Bob Healy was the lead detective on my case."

"Fuck! He was the—"

"That's right," Joe said, a sad smile spreading across his face. "Detective Robert Healy, Internal Affairs' best and brightest. He was the guy that made the case against me and Ralphy."

Even after four years, it hurt like a son of a bitch; the old disgrace rained over him like a shower of bee stings. It's how far you let yourself fall, Father John had once told him, that's the measure of a man. And Joe Serpe had fallen quite a long ways.

He thought about Vinny every day, but Joe had good stretches now, sometimes whole months, without revisiting his own fall. Now it was all back—the hearings, the testimony, the loss of his family, his shield, his pension, his self-respect, Ralphy's suicide. And all because Ma had misplaced a delivery ticket. God just couldn't resist fucking with him.

"C'mon," Frank snapped. "Drinks are on me. Lugo's, here we come."

Joe Serpe didn't have it in him to protest. He would have preferred to drink alone, but he had the rest of the weekend for that.

Frank shut down his PC, clicked off the lights and locked the door. Joe went ahead of him to check the trucks and make sure all the tank valves were in the closed position and that all the keys had been removed from the cabs. There had been a lot troubles in the neighborhood recently, minor stuff, mostly. The vandalism hadn't turned serious yet, just a few broken windows and some artful graffiti. But a misplaced ignition key and one opened valve could lead to a few thousand gallons of fuel oil on the ground. As he inspected the trucks, Joe thought he heard something moving in the yard. He whipped the flashlight around, cutting broad gashes in the darkness. He saw nothing. Seeing Healy again had really spooked him. The sooner he got to Lugo's the better.

* * *

Cain didn't pick his head up until Frank and Joe had locked the yard gates behind them. He listened to their cars pulling away. His heart was still racing from when Joe had heard him slip. Joe had shined the flashlight right over his head. That Joe hadn't seen him filled Cain with a kind of pride. His special hiding spot was so good that not even a real detective could find him. When the swell of pride vanished, Cain began to panic.

He knew Frank wouldn't fire him if he could just talk to him. Frank understood better than anybody the way it was with Cain, how he acted bad sometimes. The thing was, he hadn't wanted to talk in front of Joe Serpe. He thought Joe was still mad at him from when he had Frank take him off the tugboat. Frank swore up and down that Joe wasn't mad at him, that he had problems of his own. But Cain was smart enough to know people didn't tell the truth sometimes when they didn't want to hurt your feelings. He also knew that like his parents, people got rid of you when they were mad at you. Or, like Mr. French, they just hit you.

Now what was he going to do? He was getting so cold and hungry and everybody was going to be mad at him. Cain knew what would happen if he didn't get back to the group home soon. They would call his parents and they would get real mad. The people at the home were probably already mad, because they got in trouble when the *tards* ran away. Sometimes, no matter why you ran, they sent you to a new place. They couldn't do that to him, not this time. He had a real job, one he loved. He had Frank.

Cain noticed that tears were pouring out of his eyes and his nose was so stuffed he could hardly breathe right. He was shaking, his chest heaving. The thought of losing everything he had worked so hard for was too much to take. He had finally found a place where he belonged, where his being slow didn't mean so much. Cain knew there was only one thing to do. He had to get back to the home. That's what Frank would want him to do, to be a man.

Then, just as he began to crawl out from his special hiding place, he heard a rattling from the big padlock and thick chain that held the gate shut. He heard voices. He scooted back in his secret niche and listened. Now he knew what to do to set things right. No one would be mad at him anymore.

★ ★ ★

It was near 11:00 when Frank and Joe shook hands goodnight.

"Shit," Frank said, trying to focus on his watch. "It's Valentine's Day. My wife's gonna kill me. I hope those roses I sent her will do the trick."

"Good luck."

"You're pretty fucked up, Joe. You gonna be okay to drive?"

"It's only a few blocks. I'll be fine."

"Famous last words."

"God wouldn't let me off that easy, Frank."

"See ya Monday morning."

"Monday," Joe repeated, beginning to walk to his car. "Hey," he stopped, calling to Frank. "You ever hear from the kid today?"

"Nah."

"I still feel bad about throwing him off–"

"Forget it, Joe. Get some sleep."

★ ★ ★

Cain's eyes fluttered. Face down in a few inches of yellow-dyed diesel, he should have been coughing but couldn't. He wasn't breathing very well either. It was the weirdest thing. He knew he should be in a lot of pain, but he just wasn't. He had been beat up real bad, so bad he couldn't remember much. He was cold mostly. Only his head hurt a little. He knew he should have been scared, but he wasn't.

He had better get up, he thought. He couldn't move. His hands and feet wouldn't work. Now he panicked. He tried screaming.

"Frank!"

But when he opened his mouth, diesel rushed in. He couldn't cough. He was drowning from inside and out. His eyes were stinging and the taste of the diesel was hard to take. His tongue was thick and slow.

"Frank!" he tried again.

Again the diesel rushed in and he couldn't spit it back out.

He moved the only part of him that worked anymore. He banged his head against the tank as hard as he could, hoping morning had come and that Frank or Joe could hear him. He split his scalp wide open, his blood mixing into the diesel.

Silence.

He stopped banging. Even if morning *had* come, no one would be there. It was Sunday.

The panic was gone.

Thursday
The Day of the Funeral
February 19th, 2004

F.F.L.

Bob Healy didn't bother waiting to get back into the house to unfurl his *Newsday*. Normally he'd check the sports headlines before scanning the front page, but the Knicks could wait. No, there was a story he'd been following since Monday morning when he saw the first reports on News Channel 12. It was tragedy enough that the poor retarded boy had been murdered and tossed into an oil tank to rot, but there was another aspect of the case that Healy couldn't get his head around. Initially, he hadn't made the connection between the victim, Joe Serpe, and Mayday Fuel.

Then it clicked.

The murder was headline material again today:

NO LEADS
Funeral Later Today

Bob Healy crossed himself. Seeing Joe Serpe on Saturday had gotten to him. Maybe it was because that day had been so cold, so haunting, so full of Mary's absence. For whatever reason, Healy had taken Joe Serpe's appearance at his doorstep as a sign. He had wanted to talk to Serpe on Saturday, to say some things that needed to be said, but old ways die hard. Healy couldn't help but treat Serpe with the practiced condescension he'd cultivated over his years in

Internal Affairs. Before Healy could change his tune, Serpe's truck was rumbling down the street.

He hadn't slept at all well that night, going over his cases in his head. Until Mary's death, Healy hadn't been much of a second-guesser. It didn't suit him or his career in I.A.B. But since he had seen Joe "the Snake", all Bob had done was second-guess himself. In a lightless, lonely bedroom in the midst of a snowstorm, there's time enough to dissect the individual molecules of a case; time to rehash every decision, every question, every unkindness.

Healy went to Mass the following day, confessed his sins, took communion. He went on Monday as well, but found neither solace nor answers in the words of the priest nor in the serenely frozen face of the crucified Jesus. Then, when he got home and flipped on cable to see the story of the murder in the oil yard, Bob Healy knew what he had to do. He would have to meet with Joe Serpe. Not only was it the right thing to do, but Mary would have demanded it.

He scanned the articles in the paper, ignoring his cooling coffee. There it was, the detail he'd been searching for. He tore the article out of the paper, put his mug in the sink, and went upstairs to shower. He had to be at Mass in twenty minutes.

* * *

Joe and Frank came in separate cars, but they met in the parking lot at Kaplan Brothers. Joe was surprised to see Frank alone. He had just assumed Frank would bring Tina.

"The wife's not feelin' too good," Frank volunteered before Joe had a chance to ask.

It was a lie. Joe could see it in Frank's face, could hear it in his voice. He knew it was a lie just like he knew it was a lie when his snitches would look him right in the eye and swear they weren't using or dealing. It was *pro forma*. I say X and you say Y. I cha cha and you cha cha cha. Joe sometimes wondered why people went through that song and dance bullshit. He wasn't pointing fingers. He had been just as guilty of it as anyone. Maybe it was a basic human instinct, he thought, the need for preliminaries before the main bout.

He knew Frank was lying the same way he had known that Ralphy was lying to him over the last two years they were together. With Ralphy, it was little things at first. By the time they got busted, Ralphy'd gotten so outrageous it was almost funny. Almost. He was like the punch line to a bad joke:

How did you know I was lying?

Your lips were moving.

Joe and Frank didn't say much to each other as they walked from the parking lot into the funeral home. Besides the lie, there were a lot of other factors adding to the unusual level of discomfort between the two men. Neither was at ease in a suit and tie. Frank especially, kept adjusting his tie and shirt collar. Joe could see his boss' neck chaffed red at the constriction of a closed top button and taut knot.

Then there was the fact that Frank had never been to a Jewish funeral before. Unlike Joe, who'd grown up in Bensonhurst with a pack of Jewish friends and who had worked in the city until the troubles began, Frank was strictly a Long Island guy. In fact, his friends used to call him the Babylonian, because he had been born, raised and rarely left the village of Babylon until he started in the oil business. Even now, he was more likely to fly to Orlando than drive into Manhattan.

"Why ain't the coffin opened?" Frank got up the courage to ask when they settled into their seats at the back of the chapel.

"Tradition," Joe said. "Only the immediate family can see him and then only for a few minutes. Jews usually bury the dead within twenty-four hours, but with the autopsy … "

Joe, checking his watch, noticed the front rows of the chapel were empty. The family would take those seats. The family—they were the biggest reason for Joe and Frank's disquiet. Frank had tried since Monday afternoon to contact them. Neither parent would come to the phone and the relatives who had picked up were either crying or curt. Frank wanted to believe it was all grief, but feared it was more than that.

Suddenly, the chapel fell silent. Everyone stood. The rabbi entered and took the podium. Behind him trailed a group of about fifteen people, all red-eyed, some crying. Though he had never met Cain's parents, Joe immediately recognized them. Cain had been a fifty-fifty child—tall and thin like his dad, darkly handsome like his mom. Cain's dad practically carried his wife along, her wailing so wrought with despair it cut through everyone like jagged shards of glass.

A few rows behind the family and to the right, Joe spotted a group of about eight people he assumed were from the group home. Some seemed very distracted or alone in this room packed with people. One, a stocky girl with Down's Syndrome, was crying with an intensity and purity that Joe had never quite experienced. Her tears were so unselfconscious, Joe was embarrassed for her. Or was he just jealous? It was hard to lose family. It was hard to lose friends. Joe had lost his share of each, but if he started crying, he feared he might never stop. Somehow, crossing paths with Bob Healy no longer seemed so important.

Finally, a woman came to comfort the girl. Joe guessed she was in her early thirties, elegantly slim, with neatly cut, shoulder-length blond hair. She wrapped her arms around the crying girl, rocking her slightly, whispering in her ear. At one point, the blond woman turned her head toward the rear of the chapel. Her eyes met Joe's. Well no, his met her's, but her eyes—light brown, close-set, intense—saw through him, or maybe saw nothing. Joe looked away.

The rabbi asked that everyone be seated. Only Cain's mother and the Down's girl continued crying. Prayers were offered, the cantor sang. The rabbi said his piece. Joe liked that the rabbi had known Cain his whole life and had a funny story or two to tell. Joe had attended far too many funerals conducted by the ranks of rent-a-clergy, men in black gowns reading the deceased's name off recipe cards. The priests at Ralphy's parish had refused to conduct his service or to even let his body inside the church. Rosemarie had been forced to shop for a cemetery that would take him.

Then the rabbi asked if there were any mourners who would like to come up and share their memories of Cain.

"By our very presence here today, we acknowledge our great loss, a loss that is as incalculable as the depth of the Lord's love. Then let us not try to measure the loss. We lay ourselves open to a period of grief and mourning," the rabbi said. "So, please, if any among you would like to speak in celebration of Cain's life, step forward and share your memories with us."

No one from the front two rows stepped up. Joe understood. Even though he believed that dead was dead, no matter what kind of package it came in, he knew that murder always seemed so senseless to the victim's family that it left them deaf and dumb. A cop knows better. Murder has sense to it, just not the kind the victim's family could comprehend.

The Down's girl got up, walked to the podium. Tears streamed down her round, round cheeks. Joe was struck by her face. It was a face meant to smile, he thought, not a face for suffering.

"My name is Donna," she said too loudly, not even trying to choke back tears. "Cain was my friend. He was smart and taught me things like his boss Frank taught him. The oil place was real important to him. He told me he felt all grown up there. I wanted him to take me there so I could feel that way too, but he said Frank wouldn't like that." She looked right down at Cain's parents. "He didn't want you to be mad at him. He didn't like when you got mad at him."

The blond woman walked quickly up to the podium, but without trying to embarrass the girl. She took Donna's arm and led her outside the chapel.

Then, to Joe's surprise, Frank was on his feet, moving to the podium. He never quite made it. Cain's mother charged him. She nearly knocked Frank off his feet.

"You son of a bitch!" she screamed, clawing at him. "You and that stupid business. I never wanted him anywhere near that dirty place. You killed him! You killed him!"

Joe and Cain's father pulled her off Frank. Joe diffused the situation by taking Frank out the door of the chapel that led directly to the parking lot and the waiting hearse.

"She's right, Joe. I as much as killed the fuckin' kid."

"She's grieving. She doesn't know what she's talking about," Joe said, remembering how Rosemarie had blamed him for Ralphy's suicide. "It makes it easier if you got somebody to strike out at. Trust me on this. Inside she's probably blaming herself. Shit, if I hadn't thrown the kid off my truck ... Who knows?"

They were halfway to Frank's car when two men blocked their path.

"What a pretty couple they make," the bigger one chortled out of the side of his sloppy mouth.

Cops, Joe thought. There was something vaguely familiar about sloppy mouth. He was a good six-foot-two, in his late forties with a jowly red face and a lazy left eye. His eyes seemed bluer than they actually were, in contrast to his ruddy complexion. He had the wide shoulders and thick body of an athlete gone to seed. The partner was small only in comparison. He was a six-footer, early thirties, clear brown eyes and a trim moustache. The bigger cop was strictly a Sears man. The partner had pretensions. There didn't seem to be a stitch of polyester on him.

"What can we do for you, Detectives?" Joe took the offensive.

"Listen to him, Kramer," the big man started up again. "The Snake knows we're detectives."

First Healy and now this clown; it was the second time in less than a week he'd been called by his old moniker and neither time did he much care for the speaker's tone of voice.

"Do I know you, Detective?"

The big man stuck his face in Serpe's. "I know who *you* are. That's what's important here. But just to show you I'm a fair guy,

I'll do introductions. That handsome devil there is Suffolk County Police Detective Jeff Kramer and I'm Detective Lieutenant Timothy Hoskins from the Fourth Homicide Squad."

Neither name rang Joe's bell. Frank remained quiet, still lost in his own sense of guilt.

"Detective." Joe nodded to Kramer.

"You don't remember me, do you, asshole?" Hoskins was at it again. "I'm Rosemarie's first cousin. You remember Rosemarie? You flipped on her husband Ralphy, you fuckin' disloyal sonovabitch."

"Yeah, now I remember you," Joe said calmly. "And I remember why I forgot you. What do you want? A little far off your patch, aren't you? This is Nassau County last time I checked."

"You don't worry about whose patch is where. This case here, the retarded kid, is mine," Hoskins sneered, throwing his thumb at the funeral home.

"But you didn't catch it," Joe blurted. "You weren't even at the crime scene."

"Well, it's mine now. Imagine how happy I was to see your name in the reports. I was fuckin' thrilled."

"And you're busting my balls why?"

"Other than because I feel like it and that I can … I just wanted to rub it in your face you dickless fuck."

"Hey!" Frank snapped out of it. "Watch your mouth, Detective."

"Take it easy, Frank," Joe warned, stepping between him and Hoskins.

"Yeah, Frank, take it easy," Hoskins aped. "Your employee here suffers from selective loyalty. When push comes to shove, he caves. You wouldn't want him to cave in on you."

"Rub what in?" Joe repeated.

"We got a suspect," Kramer finally spoke.

"That's great," Frank said.

"Yeah, great," Hoskins sneered. "You'll love this, Snake. The suspect's name is Jean Michel Toussant."

"Mr. French?"

"That's right, Snake, Mr. French, the mental health aide from the group home. We got witnesses say Toussant had it in for the kid. This tard who's next door to the kid says he heard a disturbance in the kid's room Saturday morning. Apparently, Mr. French had a puffy left eye that day. Told the rest of the staff he slipped on a wet floor and banged his cheek into a wall. Since the kid was gone, there was no one to dispute his account of things. And you'll never guess what we found in the victim's room."

"Blood spatter."

"Bingo!" Hoskins mocked. "See, Kramer, he walks like a cop, talks like a cop, but—"

Serpe ignored him. "So what's Toussant say?"

"Nothing yet," Detective Kramer answered. "We'd have to find him first."

"He ran?" Frank said.

Kramer nodded. "He ran. Left work early on Saturday, complaining about the puffy eye. Didn't show for work Monday. His neighbors haven't seen him."

Hoskins glared at his partner. If looks could kill, several generations of Kramers were doomed.

Kramer yawned. Apparently, he was pretty used to Hoskins' antics.

"You got any leads?" Joe asked.

"Fuck you, Serpe," Hoskins said. "I wouldn't a told you a thing, but now I'm glad Kramer got a big yap. It gives me a chance to tell you to keep your rat fuckin' nose outta this case. Maybe if you had protected the kid like you promised, we wouldn't be standin' here at his funeral makin' nice. Oh yeah, I heard about that. He bragged to all the tards about how his cop friend Joe was gonna protect him. Yeah, well you did a bang up job, didn't ya, Snake? Relyin' on you is like a death warrant."

Once again, Hoskins pressed his face threateningly close to Joe's. "What's a matter, Serpe, nothin' to say? See, partner, he knows

I speak the truth. He sold out his best friend. Both Ralphy and the kid would be alive if they hadn't met you."

"That's enough, asshole!"

All four men turned to see Bob Healy standing behind them.

"Hey, Kramer, it's a fuckin' cheese eaters convention. Let me introduce you to Ralphy's other executioner. This here is Bob Healy, detective first, NYPD, retired. That's right, in the big city you can make first grade jamming up your brother cops. How's it feel to build your career climbin' over the bodies of good men like Ralphy Abruzzi?"

Healy shook his head. "Listen, you sorry excuse for a human being. You don't think I know that cops get weak, that they fuck up like everybody else? I know. I know better than anyone. In I.A., I saw every kinda weakness a man can see. You think we made a case on Abruzzi because he was weak? If you think that, you're an even bigger shithead than I thought.

"Let me tell you a thing or two about the blessed St. Ralphy. St. Ralphy wasn't taking free coffee from the donut shop or veal cutlet parm heroes from the local pizzeria. He was leaking confidential police information to at least three different criminal enterprises. Not one, asshole. Not two, but three. To feed his fucking habit, he was willing to put his brother and sister officers at risk. And you know what, Detective, we had information that St. Ralphy's mouth got at least two C.I.s and one cop killed.

"Oh, you didn't know that, huh? Well, now you do. Since St. Ralphy ate his ammo, the department didn't feel it would serve any purpose to let the press get hold of that stuff. He saved his family and the rest of us a lot of grief. But who's gonna pay the bill for that dead cop, Detective? You? Your partner? Serpe's paid his fair share for being loyal to his friend and partner. So why don't you get off his back and let the man mourn the loss of his coworker in peace?"

Tim Hoskins was unmoved. "Fuck you. And fuck him. It's not enough that you drove Ralphy into his grave, but now you gotta smear his name. As far as I'm concerned, you're both F.F.L.

Remember what I said, Snake," Hoskins hissed, turning to leave. "I don't care if you and the tard were blood brothers. Stay the fuck outta my business."

Kramer nodded. "Gentlemen."

"F.F.L.? What's F.F.L.?" Frank was curious to know.

Both Joe Serpe and Bob Healy answered at once. "Fucked for life."

★ ★ ★

There are awkward silences and then there are awkward silences. The silence between Joe Serpe and Bob Healy as they sat across the diner table was excruciatingly loud. They avoided eye contact, drummed the silverware, folded the corners of the place mats.

Strange, but after days of planning what he would say and how he would say it, Bob Healy was at a complete loss. He hadn't anticipated the incident at the funeral home nor had he intended to blurt out the details of Ralph Abruzzi's treachery.

For his part, Joe Serpe had re-consigned Healy to that area of his head the retired I.A. detective had occupied for the last several years. He had thought of Healy like an inoperable tumor—one that had done its damage by disabling him, but wasn't going to kill him.

"You two married?" the waitress asked, a pot of coffee in her hand.

"What?" Healy startled.

"Only married couples look as uncomfortable as the two a you and have as little to say."

"I'll have some," Serpe said, pointing at the pot.

"Yeah, me too."

Frank Randazzo, still absorbing the hurt of the day, had excused himself shortly after Detectives Hoskins and Kramer made their exit. That left Joe Serpe and Bob Healy, the two old enemies, to sort things out for themselves. They agreed to meet at the Lazy Bull Diner in Smithtown.

"So, that stuff you said about Ralphy ... " Joe hesitated. "Was it—you know ... Was it—"

"—true? You tell me, Serpe."

"Jimmy the Geek and Moesha Green." Joe spoke the names. They were the names of two of his and Ralph Abruzzi's confidential informants who'd turned up dead in the last year they partnered up.

Healy confirmed it with a shake of his head.

Serpe wasn't satisfied. "The cop?"

"We ain't going there, Joe."

Serpe stared coldly across the table. Healy had crossed a line. Maybe Ralphy was worse than Joe thought and Healy a little better, but they still had issues between them that weren't going to go away with a snap of the fingers.

"You don't call me that."

"All right."

"So, if you guys had this shit on Ralphy, why—"

"—go after you? Why make you roll on your partner? Because, like I said before, the brass wasn't eager to wash the department's dirtiest laundry in public. A cokehead cop and his partner is one thing ... Dead informants and a brother cop, that's something else."

Serpe bristled. "I.A.B. sacrificed my career and my family, so the department didn't have to—"

"Calm down!"

"Fuck you!" Serpe got up to leave.

Now they were turning heads.

"Look, Serpe, I see you're pissed, but sit back down. I'm asking you, please."

"Okay."

"Let's lay the cards down here, right now," Healy said. "Forget the dead snitches, even the cop, for the time being. You knew Abruzzi was using for years. You never came forward. Okay, maybe I understand that. He was your best friend, your partner. But when he started skimming coke and money off the top … Well, there's a point where your loyalty to the department, to the other men and women who carry the shield, becomes bigger than your loyalty to your friend and partner.

"The truth is, Serpe, you fucked yourself. Now, if in your heart of hearts, you think I'm full of shit, well, stand up and walk away. We can go back to the way things were before last Saturday; you can put that chip back on your shoulder and I can look at you like any other scumbag cop who disgraced his uniform. You can be like that dickweed Hoskins and go on singing the praises of St. Ralphy till the cows come home."

Joe Serpe didn't move. He didn't even blink. He remembered the call. Rosemarie, frantic on the other end of the line. She couldn't get the basement door open and Ralphy wouldn't answer her. He knew he should just let her call 911 or he should do it for her, but he drove over to his former partner's house that one last time. It was the Sunday before Ralphy's sentencing hearing. Prison is no place for most people. It's worse for a cop.

Rosemarie, white and shaking with fear, met him at the garage door. Rosemarie, who was godmother to his son. Rosemarie, who had spit in his face the last time they saw one another. She latched onto his forearm so tightly it felt like a prayer. She could not speak. He unfurled her fingers and told her to go upstairs.

Joe tested the basement door. It wouldn't budge. He pressed his shoulder to it. It was barricaded. He didn't bother calling to Ralph. In the garage, he found the pump action shotgun clipped beneath the workbench. Ralphy kept it just in case. Joe kept one in his garage as well. Along the way, most cops get threatened with this or that. In Narcotics, you take those threats more seriously.

Joe aimed the shotgun at where he guessed the hinges on the other side of the door would be. *Cha-ching. Bang! Cha-ching. Bang!* The door did not fall immediately away. He put the shotgun down and pressed his palms against the top of the door and pushed. The door swung up and smacked into his shins. *Christ!* Ralphy had moved the pool table against the door. Joe pushed the door onto the pool table slate and climbed over it. Ralphy was in his favorite recliner, the back of his head spread over the chair and the wall behind.

Remembering that day he found Ralphy was like a shiv in the back, and he let Healy know he wasn't pleased.

"Why, goddammit?" he barked.

"Why what?" Healy asked.

"Why now, after all these years? Why tell me this?"

"My wife died six months ago."

"That's too bad, but what's that got to do with—"

"Makes you rethink things," Healy admitted, "when you lose somebody close."

Joe thought of Vinny. "What happened?"

"Pancreatic cancer. She went quick."

"Sorry."

"Mary, that was her name. She was brave about it, but I could see in her eyes she felt it was so unfair. I wished she would have said it just once. Then maybe … "

"You'd be able to live with it."

"Exactly."

"My brother, Vinny—"

"The fireman?" Healy remembered him from court. A big, quiet fellow, but always there.

"Yeah, he died at Ground Zero."

"I'm sorry."

"I guess there's a lot of shit we carry around with us," Joe said.

The awkward silence returned, but it was worse now. What was the protocol? Who would leave first? Was there anything more that needed to be said? Joe Serpe made the first move. He threw a five dollar bill on the table and stood to go.

"I guess I appreciate your telling me," he said, unable to look Healy in the eye.

"Thanks for hearing me out."

"Should we shake hands?"

Healy smiled up at Joe. "I don't suppose it would kill us."

They shook, but to Joe it still felt slightly like treason. Scars may lighten, but never vanish. Healy lingered. He knew there was one more thing he should have said, that he would someday have to say to Joe Serpe, but the talk had turned to Mary and Vinny Serpe. He had missed his moment. Still, he hoped he would be able to sleep a bit better tonight.

Monday
February 23rd, 2004

TRIPLE D CLUB

The flowers had turned black with truck soot, withered or frozen in the corner of the oil yard. The people from the group home had come the day after the kid's funeral and laid them out as a memorial to Cain. It was a recent phenomenon, this building of makeshift memorials—flowers and crosses at the roadside wherever an icy patch and oak tree had conspired to introduce an immortal teenager to his Maker. To Joe Serpe's way of thinking, a memorial was no more out of place at the scene of a murder than at the scene of an accident. They were equal wastes of time. He was quite sure God paid them little mind.

Even the bits and strands of yellow crime scene tape that remained had aged years in the week gone by since he and Frank had climbed into the tank and found Cain's body. The cops had impounded the International and it was unclear when it would be returned. In a bizarre twist that only modern life can produce, Frank now needed that truck more than ever. Mayday Fuel was benefiting from what politicians would call the "sympathy vote." The company's phone was ringing off the hook.

Neighboring oil companies had picked up the slack, making Mayday's deliveries until Frank could get his trucks rolling again. It had happened that way after 9/11. Some local oil companies were partially owned and manned by city firemen. Many were completely decimated. No one in the oil business had been wholly untouched by the events of that day. Some had drivers, like Joe Serpe, who'd lost relatives.

Joe went over to the makeshift memorial, kneeling down to try and read some of the cards Cain's friends and housemates had left behind. He didn't get the chance.

"Any news?" Steve Scanlon wanted to know.

Scanlon, a retired city fireman, owned Black Gold Oil. It was a smaller operation than Mayday's and Steve kept his two trucks parked in the next yard over from Frank's. Though they were competitors, proximity and terrorism had made allies, if not pals, of them. Steve's partner and several of his friends had fallen victim that terrible day. Frank had volunteered to do all of Black Gold's stops during the weeks following 9/11. Because of the cold weather and the small size of his fleet, Scanlon had been unable to return the favor this past week.

"No nothing," Joe said. "The cops have a suspect, but they can't find him."

"Hear about the murder over by Babcock last night?" Scanlon asked.

"Another one, huh?"

"Yeah, another kid. Paper don't say much, no details or anything. You think maybe there's a connection?"

Joe was unwilling to speculate. "I don't know what to think anymore. Let's let the cops do their job and see what they come up with."

"I guess you're right," Scanlon said unconvincingly. "Busy?"

"As a motherfucker."

"Then I'll let you get started. Be safe out there."

"Yeah, you too, Stevie."

"All right then … "

Scanlon walked quietly away. Joe was glad of it. Not only did he have a crazy day ahead of him, he had decided—in spite of his words to the contrary—that the cops had had enough time to do their work.

Joe was going to stick his nose in where maybe it didn't belong. He owed Cain that much and, unless some horrible fate suddenly befell Mulligan, he had nothing left to lose.

★ ★ ★

Bob Healy still wasn't sleeping very well. It was almost worse now than before he spoke to Joe Serpe. Like his Irish grandma used to say, "Setting things right is God's work and he seldom sees moved to do it." But Healy had already tampered with the past and there was no longer any question of leaving things well enough alone. Problem was, there didn't seem to be an easy way out of his predicament. Unless he called for another oil delivery, which Serpe would certainly avoid, Healy could think of no comfortable way to approach Joe.

Christ, Bob figured, he'd waited all this time. He could be patient a little longer. Something would come up. He only hoped it would be soon. He didn't know how much longer he could go without sleeping the night and this business of going to Mass was starting to get to him.

He opened the paper. S.O.S.—Same old shit:

IRAQ
IRAQ
IRAQ
MURDER

Murder! While it was surely true that New York City had come a very long way from its ugly streak of 2000 plus homicides per year, murder was still more than a trace element in its chemistry. On Long Island, however, murder was still big news. It was even bigger news when two murders occurred within blocks of each other, in the same town, in a span of eight or so days.

Bob Healy read the story with great interest, though there were few details. The victim was about the same age as Cain Cohen. His name was Jorge Reyes, a nineteen-year-old illegal from El Salvador. Like the Cohen kid, he'd taken a pretty bad beating. The preliminary cause of death, however, seemed to be related to several stab wounds which Reyes received. The cops were very vague about the number of wounds, location of the wounds, etc. In fact, the cops were being rather too coy about everything. Bob Healy could read between the lines. Reyes' murder was in some way connected to an ongoing investigation. Gangs, he thought.

With newspaper still in hand, Healy walked over to the phone and dialed. It was a long shot, but when a long shot is all you have, you play it.

* * *

Joe had done thirty stops, loaded twice and wanted nothing more than to try to meld his molecules with those of his fold-out couch. In order to resist that temptation, he had been feeding himself a steady diet of caffeine in the forms of coffee and Coke. He'd gone home, showered, shaved around his salt and pepper goatee, brushed his teeth and put on some clean jeans, running shoes, and a sweater. His hair was still wet when he rang the bell at the group home.

Only about half a mile east of the oil yard, and a few blocks west of where the Reyes kid's body was discovered, the group home looked like any of the other houses in the neighborhood. It had once been a large L-shaped ranch to which the previous owners had added a full second floor. That same owner had also converted the garage into living space. Joe had driven by this place dozens of times over the last three years and only once, when Cain pointed it out to him, did he ever take notice.

"Who's there?" a fuzzy male voice wanted to know.

"Joe Serpe. I worked with Cain and … "

A buzzer sounded. A lock clicked.

"Come ahead."

Joe walked down a short hallway to a small office. The two cheap plastic plaques on the door read:

Kenny Bergman

Home Manager

Joe knocked and let himself in. Bergman was seated behind a typical state-issue metal desk. The whole office was filled with what looked like used public school furniture. Dented aluminum and scratched wood seemed to be the unifying design elements. The wood-paneled walls were covered in diplomas, certificates and pictures. Bergman's desk was covered with stacks of paper, an outmoded computer and a phone. The only up-to-date thing in the office was the row of closed-circuit monitors on the shelf over the manager's left shoulder. Serpe recognized Bergman from the funeral chapel. He was a relatively young man–in his early thirties, maybe younger. He had a mop of curly brown hair and a full beard in desperate need of trimming, but Joe guessed Bergman did all right with women. If they were his pleasure. He had a straight nose, a bright friendly smile and big hazel eyes. But strain showed at the corners of his mouth, the creases in his eyes, the folds of his brow. The look of Bergman almost made Joe guilty for feeling tired.

Bergman followed Joe's eyes to the row of monitors.

"We had a security system put in a few months ago. It's weird. We never had any problems in the neighborhood and then word got out that a private agency was looking at the area as a site for another group home. Suddenly, we became targets of vandalism. People worry about their neighborhoods becoming warehouses for the unwanted. It's a shame."

Long Island is the NIMBY capital of North America. Not In My Backyard. You can't even fart on Long Island without doing an environmental impact study. Any proposal to build public works, power plants, highways, treatment centers, community centers, schools, even parks and hospitals comes under intense scrutiny and attack. If there was the slightest chance property values would be negatively impacted, forget it. The thing wasn't getting built. Offer to build a golf course, on the other hand ...

Joe held his hand out to Bergman. The manager stood and took it. Joe thought it a solid, honest shake. Serpe had never gotten over his belief in judging people by the little things they did. Handshakes were important to him.

"You were at the funeral," Bergman said. "Cain's mom went a little crazy on your friend. That was Frank Randazzo, the owner of Mayday, right? I met with him a few times. Good man. Good heart."

"You don't have to tell me."

"So what is it we can do for you, Joe?"

Serpe collected his thoughts. He knew he had no official standing to be doing what he was doing. He tried the truth.

"The cops have a suspect in Cain's murder."

"Yes, Jean Michel Toussant. He was employed here as mental health therapy aide."

"You know Cain told me he got rough with some of the residents."

Bergman snapped. "Look, Mr. Serpe, is this about a lawsuit or something? Are you trying to put the squeeze on us? We're a state-run agency. We hire people, and if we get complaints, we have to follow union procedures. I'm sorry if—"

"Calm down, calm down!" Joe held his palms up. "You're reading this all wrong."

Bergman sat back down, but his face was still red. "Then what is it you want?"

"I used to be a cop."

"Cain told us. He told everyone. So ... "

"I want to find this Toussant. The Suffolk County cops can't seem to do it."

"What do you expect me to do?" Bergman puzzled, his tone far from accommodating.

"That's a good question." Joe let his honesty show. "I was hoping I could talk to the staff, maybe some of the residents. Maybe Mr. Fren—I mean, Toussant, said something to one of them that would help."

"We all really liked Cain a lot, Mr. Serpe, but I couldn't possibly let you upset the residents or involve this home in any vigilantism. Besides, the police have already interviewed everyone here. I don't see what you'd be able to find that they weren't."

"Okay," Joe relented. "I understand you wouldn't want me upsetting the residents. How about the staff?"

"Like I said, Mr. Serpe, I'm afraid not, but I understand your impulse to help. Now if you'll excuse me, I've been working crazy hours since—"

Bergman was interrupted by a knock at the door.

"Come."

It was her, the woman who had comforted the Down's girl at Cain's funeral. She strolled right past Joe over to Bergman's desk and handed him a manila folder.

"These are the assessments you asked for, Ken," she said in a very businesslike tone.

"Marla Stein." Bergman gestured at Joe. "Meet Joe Serpe. He worked with Cain at the oil company."

Joe was already standing, hand extended. "Pleasure to meet you."

"Joe Serpe, the ex-cop, Snake," Marla said, a crooked smile on her face. "Cain was a big fan of yours, Joe."

"Marla is our staff psychologist," Bergman explained. "She works at many of our area homes, but has put in extra time since Cain's … I'm sure you understand."

"Of course, like grief counseling at a school when something goes wrong," Joe said, letting go of her delicate hand.

Bergman wasn't finished. "Joe was offering to help find Jean Michel, but I explained to him that we couldn't possibly help him."

"That was very generous of you, Joe."

"Thanks."

"Ken, I'm heading out," she said. "I'll be in Riverhead tomorrow morning, Patchogue in the afternoon. I'll be on call for you guys tomorrow night after seven."

"Great, Marla. Thank you."

Joe saw his opportunity. "I'll walk you to your car. If that's okay?"

"Fine," she said, smiling slightly and so Bergman couldn't see. "Just let me go to my office and I'll meet you out front."

The home manager didn't look pleased, but there was nothing he could do about it. Joe thanked him for his time.

Joe barely noticed it had started snowing. He was light-headed, his heart racing. He felt nervous, his bare palms moist, his throat dry. It wasn't as if Joe had abstained since his wife had packed up Joseph Jr. and headed to the Sunshine State. On the contrary, he'd been very popular with the Triple D Club at Lugo's. Triple D: Divorced, Drunk, and Desperate. That's what the drivers called the large group of women who made Lugo's their home away from home. Some were there so frequently, their real homes were in danger of becoming homes away from home.

Joe felt no guilt over his exploits with club members. He was as divorced and drunk as any of them and maybe a little more desperate. He had come to think of his nights with these women as an odd mixture of necessary pleasure and mutual short term punishment. Not that he was complaining about the sex. Desperation is like a jet engine afterburner. It kicks things up a few notches. No, it was the mornings after that did it; the hangovers, awkward goodbyes, and the lies of possibility.

Occasionally, Joe would break the unwritten club rules and date one of the members. It never lasted. Five weeks had been the limit. There was just too much baggage to deal with. The thing about it was, there were no recriminations after the parting of ways. Two nights later, Joe'd be seated across Lugo's bar raising his glass to the woman he'd just broken up with while buying a drink for the woman to her right. Just lately though, he had been avoiding the Triple Ds. He had grown weary of hopelessness.

"Hey," Marla said, walking up to the sidewalk where Joe was waiting. "My car's across the street. Hungry?"

Not really. "Very."

"Come on. Dinner's on me."

The Seaside Grill was a cozy restaurant on Portion Road just around the corner from Lugo's. Joe Serpe didn't know it existed until the moment he walked in. For the second time in less than a week, he found himself steeped in one of those awkward silences.

"Psychologists are trained to be very patient, Joe, but if you don't say something soon I'm going to scream."

Joe took his face out of his menu. "Sorry."

"It's not the Gettysburg address, but it's a start."

The waiter came to the rescue. Marla ordered a Cosmo. Joe a pint of Blue Point lager.

"I remember you from the funeral," Marla tried again.

"Helluva line, that. I've said it a couple of times myself in the last few days."

"It's weird, isn't it? It's like running into someone at the hospital and saying, 'Hey, she's my oncologist, too.' It's sad, but it's common ground. People search for it all the time, common ground."

"I guess."

"For a handsome man, you seem awfully uncomfortable around women."

The waiter gave Joe a brief reprieve by bringing their drinks.

"Cheers," she said.

They clinked glasses.

"Not all women," Joe said.

"Gee, you're a real charmer."

He was flustered. Marla reached across the table and put a calming hand atop his.

"That's not what I meant."

"I know," she said, giggling. "I'm sorry. Tell me what you meant."

"I meant that I've been on the sidelines for a long time and I'm unaccustomed to game speed."

"Christ, men and sports analogies."

"Yeah, that was pretty dumb, huh?" He felt himself breath normally.

She asked him to just come out and say what was on his mind. To his surprise, that's exactly what he did. He confessed that he'd thought about her ever since seeing her at Cain's funeral, but that he never really expected to see her again.

"I came to the group home hoping to get a lead on Mr. French."

"What an asshole that guy was. Hit on anything in a skirt with an IQ over ninety."

"I heard he hit anything with an IQ under ninety," Joe said, the bite of criticism flavoring his words.

Marla didn't take shit. "Hey, Joe, you ever work with bad cops? You report all of them? Any of them?"

He took that one full in the belly. "You got me there."

"Look, the office walls are paper thin at the home and I heard almost every word of your conversation with Ken. I've got my issues with Bergman, but he wasn't lying to you about Jean Michel. We work for the state. Disliking someone or even suspecting someone of misconduct isn't grounds for a firing squad. The mental health therapy aides are part of a union and there are procedures."

"You're right."

"So, aren't you going to ask me if I know anything about Mr. French?"

Joe obliged. "Do you?"

"No, but I'll ask around. Professional ethics don't allow me to question any of the residents, and I wouldn't in any case. But … " Marla smiled that infectious crooked smile, her eyes lighting up. "Gossip among the staff at these homes is what keeps people coming to work day after day. A lot of the staff has worked in other places, worked for different agencies. Many times they've crossed paths before. Maybe some of them have been on staff with Jean Michel somewhere else. Have you got a card?"

Joe laughed. "Oil drivers give out refrigerator magnets, not cards."

Marla slid a pen and her drink napkin across the table to Joe. "Write down the numbers where I can reach you."

He hesitated, then felt compelled to explain about Vinny's voice on the answering machine.

"You probably think I'm nuts," he said, sliding the pen and napkin back her way.

"No," she said, "I think you're mourning. There's no twenty-four second clock for grief."

"Christ, women and sports analogies," he chided.

"I deserved that."

They never ordered dinner. Two rounds of drinks later, they were standing in the parking lot. The snow had stopped, but had left a thin white blanket in its wake.

"You haven't asked to see me again," Marla said, writing her name in the snow on the hood of the car. "I know you want to."

"Pretty confident, aren't you?"

"It's not like reading tea leaves, Joe. If you're trying to hide your attraction, you're doing a shitty job of it."

"I'm not trying to hide anything, but—"

"I get that this is the part where you try to push me away," she said.

"I just come with a lot of baggage is all."

"We all do."

"Some more than others. I'm pretty well damaged goods and—"

"Shhh." Marla pressed her index finger across his lips. "Damage is a two-way street, Joe." She stood on her toes and placed her lips softly against his. Just as quickly, she pulled back. "My career is all about damage. I'm not afraid of it."

"You can't fix me," he heard himself say.

"I don't know you. And I couldn't fix you even if I wanted to. For now, I'd just like it if you'd kiss me."

Tuesday
February 24th, 2004

COPS AND MURDER

The tugboat seemed to glide. The stops came easy, went fast. Joe smiled when passing drivers, stuck for several minutes behind his soot belching truck, gave him the finger as they passed. And all because he'd kissed a girl. That's as far as it had gone, as far as he was willing to let it go. They'd stood there for an hour talking, kissing again, talking some more. She thought he looked like De Niro.

"You talkin' ta me?"

"Not 'Taxi Driver,' De Niro. Ich! 'Heat' De Niro."

That's what she'd thought when she looked back and noticed him at the chapel. He wasn't about to argue the point, though he didn't see it himself. Frankly, he didn't care if Marla thought he was a dead ringer for a horse's ass, as long as she was partial to horses asses.

It was about 3:00 PM. Joe had seventeen stops behind him with another seven to go. He was heading up to Commack from Bayshore along Crooked Hill Road when, just south of Suffolk County Community College, his winning streak came to an abrupt end. He had seen the unmarked Crown Vic in his sideview mirror when he passed St. Andrew, but paid it little mind. The tugboat could barely make the speed limit, let alone speed. Besides, he just figured it was an unmarked trooper on his way to the barracks along the Sagtikos Parkway.

The siren broke Joe's reverie and the display of lights were several months too late for Christmas. Serpe pulled over to let the Crown Vic by. The Vic wasn't having any. The cop at the wheel did a rather too dramatic skid in front of the tugboat.

"Asshole," Joe muttered, already scrambling to get his license, the truck registration and insurance, and bills of lading to account for all the oil he had on board.

By the time he had collected his paperwork, the two cops were almost to the driver's side door of the old Mack. Their faces were familiar and definitely unwelcome.

Detective Hoskins pounded on the door. "Outta the truck, shithead."

Joe complied, full documentation in hand. "What the fuck?" He handed the paperwork to the detective who, in turn, handed it to Kramer.

Kramer smirked, nodded and began strolling around the truck.

"Gotta love Suffolk County, they even make Homicide detectives do traffic stops. I guess they want you to earn that hundred grand plus, huh?"

Serpe knew he should just keep his yap shut, but couldn't resist. The disparity in pay between city cops and Suffolk cops was a real sore point. Though it was only about thirty miles from the Queens border east across Nassau to the border of Suffolk Count—they might as well have been light years apart. They call the NYPD "New York's Finest," but they're paid like New York's finest migrant workers. Suffolk cops, on the other hand, were the highest paid police force in the state, maybe in the nation. It was perverse, almost inversely proportional to the threat level faced by the members of each force.

"It's bad enough that I have to listen to that horseshit from my neighbors on the job in the city, but at least they're cops," Hoskins barked. "From the likes of you … " He spit on Joe's boots.

Joe was tempted to wipe the spit off on Hoskins' polyester pants by thrusting his boot into the detective's groin. He couldn't afford to be weak, not this time. Serpe didn't need to be a theoretical physicist to figure out the mechanics of what was going on, that Ken Bergman from the group home had dropped a dime on him.

Joe knew he was taking a risk by freelancing, but he didn't figure he'd get ratted out in less than twelve hours. It dawned on him that if he intended to take this thing any further, he was going to have to be more cautious, maybe even get a little backup.

"All right, guys, I get the point," Joe surrendered, figuring to speed up the process of intimidation. "I fucked up. I shouldn't have stuck my nose in."

"What the hell you talkin' about, Snake?" Hoskins chided. "Hey, Kramer, you know what this guy's talkin' about? We're stoppin' you for violations. Then, when *we're* done writin' you up, we're gonna give you a police escort over to the D.O.T. checkpoint on Wicks Road. Over there, they're gonna write you so many violations on this piece a shit you call a truck, both you and your boss are gonna have to take out second mortgages."

The D.O.T., a trucker's worst nightmare. The cops were hairy enough, but getting stopped by the Department of Transportation was the ultimate bureaucratic cluster fuck. They went over every inch of your vehicle: from tire tread to turn signals, from air horn to air brakes, from mirrors to manifolds. Then they ran your license, inspected your paperwork, matched your trip sheet against your bills of lading. Since 9/11 it had only gotten worse. The government had made a point of cracking down not only on vehicles that carried hazardous materials, but also on the men and women licensed to drive them.

"What you got, Kramer?" Hoskins was getting impatient.

"Big stuff, Tim," Detective Kramer called back to his partner.

"Oh yeah, like what?"

"Better come see for yourself."

When Hoskins and Joe Serpe got to the back of the truck, Kramer was fanning himself with three tickets.

"These are for you," Kramer said, handing the three citations over to Serpe.

Joe scanned them and laughed. They were all trumped up bullshit, but he found one of the alleged violations particularly amusing. "Dirty taillights, huh?"

"Yup," Kramer answered trying hard to keep a straight face. The detective walked up and wiped his fingers across the taillights on the rear of the tank. "Filthy," he said, showing Joe his dirty fingers. "How's a vehicle following close behind you going to see if you're turning or coming to a full stop? We must endeavor to keep our truck clean, Mr. Serpe."

Joe saluted. "Aye, aye. Now can we stop it here?" he urged Kramer. "I get that I stepped on your toes last night and I was outta line. I'm sorry. I really liked the kid and—"

"You're not listening, Snake," Hoskins interrupted. "Seems like a problem for you, listening. This got nothing to do with anything but your shitty truck. Kramer, give the man back his paperwork and let's you and me escort him over to the D.O.T. Then maybe after them guys write his boss a few thousand bucks in tickets, Snake will learn to listen better when Detective Lieutenant Hoskins talks to him."

Joe looked over to Kramer for a helping hand. Kramer shrugged his shoulders as if to say, "Hey, I think Hoskins is a dick, too, but there's nothing I can do about it. Next time, just do as the man says."

"Follow us," is what Kramer actually said.

Joe got back in the tugboat hoping that the detectives were satisfied they'd made their point and would just speed off. It was too much to hope for. Hoskins wasn't a second chance kind of guy. It was time for the Christmas in February motorcade to begin. Kramer turned his siren on full bore and put on a dazzling display of lights. Too bad Joe left his Santa suit at home.

Maybe because the D.O.T. inspector resented being used by the Suffolk cops to make a point, he took some pity on Joe. The truth is, almost every truck on the road is in violation of one or more local, state or federal statute. Sometimes it's major stuff, but mostly it's minor crap. Between the Suffolk cops and the D.O.T., Mayday Fuel Oil, Inc. was in the hole for about a thousand bucks in tickets. That wasn't the half of it. Between the downtime caused by having to yank the tugboat off the road to repair the violations and the cost of those repairs, Frank was going to be out another grand. Add this to the fact that it was now too late for Joe to finish his route, and the day was shaping up as a financial disaster.

Kramer and Hoskins were waiting for Joe as he pulled onto the south service road of the Long Island Expressway. They were a little less dramatic this time, Kramer signaling to Joe to come have a private word. Hoskins stayed in the Crown Vic.

"What now?" Joe wondered.

"I'm the junior partner here," he explained. "Look, I don't know if what Tim says about you is true or not. It's not my business, but he got a hard-on for you like nobody's business. And to tell you the truth, this case is none of your affair. Keep a low profile and we won't have to see each other again. You keep poking your nose in where it doesn't belong, Hoskins is gonna have your balls on a plate. Trust me on this, he'll pull your ass over every day and then he'll start on your boss' other trucks. He's a slash and burn kinda guy, Serpe, and he gets results. He'll take your boss down just to prove a point. Consider yourself warned."

"Thanks."

"Don't thank me. Just stay the fuck outta this. I don't enjoy this bullshit."

"One more thing."

"Yeah, what?" Kramer asked.

"Your taillights are filthy."

A smile flashed across Kramer's face. When he got back to the car, he didn't linger. The rear wheels of the Crown Vic kicked up road sand and pebbles as it fish-tailed away. Joe Serpe watched the Ford disappear into the rush hour traffic. Now there was little doubt about what he would have to do.

★ ★ ★

"What did you just say?"

"I said, I quit, Frank.

"What the fuck for? We got your last stops covered."

Joe pointed to the array of tickets spread across his boss' desk.

"You didn't do nothing wrong, Joe. I can't let you do this."

"It's not up to you. And it's not gonna stop here. Dixie'll pick up the slack. He'll like the extra money from the full time gig."

"But—"

"But nothing, Frank. You saved me, buddy, and I'm not taking you down with me. I've known too many cops like this asshole Hoskins. I'll be like a cancer to you."

"I hate this shit."

"Don't worry," Joe said, resting his hand on Frank's shoulder. "Maybe it'll be just temporary."

"You can't just leave this thing with the kid alone?"

"Maybe if he hadn't died in our yard, in your truck. Maybe if the cops could find this guy Toussant. Anyway, do you really want me to let it lie?"

"Yeah."

"You're a bad liar, boss. Besides, I'm doing it for me, really. I figure I got debts to pay."

"If that's the way you want it … "

"Sometimes it's not about wanting, but about the way it is. This is one of those times." Joe cleared his throat. "One more thing … "

"What's that?"

"Now that I quit, I need you to fire me."

Frank slammed his fist onto the desk. "There's no freaking sense in this."

"Maybe in the real world this doesn't make sense," Joe confessed.

"This ain't the real world?"

"When you're talking cops and murder, Frank, it's a different world altogether."

"Okay, you're fired."

"Not now."

"Not now what?"

"Don't fire me now."

"When?"

"Tomorrow morning."

"You have a time in mind?"

"Around 7:30, I guess."

"Why 7:30?"

"I want a very public execution."

"Public execu—"

"Trust me, boss. I know what I'm doing."

Frank threw his hands up in surrender. "Yeah. Yeah. Cops and murder, a different world altogether."

★ ★ ★

The red rectangle blinked three times at Joe when he walked into the basement apartment he had shared with Vinny for less than a year. They had shared a room all through their childhood and Joe remembered how much he wanted to get out, to finally get some space of his own. There were many nights during his marriage that Joe found himself wondering whether it was true love or his desire to get out from under that motivated him to buy an engagement ring all those years before. Whatever the reason, he got out, all right.

Then, when Joe was making an Olympic sport of being kicked out of everything from his house to his marriage to his career, Vinny was there to take him in. Joe's heart still ached at the memory of Vinny, stuttering madly, promising not to drive him away like he had when they were growing up. That's one thing Joe had set right before 9/11. Even in the depths of his misery, maybe because of it, he and his little brother had come back together. They were comfortable together in that basement apartment. Joe could have afforded to move to a better place a few years ago, but he couldn't bear the thought of leaving.

The three blinks of the phone machine were all messages from Marla. Joe's heart raced at the sound of her voice, her words barely registering. His response was so beyond voluntary that it frightened him. Maybe he couldn't control the beat of his heart, but he could control the speed at which things moved along. He was determined to take it slow with Marla.

By the second message, Joe could hear her words.

"Me again. Listen, there's a woman who drives a van for our group home in Patchogue who dated Toussant for about a month when they both worked for a private agency in Oceanside. She told me some stuff. I don't know if it'll help you, but … Give me a call."

"Hey," he said. "It's me."

"Hey, me. You got my messages?"

"Got 'em. So what's this about a woman—"

"What?" Marla interrupted. "No declarations of eternal love?"

Joe didn't know what to say. "I … I … Um—"

"Calm down, Joe. I'll settle for assurances you'll take me out Saturday night."

"I think I can manage that."

"Kissing. I'll need kissing."

"I can almost guarantee you that."

"Almost."

"Okay, I'll kiss you."

"Promise?"

"Needles in my eyes if I don't."

"Fair enough," she said. "So I guess you'll want to hear about what Corral had to say."

"Corral?"

"Corral Lofton. She's the van driver at our Patchogue home. She said she dated Jean Michel for about a month last year."

"Did she tell the cops this?" he asked.

"No."

"Why not?"

Marla hesitated. "She's married and … "

"And what?" Joe was impatient.

"He raped her."

"He raped her? Why didn't she—"

"—go to the cops?" she completed his question. "Come on, Joe, you were a cop. Do you really have to ask?"

"Tell me anyway."

"Like I said, she's married."

"Unfortunately, married women are raped all the time."

"But she lied to her husband about where she was that night," Marla shot back. "Corral told him she was going to the movies at the Green Acres Mall with her friends from work and then spending the night at her sister's apartment in St. Albans. It would have been difficult explaining how she wound up being raped in Brooklyn by a man she worked with. And there's other reasons."

"Brooklyn, huh?"

"That's the thing, Joe."

"What is?"

"The thing that might help you find Jean Michel."

"Brooklyn?"

"Jean Michel took her to an after hours club called *Rien*."

"*Rien*?

"*Rien*," she repeated. "It means nothing in French."

"Nothing nothing or like *nada* in Spanish."

"The latter. Apparently, Jean Michel's cousin owns the place."

"Did she tell you where in Brooklyn it was?"

"Not exactly. Corral said it was on Flatbush Avenue somewhere, past the junction. Does that make any sense to you? I don't know Brooklyn."

"I know the area. Great. Thanks. I think I can really do something with this."

There was silence on the other end of the phone.

"Is there's something else?" Joe prodded.

"Jean Michel's a sick fuck."

"Learn that term in graduate school, did you?"

"I'm human, too, Joe."

"Sorry. That was stupid of me. Go on."

"He drugged her, brought her to a room above the club and videotaped himself raping her. And ... And he—" her voice cracked.

"Okay, okay, I know this is hard for you, but it's important I hear all of it."

"He let other men have her, Joe, two at a time."

"I get the picture."

"It gets worse."

"Worse! How?"

"He showed her the tape."

"He what?"

"He made her watch it the next morning, all of it, while he masturbated in front of her.

And he threatened to send it to her husband if she went to the police. He still has it. So, if you find him, you can't let on how you–"

"I understand. He won't know how we found him."

Marla was confused. "We? Who's we?"

"I'm still working on that. How did you get Corral to tell you this? It couldn't've been easy."

"But it was, Joe. I'd like to think it's because I'm good at my job, but that's not the reason. I just happened to be a person she trusts and I gave her an opening. She's been dying to tell someone for a long time. It's hard carrying shame around with you."

"No one needs to teach me that lesson. Listen, I want you to hear this from me."

"Uh oh. What?"

"I quit my job today," he said.

"But you told me you love Frank and—"

"That's why I quit. It's a long story. I'll tell it to you Saturday night, okay?"

"Okay. Kisses guaranteed, right?"

"Try and stop me."

Joe found himself staring at the phone several minutes after he hung up. It wasn't about Marla this time. He was disgusted with himself. He was disgusted with himself because of all the emotions he could have felt for Corral Lofton, anger was the most prominent. If she hadn't cheated on her husband … If she had gone to the cops … Did Mr. French kill Cain? Maybe, maybe not. But Corral Lofton knew what a violent, horrible man Toussant was and instead of protecting other women or the people she drove in her van, she chose to protect herself.

That was life. People protected their own or themselves. It wasn't Joe's place to judge them. He had just forgotten how gray a cop's universe could be. When you go into the academy, you're certain there's a right and a wrong. Once you're on the job a while, the distinctions blur. When you're a narcotics detective, the distinctions get to be as fine as camel hair. Sometimes there are no distinctions at all.

Corral Lofton had lost a lot that night in the room above the club. She just couldn't afford to lose anything else. When he thought about it that way, Joe understood completely. Loss and Joe Serpe were far from strangers. What he had lost was gone forever, but Joe made himself a promise to try and get back some of what Corral had lost.

Out of the shower, he sat down on the couch to make a list of the people he could ask for favors. Mulligan snored loudly on the back ledge of the sofa. Joe made another list of cops and ex-cops he might ask to act as backup for him during his ride into Brooklyn. Neither list took long to complete. If Joe hadn't testified against Ralphy in open court, both lists would have been quite long.

If he had been willing to go to prison for Ralphy's sins, his old buddies would have respected that. That he had paid for his crimes of omission with his career, pension, family, house, and marriage wasn't enough. That Ralph would have gone to prison with or without Joe's testimony was of no consequence to the guys on the job. Joe was a rat. Period. No respect. No understanding. No second chances. In the course of a few short months, Joe Serpe had gone from prince to pauper. Not only wasn't there anyone to go to for help, there wasn't anyone who would even speak to him.

When he went back into the bedroom to collect his oil clothes and put them in the hamper he kept in the landlord's garage, the stink of them gave him an idea. It was an idea that ten days ago he wouldn't have believed was in the realm of possibility. That was before the world had changed on him again.

Ash Wednesday
February 25th, 2004

PRETZELS

The sun was almost warm on the skin, the sky cloudless. It was one of those rare February days when the weather implies that Spring might actually come. During cold, snowy winters, oilmen savor such days as this. Business slows down just enough to let you catch your breath. Your movements become less robotic. Lugo's would be packed later. In the meantime, it was a lovely day for an execution.

The yard was busy, but in a more relaxed way than it had been for weeks. When the weather's bad, the activity is all business. There's no wasted movement. Trucks are warmed up and moved out. Conversation is kept to a minimum. Greetings are grunts, nods, and waves. Today, guys from the truck repair shop and auto body shop next door to the yard were stopping by to shake hands, tell stories of their latest conquests, and near misses, but Cain's murder was still on everybody's mind, if not on their lips.

Frank was miserable. It wasn't an act. Still reeling from the kid's death, he hated to lose Joe, too. Dixie was a good driver, maybe better than Joe, but he was a real yahoo from the Florida panhandle who'd come up north on a football scholarship. He quit after one semester and stayed because he was too embarrassed to go on home. That was 1998. Frank liked Dixie well enough, although they had about as much in common as Robert Oppenheimer and Richard Petty. One of the barriers between Frank and Dixie had been removed by fate. Dixie never hid the fact that he didn't much care for "having that retard boy around." Truth was, Frank had had business enough for months to put Dixie on full time in his own truck, but he didn't care for Dixie's attitude toward Cain.

Promptly at 7:30, Joe Serpe strolled into the yard as if it was a day like any other. The timing couldn't have been better. Jesus from the truck repair place, Steve Scanlon from Black Gold, Dixie, and Pete from the deli were all there as witnesses.

"Don't bother, Joe," Frank spoke his lines with little enthusiasm.

"Don't bother what?"

"Coming into the office. You're done."

"Frank, what are you talking about?"

"You're a habit I can't afford, Joe."

"I'm fired?"

"I'm sorry, but yeah, you're fired. Here, this is for you." He held an envelope out to Joe.

"Why, because those asshole cops gave me those tickets? "

"Like I said, Joe, I can't afford this shit. This is business. Maybe if things settle down, I'll take you back. But this is costing me too much money."

"Fuck you!" he growled, smacking the envelope out of Frank's hand. "And you can shove your thirty pieces of silver up your ass."

"I'm sorry you feel that way, Joe, but I got no choice."

Joe flipped Frank the bird and turned to go. Although he knew it hurt Frank to go through this charade, Joe smiled to himself. Now if the cops came sniffing around, there'd be enough witnesses to insulate Frank. If there was fallout—and Joe knew there probably would be—from his going after Toussant, Hoskins and Kramer couldn't justify punishing Frank and Mayday.

Before he could get to his car, Joe was stopped by Steve Scanlon.

"Joe, Joe!" Steve called to him.

"Yeah, what's up?"

"Can we talk?"

"Why not?" Joe laughed. "I got nothing else to do with my time."

"Come on over to my office."

"Sure."

* * *

Bob Healy was getting impatient. Now not only did he have the old baggage he was carrying around for Joe Serpe, but he had information about the kid's murder. His suspicions were correct. There *was* an ongoing investigation. That's why Detective Lieutenant Asshole had been so rough on Serpe. He didn't want anyone stumbling into the trap that he had so carefully set, especially not a street smart ex-cop like Serpe. It had nothing to do with that Toussant guy.

Healy knew all about ongoing investigations. They become your babies. You nurture and protect them. You sacrifice for them. Trouble is, sometimes you lose perspective. Yeah, sometimes you ignore facts staring you right in the face. Sometimes you bend the rules into pretzels if it means keeping your baby alive. With the Serpe/Abruzzi Case, Bob Healy had mangled the rules beyond recognition. By the time Ralph Abruzzi killed himself, there were no rules.

One more day, Healy told himself. One more day. Then he would go find Serpe himself and lay it out for him. It was almost funny, the retired detective thought, that had Serpe not delivered his oil that day, he would have taken this to his grave. During a long, distinguished career, Bob Healy had prided himself on never sinking to the depths the renegade cops he hunted were willing to go. Once, and only once, *he* had taken the plunge. And that one time had led to suicide and disgrace. He caught sight of himself in the hallway mirror, the ashes on his forehead still fresh. If Bob Healy was ever going to get clean, he would need Joe Serpe's cooperation.

* * *

Black Gold's offices were in an old construction trailer dumped unceremoniously in one corner of the adjoining yard. You wouldn't think there could be much difference between rectangular plots of dirt where men parked big trucks, but you'd be wrong. Everything about this yard was second class to the one where Frank kept his trucks. Although he didn't own the land, Frank had paid for a layer of crushed concrete to be spread and tamped down over the dirt of his yard. This way, the trucks didn't create ruts in which water could collect. No water, no mud, no big patches of ice.

In summer, Steve Scanlon's yard looked like something out of the Oklahoma Dust Bowl. In winter it was an obstacle course of mud puddles and black ice. It wasn't even his yard, really. He was forced to share it with Harry's Truck Repair and Hot Tar Paving.

"So what is it I can do for you, Steve?" Joe wanted to know.

"It's the other way around, Joe. It's what I can do for you."

"Yeah."

"I saw what just happened."

"You and half the population of Ronkonkoma," Joe said.

"How'd you like to come drive for me?"

"Thanks, Steve, but I—"

"No, Joe, hear me out, okay? I'm thinking of expanding my operations. I've had two solid years and, truth be told, I need a guy who isn't constantly working around his firehouse schedule like my other drivers."

Joe understood. Steve made no secret of his distaste for the driving aspects of the business. He'd done his twenty years in the fire department, built Black Gold up, and didn't want to work as hard anymore. And since 9/11, he had never been completely thrilled with the drivers he had recruited from his old firehouses. Nearly all New York City firemen, because of their flexible schedules, have second jobs. Flexible or not, there were just too many times Steve was stuck with driving chores.

"I'm listening."

"Like I said, I've had some good years. I'm gonna invest in some new equipment. You and me both know my old Fords are falling apart. I've already got orders in for three new Sterling automatics. I'm gonna buy a piece of land with a building on it. I'm sick of this paying rent bullshit. If I could have a solid driver like you on board, it would free me up to work on my expansion. I'll give you twelve bucks a stop and load, plus an extra fifty bucks a day if you route the other drivers for me. I would also think about getting you some health in—"

"Let me think about it, okay?" Joe cut him off.

It was a very tempting offer and one, if only for appearance sake, Joe couldn't afford to dismiss out of hand. He couldn't risk raising suspicions that his firing had been a sham.

"I really wish you'd take it."

"I'm still taking in getting fired, Steve. Besides, I've been working six days a week, fifty weeks a year for the last three years running. Gimme a few weeks. Fair?"

"Fair enough. I'm telling you, Joe, I'm gonna be big. No reason you can't come along for the ride."

"We'll see."

They shook hands. As they did, Joe got an idea almost as crazy as the one he'd had the previous evening. He was so taken with it he neglected to let go of Scanlon's mitt.

"Everything okay with you?"

"What? Oh!" Joe let go. "Steve, in the city, can the fire department do building inspections without prior notice? Like in an after hours club or something?"

"Shit yeah. Especially in those joints. They do all sorts of illegal crap like blocking exits, barring windows … All kindsa stuff that'll get people killed. Remember that fire killed all them Salvadorans? Why you ask?"

Joe reached into his wallet and removed a scrap of paper. There was an address scrawled on the paper. He handed it to Scanlon.

"You still know anybody in the house that covers that neighbor-hood?" Joe asked.

"Of course," Steve said. "My last firehouse was in Coney. The captain over in Flatbush's a good buddy a mine. But that still don't answer my question."

"Steve, how would you like to gimme real incentive to come work for you?"

"What's one thing got to do with the other?"

"I was just getting to that."

* * *

Bob Healy had fallen asleep, the clicker wedged under his chin. He was never the type of man to nap, but since Mary's passing he found rare comfort in the occasional afternoon snooze. Now that he wasn't sleeping well at night, Healy was nodding off with far greater regularity. Unfortunately, he'd usually startle awake. He hadn't startled awake this time. No, this time, it was the doorbell.

He let the clicker fall to the floor, rubbed his stiff neck, wiped the drool off his chin with the sleeve of his shirt. The bell demanded his attention. He started for the door, but went back to shut off "General Hospital." It wouldn't do, having to explain his new addiction.

"For chrissakes! I'm coming. I'm coming," he screamed.

When he pulled back the door, he couldn't quite believe his eyes. It was Joe Serpe. And before Healy could invite him in, Serpe said, "I need your help."

Thursday
February 26th, 2004

GOOD DEEDS

ebruary was back to prove spring would never come. One of the great advantages of sub-freezing cold is that it keeps the stink of garbage to a manageable level. Both men were thankful for that much as they crouched near the dumpsters in the alleyway behind Jerk-It-Out Caribbean Palace. Buzzed as they were with a potent mixture of fear and vengeance, neither's stomach would have held up to the stench of rotting goat.

Still, they were getting impatient for their cue, dressed in their Halloween costume versions of firemen's uniforms. It wasn't the restaurant they were interested in, but the adjoining business. From Flatbush Avenue it seemed harmless enough—just another storefront with its front window and door blacked out. Maybe it was vacant and the "To Rent" sign had fallen away. Could be the windows were blacked out because there was construction going on and the owners didn't want the public to get a peek until grand opening day. Could have been a lot of things that it wasn't.

Joe Serpe knew exactly what it was and who was occupying the apartment above. Once Healy had agreed to help, Joe drove into Brooklyn and spent the better part of the evening parked across the street from the little storefront. Around 1:00 AM, a man fitting Cain's description of Mr. French strolled out the front door of the club. If Joe had any doubts about his identity, the man's nervous behavior gave him away. Joe followed him from across Flatbush Avenue. As the big man walked, he constantly checked behind him. He ducked into a doorway when he heard a siren. Walking back from the bodega, he kept in the shadows.

Click.

There it was. The lock release bar to the rear exit door of Rien had been pressed. Healy got out of his crouch, but Serpe held him back.

"Easy. We don't want anyone to see us if we can avoid it. Especially not the firemen."

"Right."

Joe counted backwards from ten.

"Let's go!"

They walked quickly across the alleyway, Healy's Glock at his side. It galled Joe more than he would have believed that he was unarmed. His carry privileges were yet another of the losses he'd suffered during the troubles. At the time, it seemed the least of his worries. He suddenly felt quite naked without a gun.

Healy pushed the door back and stuck his head in. Clear. They tip-toed into the bare-bulb hallway, a staircase to the left. The place smelled of next door's cooking, stale beer, and piss. Cases and cases of Red Stripe empties lined the walls. They could hear the less-than-cordial exchange between the firemen and a thickly accented man who Serpe assumed was Toussant's cousin.

Healy nodded at the staircase. Serpe shook his head yes. They didn't have much time and scurried up the steps. As they did, Healy clicked on the safety and buried the 9mm between the waistband of his pants and the small of his back. Near the landing, Joe pointed to his chest to indicate he would go in first. Healy didn't disagree. But even before they reached the top of the steps they could hear a woman moaning her way up the orgasm scale. Their job just got a little bit easier. At the very least, Mr. French would be preoccupied. If they timed it just right, he'd be downright distracted.

Although it had been several years, Joe's police skills hadn't completely eroded. He fingered the doorknob and gently tested it. He gave Healy the thumbs up. Then made a gun of his thumb and forefinger. Healy retrieved the Glock, released the safety and showed it to Serpe.

Serpe nodded, putting his index finger across his lips. Healy mouthed the word "Quiet." Though given the intensity of the woman's approaching orgasm, they probably could have set off a small atomic device and gone undetected. Serpe held up his right hand, fingers spread. He mouthed, "Five. Four. Three. Two. One. Go."

The doorknob spun easily and the door opened without much effort. Serpe stepped inside.

"That's it, baby! Yeah. Oh. Oh. Yeah. Yeah. That's it, baby! Just like that! I'm coming! Fuck me harder! Fuck me! Fuck me! Fuck—" her demands exploding into an aria of squeals and breathless moans.

"Oh fuck," Toussant groaned. "Oh fuck. *Moi aussi*, bitch."

If it wasn't so hideously perverse, it might have been funny. For there was Jean Michel Toussant, stiff dick in hand, shouting at the 52" inch plasma TV. On screen, the opera singer, a twenty-something leather-bound silicon blond, was coming to the end of her aria.

Healy aimed the Glock at Mr. French's most obvious target. It got very small very fast.

"My name is Serpe," Joe whispered. "Cain's friend."

Toussant's eyes got wide just before Serpe's fist connected with his jaw. Toussant was a big man, but he crumpled. Joe stopped with that punch. It was meant as a calling card.

"I don't kill 'im," Toussant pleaded, the side of his jaw already puffing out. "I 'it 'im, sure, dat is why I run, but I don't murder 'im, the monkey boy."

"Where are the videotapes?"

Mr. French was now completely confused. "What video—"

"The rapes, asshole!" Joe said. "All of them!"

Toussant was scared, really scared, and moved too quickly for Healy's liking.

"You flinch like that again and I'm going to kill you," he said. "Understand?"

French shook his head vigorously that he did.

"Videotapes?" Joe repeated.

"There," Toussant said, bobbing his head at a cardboard box at the side of the TV.

Serpe stood and checked it out. There were fifteen or so tapes in the box. Most were store-bought porn tapes. Three were homemade. Joe could not believe that these were tapes labeled: Anne, Corral, Kisha. He took the whole box. He also noticed a cell phone by the TV and slid that into his back pocket.

"Throw on some clothes, you sick fuck. We're going to have a little talk."

Panic again spread across Toussant's wide face.

Healy gave his best motivational speech. "Thirty seconds before I shoot your balls off."

Toussant threw on a sweater, jeans and slipped on a pair of ripped white socks. Without explanation, Joe told him to take off one of the socks. After Toussant complied, Healy handcuffed his wrists behind his back. Serpe tossed a beat up old Army jacket over Mr. French's shoulders. As he did, Joe slipped a Glad bag filled with several small vials of crack cocaine into the pocket. Neither Toussant nor Healy seemed to notice. That done, Serpe shoved the balled sock into the big man's mouth. Toussant gagged, but a look at Healy's sidearm convinced him not to spit it out.

Toussant's cousin was still arguing with the fire inspectors as the three men came down the stairs and out the backdoor. In total, it had taken less than five minutes from the time they entered the rear door of Rien till they were at Joe's car. As best they could tell, no one had seen them. Healy and his Glock kept Mr. French company in the backseat. The timing couldn't have worked out much better. They would make their destination at full nightfall.

Joe Serpe had no clue as to what Scanlon had told his captain friend to get him to cooperate. He didn't need to know. Whatever line of shit Steve had passed along, the backdoor at Rien was opened when it was supposed to be and now they had Toussant. Serpe wasn't too worried about there being any repercussions from their snatching the big man. He doubted Toussant's cousin would want to advertise the fact that he'd been harboring a murder suspect. Unfortunately, Joe had had to tell Scanlon a rough approximation of the truth. He was more than eager to help, saying he had always liked Cain.

Getting Bob Healy to cooperate hadn't been quite so easy. Especially after Healy had explained about the things he'd discovered on his own since their uneasy meeting at the diner.

"You know about the G.A.T.F.?" Healy asked.

"The what?"

"Gang Activity Task Force. It's a joint NYPD, Nassau, and Suffolk task force. You read the papers, don't you?"

"I stopped reading the papers or watching the news when they were harassing my wife and kid. They actually followed my son to school and asked him about what his dad was doing to his Uncle Ralphy."

"Sorry," Healy said. "I guess it was pretty rough on your family, the trial and everything."

"Rough's one way to describe it," Joe agreed. "Hell is another. The last time I watched the news was to get info about Vinny. I was out delivering that day and some guy, his face as white as a sheet, invites me to come into his house. That's when I saw the first tower collapse. I didn't know it, but I was watching my brother die."

"Look, Serpe, I didn't mean for the conversation to go this way."

"I realize that."

"Why I asked about the papers is that if you read them regularly, you'd know there's been a huge increase in gang violence on the island. With the influx of all these illegals, it was bound to happen. It was the same when your people and my people came over. For a long time the only Hispanic gang on the island was the Latino Lobos."

"I know all about them," Serpe said. "They started in the city. Mostly Puerto Ricans and some Dominicans. Big into dealing and protection. I arrested plenty of 'em. But I've been outta the loop for a while, so I didn't know they'd spread out here."

"Yeah, mostly to places like Freeport and Bayshore. It was pretty much contained until the big influx of day laborers from Mexico and El Salvador the past couple of years. Now you got big Hispanic populations over in Farmingville, C.I., Brentwood, and Huntington Station."

"The cops gave Frank a warning a few weeks ago about an increase in vandalism and stuff, but they didn't make the particulars clear. So now there's competition between gangs?"

"Exactly. I've always followed the news real carefully," Healy said. "And over this last year there's been a big increase in violence between the Lobos and the MSS, the MexSal Saints. But it was mostly them killing each other. You know the old cop philosophy."

"As long as they kill each other, who gives a shit?" Joe laughed.

"That's the one. But violence spreads. Always does. Some civilians have been getting caught in the crossfire just lately."

It hit Joe. "Cain?"

"Well, yeah, apparently the cops think so. It didn't occur to me until that Reyes kid was killed, then I did some checking. Did you take a good look at the truck you guys found the boy's body in?"

"What do you mean take a good look? I saw that truck every day."

"But the day you found him, did you see anything unusual by the truck or some spray paint on the truck itself?"

"No. I was a little preoccupied that day," Joe said, sarcasm leaking in. "Why?"

"Cops found cans of red and black spray paint and a faint black spray on the tank itself. It was there under the snow, I guess," Healy said. "The Saints' colors are red and black and their symbol is a black dagger surrounded by a blood-dripping red halo. I think you can see where I'm headed with this."

"You don't have to draw me a map. Cain tried to stop them from fucking up the trucks and got killed for his troubles. It's just the kinda shit he would pull, too. Fuck!" Joe slammed his fist into his thigh. "He got real attached to things, like this dumb shirt I had made up for him. I could just imagine what he'd do if he found someone screwing with the trucks."

"The Lobos and the Saints are like rival tigers pissing on trees in the jungle. Marking territory is part of their initiation rites. Rumor has it that another part is—"

"—killing a rival member. But—"

"That's right. Whoever was in your oil yard that night didn't do either job right. This Reyes kid, the cops think the Saints killed him because he fucked up, brought dishonor on them."

"Where did you get all this shit, Healy? I'm thinking it didn't all come from *Newsday*."

"My little brother George works in the Suffolk County D.A.'s office. He hears things."

"Hoskins and Kramer part of this task force?" Joe asked.

"Bingo. That's why they're on the case even though they didn't catch it. The minute word got back about the spray paint and the paint on the truck, the case was theirs. So you see, going after this Toussant guy isn't worth it."

"I never really thought he did it," Serpe confessed. "But you can't tell me he didn't hit the kid. Trouble was brewing between them for weeks. Besides, whatever went on between Cain and Toussant started the whole chain of events. I can feel it in my guts. I'm going after him whether you come or not."

"Look, Serpe, I'm not saying the guy's not a total piece a shit, but—"

"But what? You think it's too thin, right? It's not worth the risk. You fucking I.A. guys kill me. You have any idea how many times me and Ralphy risked our necks for nothing, to go after some little pissant dealer who wasn't half the—"

"Whoa! Whoa!" Healy put up his palms. "The last time I looked, there wasn't a cop of any kind in this room. We're just two private citizens here and that's all we are. There's a lot of mutts and skells out there on the street, a lot of them worse than this scumbag Toussant."

"You think so, huh? You wanna ask Corral Lofton?"

After Joe recounted what Marla had told him, Bob Healy didn't need any more convincing. But after he agreed to help, Healy did say one thing to Serpe that stuck with him and probably always would.

"You know, Hoskins was right about one thing. We *are* both fucked for life. And we can't buy our souls back with good deeds."

About twenty-four hours had passed since that conversation. Now they rode a long way in silence, Healy occasionally interrupting the quiet to reassure Mr. French. "Just keep calm and nothing's gonna happen to you. It's the Suffolk Police you have to worry about."

As he steered the car through the setting darkness, Serpe noticed his right hand had swelled considerably. He flexed it with no small measure of difficulty. Only in the movies, he thought, could you smack a man square on the jaw with your bare knuckles and suffer no damage yourself. But that was the thing about movies, wasn't it? There weren't any consequences, not really. In make-believe, there never are. Trying to shake some of the pain and stiffness out of his puffy fingers, Joe understood there would be consequences to what he was planning to do.

"We're almost there," he said, half-turning to the backseat. Then he refocused, trying to find the turnoff for the unmarked road.

Getting Toussant out of the car was no mean feat. They literally had to drag him out, but neither Serpe nor Healy could fault him for resisting. Most people don't suffer their impending executions gladly. Once they'd gotten far enough into the woods, Joe removed the sock from Mr. French's mouth. He screamed. *"M'aidez.* Somebody 'elp me."

Serpe was amused at the irony in that. "Scream your head off, asshole. Unless the local deer figure out how to dial 911, you're fucked."

Next, Toussant did the second most logical thing after screaming; he ran. At least he tried to, but Healy slammed his right leg across the back of Toussant's knees. The Haitian's legs went rubbery. First he teetered back, then pitched forward. The two ex-cops let him lay face down in the frozen compost of fallen leaves, bark, and squirrel droppings for a minute before propping him up into a squatting position.

His first two options gone by the boards, Toussant went to his third; a combination of begging and bargaining. Between pleas for his life to be spared, promises of an impending religious rebirth and feeble claims of innocence, Toussant rolled over on his cousin for dealing Ecstasy and coke out of his club.

"Just shut up and listen," Healy barked.

Serpe took over, kneeling close to the big man, whispering in his right ear. "I wanna know exactly what happened that Saturday morning, minute by minute. I wanna know what you did to Cain, when you last saw him. The first time I think you're lying to us, I'm gonna nod to my partner over there and he's gonna press that gun right up to the back of your head. Its muzzle will be so close that when he pulls the trigger, it'll light your fuckin' hair on fire. Luckily, you'll be too dead to give a shit."

Toussant didn't hesitate. As he had admitted back in Brooklyn, he said he had hit Cain, but claimed that the kid had taken the first swing. Pressed for a reason why, Toussant confessed to goading Cain into it.

"I call 'im names. I tease de monkey boy about 'is big cop friend and 'is boss. I say it stink in 'is room."

Joe Serpe had no trouble believing Cain would have had a go at Toussant after that. But even with the kid's surprising strength, he'd be no match for a man like Toussant.

"Firs' 'e punch me across the face, then the eye. I 'ave to defend myself. You would defend yourself, no?"

Healy and Serpe let that question hang in the air like the smell of rotting undergrowth. That made Mr. French nervous. He started talking. Whining. Complaining about how hard his life was.

"These retards, you think it is a joy to work with them? They are terrible, dirty and stupid."

If he was trying to win his captors over with his charm, he was doing a poor job of it.

"So why do you work at these homes if you hate the residents so much?" Healy was curious.

"Women." Toussant blurted out before he could stop himself.

"You fuckin' piece of shit!" Serpe backhanded Toussant with his good hand, sending him sprawling. Joe wanted to grab the gun out of Healy's hand and do the world a favor. There was evil in the universe, enough of it so that removing Toussant would go unnoticed. Joe wasn't interested in whether Mr. French was born a violent pig or if he developed into one.

"Take it easy, Serpe," Healy warned, seeing the brewing storm in Joe's eyes. "Let's get this over with."

Joe took a deep breath. "Okay, Toussant, what happened after you hit the kid?"

"'e was difficult to control at first, but I learn 'ow to 'andle such people. The monkey boy is crying, threatening me you will kill me."

A broad smile crossed Serpe's face. "Yeah, and then … "

"I keep 'im restrained until 'e calm down a little. I say for 'im to forget it if 'e knows what is good. Then I leave the room and I never see 'im after that."

"And what time was that?" Healy asked.

"Please, I beg that you don't kill me. I 'ave many children. I—"

"What time, shithead?" Serpe screamed.

"I don't remember, early. Seven-thirty maybe. I don't know."

Silence again dominated the night.

Healy and Serpe propped Toussant up once more. The big man was now beyond begging. He body trembled in their hands. Reluctantly, Healy handed the 9mm to Serpe. If ever there was a test of trust between two men, this was it. The sight of the gun changing hands was too much for Toussant. Vomit spewed from mouth in a steady stream and, his hands still cuffed behind him, he fell forward right into his own puke.

Healy straddled Toussant to remove the cuffs, but the Haitian's panic got the better of both of them. He squirmed and bucked, knocking Healy off him. Serpe pressed his boot down on Toussant's neck. That seemed to take all the fight out of him. Healy took off the cuffs. They both stepped away from Toussant.

"Okay, shithead, start running," Joe said.

"You are going to kill me?"

"Ten, nine, eight, seven … "

Jean Michel Toussant didn't need to be told twice. He ran wildly, further into the woods.

When they got back to the car, Joe Serpe retrieved the cell phone he'd lifted from the room above the club. He dialed 911.

"Hurry," he said breathlessly when the operator got on. "There's a crazy man assaulting people along the nature trails in Bethpage State Park. Hurry."

As they approached the Seaford-Oyster Bay Expressway, Serpe tossed the phone down a storm drain.

They were nearly to the Sagtikos Parkway before anything but ambient engine noise and talk radio could be heard in the car. Both men had kept their very loud thoughts to themselves. Serpe, feeling unexpectedly guilty, could not get Healy's admonition about the relative merits of good deeds out of his head.

"You trusted me with your piece back there," Serpe said. "I appreciate that."

"Yeah, especially since you wanted to kill him."

"You noticed that, huh?"

"I noticed."

"Then why'd you do it?"

"You're not exactly a stranger to me, Serpe. You never struck me as the executioner type," Healy answered.

"If anyone ever deserved executing, that piece of shit did."

"I don't disagree, but you're still not a murderer."

"What am I, then?"

"A guy who plants a little evidence, maybe."

"You saw—"

"Yeah, I noticed that too."

"I couldn't just let him walk away."

"I suppose not. What are you gonna do with the tapes?"

"Me, I don't know what to do with them, but I think I know someone who will."

"Okay. So what's our next move?"

Serpe was shocked. "*Our* next move? There isn't a next move for me or you. The cops will pick up Toussant and our part in this will be over. I guess G.A.F.F. or G.A.F.T. or whatever the fuck the name of that task force will have to do the rest."

"Yeah," said Healy. "I guess."

When they pulled up in front of the lonely split ranch at 89 Boxwood, Healy hesitated, staring at the house as if for the first time.

"I used to love this house," he whispered as much to himself as to Joe Serpe. "Now, when I leave it, I almost hate to comeback. I hate it."

"You don't hate the house," Joe said. "You hate that she's not there waiting for you. You forget sometimes, right?"

"Less now than I used to."

"It gets easier, but it never gets easy."

Healy shook his head, unconvinced.

"So thanks for helping me out." Joe offered his hand. "You did a good thing today."

"I was glad to help." He shook Serpe's hand. "Listen, I'll have the shirt dry cleaned and mail it back to you," Healy said, referring to one of Vinny's shirts Joe had lent him as part of their charade.

"Keep it," Joe said. "Or give it away. I've been hanging on to some of my grief a little too long also."

"You sure?"

"I'm sure."

Bob Healy waited until the car was completely swallowed by the night before stepping toward his house. He never did tell Joe what he had meant to, but he wasn't terribly bothered by it this time. In spite of Serpe's words to the contrary, Healy knew they would be seeing each other again, and soon.

Friday
February 27th, 2004

Friday
February 27th, 2004

ON THE WATERFRONT

It had been a long time since Joe Serpe picked up a *Newsday* with his twenty-four ounce coffee at the 7/Eleven on Portion Road. Sometimes he couldn't avoid a glimpse at the screaming headlines of the New York daily rags as he passed the rack on his way to the coffee pots, but that was about the extent of his media interest. Blessedly, the tugboat had no radio and he never watched TV news. As far as he could tell, he was none the worse for his less than encyclopedic knowledge of world events.

After Vinny's death, Joe's life had gotten very small. He liked it that way. With his family gone and his brother dead, the outside world couldn't touch him. He had Mulligan, his sack time with the Triple D ladies, and his work. In the last three plus years, the only aspects of his life that ever really changed were the faces of the women he slept with and the price of oil. And with oil, price was almost beside the point. It was like food in that respect. People had to eat and they had to heat.

Ossie, the Pakistani counterman, gave Joe his usual broad smile, but this morning mixed with a tinge of confusion. Joe noticed a questioning look in Ossie's eyes. This was not lost on Joe. When he worked undercover, his life had often depended on his ability to read people's faces. If he couldn't detect a situation going sour from the tiniest changes in a dealer's demeanor, all the backup in the world would have done him no good. There was less at stake this morning. As Joe slid a five dollar bill across the counter, he mumbled something about movie listings.

Serpe sat in his car, sipping his coffee, scouring the pages for word of Toussant's arrest. Joe smiled as he turned the pages, once again enjoying the feel of the paper in his hand. Before the troubles, he had been a newspaper junkie, reading two, sometimes three papers a day. It used to drive Ralphy crazy. Suddenly aware of his pleasure, Serpe also began to realize how he had let his life atrophy. In a weird way, Cain's murder had given Joe his life back. The long sleepwalk was over.

He had purpose. He had Marla, he hoped. And strangest of all, he had Bob Healy. Though Joe had no idea how to characterize their relationship, they definitely had one. As much as Joe liked Frank and as close as they had become, it wasn't a cop thing. In an inexplicable way, Joe had felt closer to Healy during their silent ride from Brooklyn to Bethpage than he had felt to Frank in the whole time they were acquainted. When this all got sorted out, he'd have to have a long sit down with Healy. Not only to thank him for his help, but to finish up their business.

As forthcoming as Healy had been about what had transpired four years ago, Joe got the sense that the former I.A. detective had more to tell. Last night, and when he came to ask for help, and even at the diner that first time, Joe sensed Healy on the verge of saying something, but he seemed never to find the words. There were still details missing. Joe had questions that begged for answers, itches that needed scratching. That he and Ralphy had been targets of the I.A.B. was pretty fucking self-evident, but why, he wondered, and for how long? Who initiated the investigation? Was it Ralphy's carelessness or Joe's covering for him that had gotten I.A.'s attention? None of that ever came out at trial. But as ready as Serpe was to finally hear everything there was to hear about those dark days, he knew he could wait a little while longer. He had something else to take care of first.

Toussant did not make the paper, at least not *Newsday*. Joe wasn't particularly surprised by this. First off, he had no idea how long it had taken the cops to track down Mr. French, there in the wilds of Nassau County. With its five golf courses, polo grounds, tennis courts and nature trails, Bethpage State Park was pretty damned expansive. If the cops hadn't gotten to him quickly, a shrewd and desperate man like Toussant might be hard quarry, even if he was as big as a house and stank of vomit. Secondly, he hadn't been big news to begin with. Like Healy said, the Suffolk cops had lost interest in him. Gangs had become the focus of their investigation.

And now they were the focus of Joe Serpe's unofficial inquiry as well. In spite of what he had said to Bob Healy last night, Joe had no intention of letting this go. Group blame gave him no comfort. No, someone, a person, had killed Cain. To Joe, murder was a kind of robbery, the worst kind, the kind that takes everything away. It didn't matter whether the killer was a Shriner, an alien, or a MexSal Saint. Responsibility lay with the individual, not with a group. Joe couldn't help but remember Abe Hirsch, the old guy who owned the candy store on Avenue P back in Bensonhurst.

Joe was about ten when he became aware of the funny numbers tattooed on old man Hirsch's forearm. When he asked his dad about it, Joe Sr. explained about the concentration camps during WWII. A few years later, Joe got up the nerve to ask Mr. Hirsch about the camps. Initially, the old jew was shocked that this skinny little Italian kid should be so interested in the camps.

"Nazis, Nazis, everybody blames the Nazis," Hirsch had said. "Vas is a Nazi but a man in a uniform? It was men killed us, not Nazis. I blame the men, not the uniforms."

Until Healy had spoken about the potential gang involvement, old man Hirsch's words had never quite struck home. Now, at this late date, he understood. Maybe Cain had interrupted this Reyes kid spray painting the trucks. Maybe he had killed Cain. Maybe he had some help. Joe had his doubts. Whereas Cain was no match for a guy like Toussant, he'd give almost anyone else a hard time. In any case, Joe was going to find out. He put the paper down, shifted into reverse and headed east down Portion Road toward Farmingville, where it turned into Horseblock Road.

There in front of the convenience store on Horseblock Road stood a hundred squatty, brown-skinned men, their mouths and nostrils pumping clouds of foggy breath into the air like little chimneys. There were few hats in the crowd to cover the heads of uniformly black hair. Many of the men wore inadequate clothing against the biting cold. The standard uniform seemed to be a denim jacket over a hooded sweatshirt, dirty jeans and dusty work boots. No gloves but work gloves. Some men wore uncomfortable smiles. Some laughed as a hedge against the grind. Mostly there was blankness in the round faces of these men descended from Aztec, Incan, Mayan, and Spanish blood. But in their eyes Joe Serpe thought he spotted a toxic mixture of hope and bitterness—the incremental destruction of one leading directly to the other.

Joe had seen this spectacle several times as he often began his days with a few deliveries in Farmingville or Selden before doubling back west into Brentwood and Bayshore. But he had never before taken the time to witness it. Before today these men had simply been part of the scenery, not unlike the mailboxes or utility poles he passed as he drove from stop to stop. Now they had been transformed from things to people. Each had a name. Each had a heart and blood and a story.

Serpe parked his car and watched as pickup truck after pickup truck pulled to a nearby curb. A white man would get out of the truck, talk to a chubby man at the curbside, then bark something at the huddled brown men. The heavyset man would translate. Hands would go up in the crowd. The white man would wade through them like a rancher culling his herd. He would select one, two, three of the men. These were the lucky ones, the ones who would work ten hours for lunch, a hundred bucks cash and maybe a *cervesa* at day's end. The luckiest of the lucky would ride in the pickup cab with the contractor. The others would secure their sweatshirt hoods, lift their futile jacket collars and hunker down together against the bed walls of the pickup.

Joe wasn't close enough to hear, but he didn't have to be. He understood the nature of these transactions. This was a shape-up right out of "On the Waterfront." Scenes just like it were being repeated with increasing regularity all over Long Island. There's always a hungry market for cheap labor and just below our southern border were millions of impoverished people eager to cast themselves into its maw. There wasn't a landscaper, contractor, builder, concrete man, roofer, or mason on the island that didn't avail himself of their services. They came cheap, worked hard, didn't bitch. You didn't have to pay their taxes, supply insurance or follow safety regulations. They were like little brown-skinned *fuck you's* to OSHA, Social Security and the IRS.

Across the street from the shape-up, close to Joe's car, were a second group of about ten people, very angry people. This group was comprised of an equal number of white men and women ranging in age from twenty-five to sixty-five. They were better protected against the weather, if only by their rage. They spat a constant stream of insults, slogans, and taunts across Horseblock at the workers. They carried a mixture of printed and handmade signs which bore slogans like:

AMERICA FOR AMERICANS
MEXICO FOR MEXICANS
or
CHEAP LABOR=
LOSS OF JOBS,
LOSS OF PRIDE,
LOSS OF COUNTRY
or
STAND UP TO THE BROWN TIDE
RESIST THE SILENT INVASION

And those were the friendly ones. A man with a bullhorn stepped into the midst of the ten angry citizens, adding his voice to theirs and fuel to the fire.

"We are being invaded, degraded and infiltrated," he bellowed. "And the worst, most unholy part of it all is that our own government, the men and women we elect to represent us, have sold us out for a plate of rice and beans. Do they care that with cheap labor comes costs to our schools, our hospitals? Do they care that these people come with their violence, their gangs? Ask your congressman, your state senator, your governor, ask them if they are aware that these people are here illegally. Of course they know. They admit it. But what do they do about it? They want to take your tax dollars and build these invaders a hiring hall. How dare they? How dare they?"

Joe lost interest in the demagoguery. He felt sorry for everybody except the asshole with the bullhorn, who, Serpe was willing to bet, had come from out of state. He was sure the people in town had some valid worries and complaints, that most of them probably wanted nothing more than to lead quiet, peaceful lives watching their kids and property values grow at a healthy clip. He also had little doubt that the men across the street would have liked nothing more than to go back to their families, to warm weather, and to steady work.

As badly as he felt for the parties involved, this wasn't his fight. He had the kid's murder to worry about. Joe waited for the traffic to pass and made a u-turn across the wide boulevard. It was his turn to choose men from the crowd, but not to clear a lot or put on a new roof. What Joe wanted was information.

"Two men," he said, wading into the crowd. "Speak English. Good English."

Some of the hands that shot up with Joe's first demand, went down just as quickly at the second. All the men eyed Joe with suspicion. Sure, the yankee looked like a working man in his Carhartt jacket, stained coveralls, Mack baseball hat, and boots. He walked like a working man, maybe even smelled like one, but his car was all wrong. Two years back, a few of the day laborers were lured to a deserted work site and nearly beaten to death. Then, only a few months ago, some neighborhood kids had set one of their houses on fire. They didn't need the protesters across the street to remind them they were targets. Nor was Joe under any illusion that he was fooling any of these men, but he also understood the allure of money. He had little doubt that these guys had taken precautions.

Joe was presented with a group of about ten men from which to choose. He didn't realize how ill-prepared he would be for the task. There was nothing in his past that would have readied him for it. He couldn't give a quick English exam or ask which of the men knew the most about the Latino Lobos and the MexSal Saints. It reminded him of the time he'd had to pick out his mother's coffin. There he was in the basement of Gargano & Sons, the funeral director in tow. How do you choose, he wondered? You can't kick the tires or take it for a test drive. Caskets didn't appreciate in value like diamonds or real estate. In the end he'd picked one based on price and the fact that the coffin matched the wood of his mom's living room set.

Joe pointed randomly at two men. "You and you. Come on."

Both men smiled cautiously, but hesitated. Understanding their reluctance, Serpe removed a dollar bill from his wallet and a pen from his jacket pocket. He scribbled his name and license plate number down and handed the dollar note to the heavyset man at the curbside who seemed to be in charge of the shape-up. The man smiled. He didn't need an explanation and nodded for the two men Joe had selected that they should go ahead. As they drove away, Joe noticed the people on the other side of the street giving him the finger. He couldn't hear what they were screaming, but it didn't take a mind reader to figure it out.

★ ★ ★

"So, what are your names?" Joe asked, as the waitress left.

"Jose and Hose B," the younger of the two men joked.

"No, really," Joe prompted.

"Miguel," the older man piped up. He was probably thirty, but looked forty.

"Paco," said the younger. Joe figured him for twenty, tops. "What's your name?"

"Joe."

"Hey, Joe, what kind of work you got for us?"

Miguel glared at Paco. Serpe guessed this must have been a breach of day laborer etiquette. You don't want to scare off the man paying your way by making him think you were picky or couldn't do certain kinds of jobs.

"To tell you the truth guys, I just wanna talk," Joe confessed, peeling off two one hundred dollar bills, but not handing them over.

"Talk?" Paco was curious, never taking his eyes off Joe's money.

"I'm a writer," Joe lied. "I'm interested in what your lives are like, where you came from, what—"

"Work," Miguel interrupted, "not talk."

Paco ignored Miguel. "Talk about what?"

"Look, in this country we all came from other countries, right?" Joe leaned across the table as if he were sharing secrets. "When my people came over from Naples, there were men here who took advantage of them. That's what I'm interested in. The men who take advantage of you guys, the gangs like the MSS and the Lobos."

Miguel, distracted and disinterested up to that point, nearly snapped his neck at the mention of the gangs. He stood up and fairly ran out the door. Joe made an attempt to go after him, but Paco waved him off.

"Let him go, Joe. He was no good to you, anyway. He probably spoke five words of English and four of them were work."

"You seem to have no problem with English, Paco. Where you from?"

"I was born in Mexico City, but I grew up in East L.A."

Joe was suspicious. "L.A., huh? Why come out here and break your back to make the same money you could in California?"

"I like the change of seasons."

"A comedian."

"No comedian, but I got my reasons."

"Like?"

"That's my business, Holmes."

"Holmes?"

"Yeah, like Sherlock. C'mon, man, you're a writer like I'm Oscar de la Hoya. You got cop written all over you, but you got working hands. So what's your deal?"

"That's my business, Paco."

"That's fair. What you need to know?"

"This Reyes kid that was murdered last week, did you know him?"

"A little," Paco said, his eager expression unchanged.

"A little?"

"We didn't live together or hang together, but we worked some landscaping jobs a few months back, clearing leaves and shit. We drank at the same place sometimes."

"He was nineteen and I don't figure you're much older. Where'd you guys drink?"

"We're here illegally, Joe, you think anyone's going to bust our *cojones* about underage drinking? Anyways, you never see white faces where we hang, not even cops."

"And where's it you hang?"

"A little shithole on Portion Road in Ronkonkoma called Iguana."

Joe knew the place. He drove by it all the time. It was a bar/ restaurant in a near-deserted strip mall two minutes from his apartment. There was a hand-painted sign above the threshold and there never seemed to be any cars in the parking lot.

"That's the place," Paco confirmed. "You should check it out sometime. The food is authentic and the beer is cold. On Friday and Saturday nights they have shows."

"Shows?"

"It's hard to explain. Just come and see."

"So about Reyes, you knew him a little. Rumor is he was trying to get into the MexSal Saints. Was he?"

Paco rubbed his hand across his cheek as he considered. "Maybe. He was lost here, lonely. He was a country boy from El Salvador. For me it is easier than for most of these men. I'm more American than Mexican. You can't understand how foreign this world is to them."

"Was Reyes a tough kid?"

"Depends what you mean by tough. To do what we do, to live like we live, you have to be tough. Was he tough tough, violent, I don't think so. But, like I say, I don't know him so well."

"Was he strong?"

"Not very strong, no," Paco said without hesitation. "He worked hard, but he wasn't so strong. Why you interested?"

Joe slid one of the hundred dollar bills across the table to Paco. "That's still my business, okay?"

"Okay, *jefe.*"

"Can you do some checking around for me, act as a translator if I need one? I'd like to meet his roommates, his buddies, find out as much about him as I can."

"As long as the pay is good, I'll check around. But how will I get in touch with you?"

"Here are my numbers," Joe said, scribbling them out on a napkin. "Call me any time. *Any* time!"

"I got it, Joe."

The waitress brought their eggs, Paco eyeing Miguel's unspoken for platter. Joe noticed, but didn't say a word.

★ ★ ★

Bob Healy had slept well, maybe better than he had since burying Mary, but as he closed the morning paper, his coffee turned sour in his mouth. Maybe, he thought, his newfound comfort had come a bit prematurely. There was plenty of mention of the Knicks new President of Operations, Isiah Thomas. The names Bush, Rumsfeld, and Wolfowitz got lots of play. Yet no matter how many times he went through the paper, Healy could find no mention of Jean Michel Toussant. Unlike Serpe, Healy was unnerved by this.

Healy dialed the D.A.'s office. George was in, but didn't give his big brother any reason for optimism. As far as he knew, the Suffolk cops didn't have Toussant, nor did Nassau's finest. There was a chance that the state police might have him, maybe even the park police. He'd have to check.

"Gimme an hour."

Bob Healy didn't like having to wait, but he had no other options. A man with all the time in the world hates waiting most of all.

★ ★ ★

Joe dialed Marla's cell phone. They hadn't spoken since Tuesday. Marla was right in her assessment of him. Several times during the week, he had considered canceling their date, pushing her away. But somehow, he couldn't bring himself to do it. The thought of her made him a little lightheaded. She didn't pick up. He left a message:

"How about Mexican food and a show? Call me. By the way, I've got a surprise for you, sort of."

Saturday Evening
February 28th, 2004

NELSON

Iguana was both more and less than what Joe had expected. It was clean, but its decor was a mishmash of the failed restaurants that had come before it. There were red and gold Chinese lamps, murals of Venice canals, steer horns from a short-lived steak house and one blue and white wall that was painted with the Greek flag. The current owners had obscured the flag with travel posters of Mexico, El Salvador, Guatemala, Honduras, and Panama. Flags from these countries adorned the back wall of the bar, which, in its fake bamboo glory, looked like a refugee from a beachfront Tiki hut.

The food, as Paco had promised, was authentic and hearty. Marla's chicken in mole was amazing—the chicken moist and the chocolate pepper sauce paradoxically fiery and sweet. Joe's beef and cheese enchiladas were delicious. The mysterious red sauce in which they were baked was nothing like he'd ever tasted before. The start of the evening had been a bit bumpy as the hostess didn't know quite what to make of them. She sort of stared at Joe and Marla as if someone were playing a joke on her. Marla, in perfect Spanish, assured her they were only here to eat.

The hostess wasn't the only one in the joint who found their presence a curiosity. A strange silence had fallen as the other diners noticed the two them being shown to a table.

The silence was replaced by a low murmur and pointing fingers.

"How uncomfortable is this?" Joe whispered to Marla.

"Psychologists learn to trust discomfort. It can be a very good thing and I'm kinda enjoying it."

"You would. Besides the hostess and the waitresses, you're the only other woman in here."

Joe was right. Though not full up, there were about thirty other customers in Iguana; ten at the bar and the rest at tables. They were all men between the ages of twenty and forty. And though they were still dressed in jeans, boots and t-shirts, they were almost all clean shaven, well-groomed and respectful of the women serving their food.

"God, what a strange existence," Joe said.

"Yes and no. They're no different than any other ex-patriot community. In some ways I think it's better than being alone in a foreign country. At least they have each other."

As they ate, the place filled in. Men now stood three deep at the bar and the tables were all taken. There was a palpable sense of excitement in the air. Joe and Marla were seated close to the bar. Directly across the dining room from where they sat was a raised platform. There were no tables on it and no one in the place seemed to even notice it existed.

Then, promptly at nine-thirty, the mariachi music which had played quietly yet noticeably in the background all evening long was turned off. Lights came up on the platform across the dining room. The darkness and shadows had hidden a beat up P.A. system that looked like it was salvaged from an old school auditorium. Also on the stage was a DJ stand, featuring two microphones and double turntables. The hostess stepped on stage, grabbing one of the microphones. She was greeted by a round of polite applause and a few whistles. She blushed and curtsied. How long, Joe wondered, had it been since he'd actually seen a woman curtsy?

She launched into some rapid fire Spanish of which Joe understood little. Marla translated: "It's show time."

Next came a second volley of Spanish. This time, Joe caught a word here and there. But the last word the hostess-turned-emcee said sounded like the name Nelson. Only when she said it, it came out NEL-sown. Apparently, NEL-sown was quite popular, because when she mentioned him the crowd went nuts. They began to rhythmically stomp their feet, clap their hands and whistle.

"NEL-sown, NEL-sown, NEL-sown," they chanted. "NEL-sown, NEL-sown … "

The stage again went dark, but this time when the lights came up the hostess was nowhere in sight. On stage stood a pot-bellied, middle-aged man with sleepy eyes and a salt and pepper mustache. He was dressed in too-tight black suede pants trimmed in silver sequins, a matching bolero jacket, a frilly white shirt, black snakeskin cowboy boots and a black suede sombrero the size of Staten Island.

He removed his sombrero and bowed to the crowd. They started shouting to him. He cupped a hand around one ear.

"They're shouting requests to him," Marla said.

"I figured that one out for myself."

Nelson heard something he liked. He moved behind the DJ setup, threw a disc on the turntable and rushed out to center stage. When the music came up, Nelson added the vocals, strutting and dancing about the stage, snapping his fingers, clapping his hands. The crowd was beside themselves. In between refrains, Nelson would scream out "A-cha!" or "Ya-ha!" sending the audience into a frenzy. It was a bizarre mixture of karaoke, Lord of the Dance, and *The Cisco Kid*. But Joe and Marla had to confess they had rarely seen an audience enjoy themselves so unapologetically. By the third number, they had ceased being observers and were screaming wildly themselves.

In between each number, Nelson would work the crowd. He would tell jokes, stories. He would ask members of the audience where they were from, if they had family back home—which they all did—and what it was they dreamed of doing when they had earned enough money in the United States. Both Marla and Joe were surprised and happy to hear that many of them dreamed of bringing their families to the U.S. and becoming citizens. That they didn't view the U.S. as a place to earn a few bucks and to be abandoned and forgotten.

Before the fourth song, Nelson pointed toward the bar area. All eyes seemed to be on Marla and Joe. Nelson removed his sombrero and whispered into the mike.

"Even I understand that," Joe said. "A song for the beautiful lady."

It was a lovely ballad, not unexpectedly about a boy who goes off to war and leaves his betrothed behind. She waits for him to return, each evening preparing a dinner they will never share. She grows old and the children of the village tease her. Yet when she dies, the people of the village honor her belief in love by setting an extra place at their tables every evening. There were very few dry eyes in the place. Remarkable, Joe thought, given the emphasis placed on machismo in the Latino community.

"You're mistaking our sense of machismo for theirs," Marla chided.

After another round of drinks and a few more numbers, they left. Joe slipped a ten dollar bill to the hostess to give to Nelson. He promised to return. She seemed pleased at the prospect.

Outside, Joe didn't wait for prompting. He took Marla in his arms and kissed her hard on the mouth. She seemed to mold her body to his as they kissed. Although she seemed so small and delicate, she was in fact muscular and surprisingly strong. That feeling of her muscles pressing against his was intoxicating. It was a good five minutes before they came up for air.

"Okay, you've gotten dinner, a show, and kissing," Joe said. "See, I keep my promises."

"A surprise. You mentioned something about a surprise."

"Yeah, that's one word for it. C'mon."

* * *

Mulligan was so pleased to see any other human being besides Joe he nearly nuzzled Marla's ankle to the bone. Women and male cats, it was amazing. When Marla found a spot on the couch, Mulligan nestled into her lap, squinting his flirty green eyes at her, and purring like a motorboat.

"You can be gotten rid of, cat," Joe warned, handing Marla a bottle of Blue Point.

"What's that smell?" Marla asked, raising up her nose.

"The finest number two home heating oil mixed with just a hint of kitty litter. Sorry, I guess I don't smell it anymore. Let me light a candle or something."

She didn't protest. Joe dug out a scented candle one of the Triple Ds had brought over several months back. Its cellophane wrapper was still intact. That was par for the course. There was often a pretense of atmosphere with the women Joe had been with since the troubles; candles, champagne, dress-up. But the hunger would usually overtake them before the candles could be lit or corks popped or layers of clothes peeled away. Joe was happy to have made a move to leave that sort of rawness behind. The pleasure in it was so fleeting.

"Vanilla," Marla said. "Thank god it wasn't something embarrassing like potpourri."

"Yeah, vanilla's embarrassing enough."

He leaned over and just brushed his lips against hers. It was intimate and shy all at once.

"One second." Joe stood up, went into the closet that had once only held Vinny's uniform shirts and retrieved a large shipping envelope.

"What you got there?"

"It's a surprise, a good surprise, but it might be a bigger surprise for other people."

"Now I *am* intrigued."

Joe handed her the envelope. "Go ahead, open it. But remember, I warned you."

Marla undid the clasp, pulled up the flap and removed three video cassette tapes. She opened her mouth to ask for an explanation when she noticed the labels on the tapes. "Oh my God! You got—These are tapes of—But how?"

"Do you know the other names?"

"Anne, I'm not sure. Could be a few people, but Kisha, yeah. She worked as a cook for us, but left suddenly last year."

"I think maybe we know why she left in such a hurry. Do you think you could find her if you had to?"

"I'll try," Marla said, obviously still stunned. "How did you get these?"

"I guess as a shrink you think no question should go unasked and that no areas should go unexplored. But with this … Well, it's the kinda thing you shouldn't ask, okay?"

"Okay. I guess I see."

"I didn't know what to do with them, but I figured you'd have a better idea. If you want me to destroy 'em–"

"No, Joe. This man did more than rape them. He took away part of these women's lives. He took away a sense of control. I think maybe I can help them get some of it back. Determining what to do with the tapes should be their decision. Can you understand?"

"I do. Look, I'm sorry I ruined your evening, but—"

"You didn't ruin anything." Marla stood close to him, folding herself into his arms. "I've never known another man like you. Guys always talk about what they've done or would do, but this is something—I just don't have the words for it."

"Then let's not talk about it anymore."

And with that, he kissed her until it hurt.

* * *

Vinny was talking to him. He could swear it. It wasn't a dream because he could still taste Marla on his lips. The suffocating stink of vanilla filled the air. Joe Serpe forced his eyes open. Marla was next to him, naked and asleep. So much for taking it slow. He stared at the smooth curves of her body in the sputtering candlelight. Just seeing her there excited him. Vinny interrupted:

" … if it's gone to three alarms and you're still in the house making this call, bend over and kiss your ass—"

Joe looked at the clock, picked up. "It's three-fifteen, for chrissakes," he whispered. "Who the fuck is it?"

"You told me to call any time, right?"

"Who is this?" He was more insistent.

"It's Paco. Sorry, man, I'm just doing what you asked. You remember me?"

"East L.A."

"That's me. So, you want to meet Reyes' boys?"

"Now?"

"Hey, you didn't tell me banker's hours only, *jefe*. So, you interested?"

"Very."

"Good. Meet me in the parking lot in front of Iguana in ten minutes."

"Twenty."

"Twenty," Paco repeated.

Click.

Joe moved quietly into the shower, shut the bathroom door behind him. He didn't want to have to explain his skipping out on what had been a perfect night. Marla had other plans, silently sliding in behind Joe. She pressed herself against his back, wrapping her arms around him. By the time Joe turned around he was already hard. Marla knelt down, taking him in her mouth, Joe's back shielding her from the water. He let his left hand fall on top of her hair, stroking, twisting it in his fingers. As he did, Marla let out little sighs. Her mouth was moister now and her motion more insistent.

He stopped her, pulling her up by the shoulders, kissing her hard on the mouth.

"I've gotta go," he said, brushing the shower spray off her face. "And if I don't stop you now, I'll never stop."

"Then let's never stop."

He kissed her again. "You can stay here if you want, but I don't know when I'm getting back."

"What do *you* want?"

"I want you to stay."

"Then ask."

"Stay."

"Okay." She rested her cheek on chest. "Why are you going?"

"It's important."

"Oh," she said, "another one of those things I'm not supposed to ask about."

"Maybe later you can ask. It may turn out to be nothing."

"I'll be here."

He stepped out of the shower and toweled off.

* * *

The lone car in front of Joe's kept kicking up debris into his windshield. Though no snow remained from the heavy winter crop, a sheet of dust, pebbles and loose gravel covered the near-empty streets. Snow always disappeared if given enough time, but the plowing, the salt and sand used to deal with it did far more damage. In the end, the cure was worse than the disease itself. When he was a cop, Joe never gave this kind of thing much thought, but when you drive a truck for a living, you learn to pay attention to the roads beneath your tires.

Iguana was dark, the parking lot empty. Portion Road was well lit, but the night was deadly still. Joe checked his watch. Twenty minutes exactly. Joe wondered about getting out of the car to wait. His hair still wet; he decided he'd stay warm. Then, in the black doorway of the restaurant, a flame. Someone had struck a match. Now there was a flame and a red point of light. The flame was out. The red point of light remained. Paco, a cigarette dangling out of the corner of his mouth, walked up to Joe's window. He rested his forearms on the door ledge. Joe cranked the window.

"Hey, Paco. So what's the deal?"

Paco pointed toward the passenger window. "Look over there."

Joe turned his head right. If there was something there to see, he was missing it. When he turned back, however, he got the idea. The muzzle of a Desert Eagle was pressed against his left cheek.

"I like you, boss," Paco said calmly. "So don't make me have to blow a big, fat hole through the side of your face, okay?"

"Okay."

Paco whistled and two men stepped out of the shadows. Both held handguns at their thighs.

"Step out slowly and put your hands on the roof," Paco instructed Joe. Then he let go with some Spanish.

Joe did as instructed, not bothering to try and talk his way out of this. First, he wanted a sense of how this was going to play out and he didn't want to piss anybody off. One of Paco's men sat in the backseat, the other walked up behind Joe and wrapped a thick piece of duct tape across his eyes. Joe felt the barrel of a gun in his ribs and followed its directions carefully. He couldn't see, but he knew he was in the backseat between Paco's buddies.

"Relax," Paco said.

"When I used to tell people to relax, it usually meant they were fucked."

Joe knew the area roads better than most, but after a few turns he lost track. His mind was on other things. He couldn't get the thought out of his head that he might never see Marla again. It seemed so strange that he should worry about her most of all. Maybe not. He thought of Healy, too. Man, his life had changed a lot in two weeks. He tried calming himself with the notion that he had at least gotten a life back. That and the fact they'd blindfolded him gave him some room for hope. No need to blindfold a man you were going to kill. But reminding himself about God's sick joy in kicking the same dead horse, Joe was careful not to get his hopes up too high.

The car came to an abrupt stop. Unlike Jean Michel Toussant, Joe didn't make a scene of exiting the car. All it took was a nudge in the ribs and he climbed right out. Someone rapped on a door, a metal door. There was an exchange in Spanish. The door opened. Another nudge. Joe stepped through the door. Another exchange. Hands slapped together. Backs were patted.

"Careful," Paco warned. "There are stairs. Go down slow."

One of Joe's back seat companions took his arm and made sure he didn't tumble. The door closed behind them. One step and another and another and … Twelve steps. Too bad he wasn't an alcoholic.

"Whachu smiling at?" a strange voice asked.

"Inside joke," Joe said.

"He got some *cojones* on him, this guy."

A hallway. Linoleum on the floor. Joe had lots of company. He could hear their footfalls and shuffling, their breathing. Another door closed, wooden this time. He was shoved into a seat. The tape was ripped off his eyes. *Fuck*! Whatever became of him, there'd be no need for the undertaker to tweeze his eyebrows.

The light in the room was low. There were four men in plain sight: Paco, his two car mates and a short, barrel-chested man with skin like the moon and cold, black eyes. When full focus returned, Joe noticed that Moon-face and Paco's two friends had tears painted under their eyes. No, not painted, tattooed. Moon-face must have been particularly sensitive as he had the most tear tattoos. Some of his tats were black, some red. Paco's buddies featured two red tears below their left eyes. Although Joe could see only these four men, he sensed at least one other lurking in the shadows or standing somewhere behind him.

"Whachu wanna know about Reyes for?" Moon-face asked, his mouth barely moving.

There were a few ways Joe could go with this. He could try being cute and get himself tortured before being killed. He could play it halfway, still get tortured, and get killed. The fact was, he could tell the gospel truth and get tortured and killed.

"Did you guys kill my friend?"

Paco didn't look happy. He shook his head at Joe and mouthed, "Bad idea."

Moon-face grabbed Joe by the throat and lifted him out of his chair.

"Put him down, Nardo." A disembodied voice came out of the shadows. Joe had guessed right. There was someone else in the room.

Nardo let go. Joe didn't have far to fall and he enjoyed breathing again.

"Hey, cop," the voice from the shadows continued, "just answer the question."

"I'm not a cop."

"Used to be a cop," Paco corrected. "Same thing. You were a very bad boy, *jefe*, no?" Paco pantomimed snorting coke. "We know all about you, your partner, and your disgrace."

"The MexSal Saints have a research department?" Joe said.

Nardo took exception to Joe's tone and laid an Asp across his thighs.

"Fuck!" Joe doubled over and fell out of the chair.

"America's a great country, Mr. Serpe!" said the man in the shadows. "They sell computers and internet service here to anyone, even scum from south of the border. You should visit our website: *www.wetback.com*."

Paco laughed. The red tears boys lifted the corners of their mouths. Nardo just got uglier.

"Pick him up."

Joe was put back in the chair.

"You know what the tears mean, Mr. Serpe?" Shadow-voice asked.

One whack across the thighs with a metal pipe was enough for Joe, so he answered as best he could.

"They're either badges of honor for stretches inside or like notches on a gun."

Nardo's black eyes seemed to light up.

"Very good, Mr. Serpe, like notches on a gun. I like that, that's good." The unseen man was pleased.

"What's the difference between black tears and red?" Joe was curious.

"Both mark death," Paco explained. "If I killed you, boss, there'd be a black tear under my left eye. Now, if I were to kill—"

"Nardo!" came a shout from the dark.

Without any wasted movement, Moon-face slammed the Asp across Paco's ribs. The wind went out of the boy in an explosion of air and saliva. Some of the spray caught Serpe in the face. Paco rolled around on the floor, gasping for breath and holding his ribs.

"Paco is young and talks a little too much for his own good," Shadow-voice said.

"He'll learn," Joe said.

A laugh that had no relationship to warmth came out of the dark. "Yes, he will learn. He will have to. Now, I ask you again, why do you want to know about Reyes?"

Joe told him about Cain, about the spray paint, about the cops and their theories. Serpe could hear that the man in the shadows was pacing, taking in what he had said.

"I am sorry your friend was killed. It is one thing to die for a cause, but to die for nothing is bad. You say he was retarded."

"He was."

"We don't kill the weak."

"He was slow, not weak. If he caught someone trying to graffiti the trucks, he would have been hard to deal with. Would Reyes have panicked? Would he have—"

"Reyes!" Even Nardo was incredulous.

"Reyes was a clown, a … " Shadow-voice hesitated. "How do you say it?"

"A wannabe," Paco answered, now on his knees.

"Still, he brought dishonor on you. Did you kill Reyes?"

"We are serious men here. We do not kill retards and clowns. He could not have dishonored what he was not a part of."

"But the cops—"

"Fuck the cops, man. They all bullshit." Shadow-voice said. "On my honor, we did not kill these men."

"Why bring me here? Even if I believe you, what does it matter? I'm nobody."

"You carry the message for us."

"Me? The cops wouldn't believe me if I told them the sky was blue."

Nardo laid the Asp on Joe's right kneecap. Once again, Serpe got up close and personal with the floor.

"What the fuck was that for?"

"It wasn't a request, *jefe*," Paco said. "You carry the message!"

"Okay, I'll carry the message, but it would be a lot more convincing if I could give the cops something to back it up. Give me a name, some proof, something." Joe put himself back into the chair. "Give me a Lobo. You think they did it anyway, right?"

"The Lat Lobos are *putas*, but they have no need to kill the clown either. You think maybe the America for Americans people are crying for Reyes or your friend? Could these two murders serve them any better?"

Joe was silent. There was logic in what the man in the shadows had said. It was a perfect scenario to whip up anti-immigration sentiment and, while Joe Serpe was anything but a conspiracy nut, he had been involved with people who had done much worse for much less.

"I'll do more than carry your message," Joe said. "I'll look into it. And if I need your help … "

"What help? This is all the help you gonna get."

Joe stood and walked toward the silhouette. "Okay, but if I find out you're lying to me—"

Joe could still not make out the man's face. A hand and forearm emerged from the shadows. Nearly all of its skin was covered in tattoos. Some were expertly done, like the black dagger surrounded by a blood-dripping halo. Others were less skillful prison tats.

"On my honor, I am not lying."

Honor. Honor. Honor. What a load of crap. The powerful preached it to protect their own asses. Joe had heard this line of shit his whole life. It was the same with the mobbed-up guys in his old neighborhood or with the Colombians or Jamaicans. There was no honor, only fear. When the leaders are facing a long stretch in prison, honor goes right out the fucking window.

Joe shook his hand.

"Take Mr. Serpe where he wants to go." Shadow-voice released Joe's hand and retreated into the darkness.

"Sit down, boss, we got to blindfold you again," Paco said, holding his hand against his bruised ribs.

"Nice way to treat the help," Joe said.

"Nice!" Paco smiled in spite of the pain. "Nice has nothing to do with it."

* * *

Joe passed out on an old recliner, makeshift ice bags on his knee and thigh. Marla was asleep when he came back in, still asleep when he woke up. Never a late sleeper to begin with, working for Frank had trained Joe's eyelids to snap open between 5:00 and 5:30. Minus a hangover, like on the Monday they found Cain, he was up before the sun. Not even the mix of intense sex, kidnapping, and mild torture could keep his eyes shut. The ice had gone to water and the gallon Glad Bags had flopped to the floor. Joe didn't have to see the wounds to know they'd swollen up pretty bad and turned an ugly shade of purple.

The soreness had spread out from where Nardo had laid the telescoping metal baton across his legs. Joe could only imagine the kind of damage old Moon-face could have done if he was really mad and not tethered to his master's leash. His only consolation was that he was sure Paco's ribs hurt a lot worse than his legs.

It was time to shit or get off the pot, as Joe's dad had loved to say. Joe got the recliner in an upright position, braced himself against one of its arms, and pushed himself up. Standing was not nearly so bad as he anticipated. Walking, however, was worse. But Mulligan was meowing his head off to be fed and Joe really had to pee. As he stiff-legged across the linoleum, Joe was sure he looked pretty ridiculous.

He took care of Mother Nature's calling, showered without disturbing Marla, then threw some dry cat food in Mulligan's bowl. If his cat had possessed a middle finger, he would have flipped Joe the bird. As disenchanted as the cat was, at least he shut up. The shower had loosened Joe up some and his walk back over to the convertible sofa was somewhat less of a struggle. He climbed onto the foldout bed as stealthily as possible. Marla stirred a little, but not to full consciousness. Joe was glad of that. He just wanted to be near her and watch her sleep. It had been several lifetimes since he'd gotten pleasure from watching a woman sleep.

★ ★ ★

So much for sound sleep. Insomnia had reinserted itself into Bob Healy's life. That was why he felt such relief to have drifted off, even for a few brief moments. His eyes closed just before Jean Michel Toussant's face had appeared on screen.

Sunday
February 29th, 2004

PAVING STONES

His lids may have risen before the sun, but sleep had retaken him. When he opened his eyes again, Marla was gone. His heart sank. Then he found her note.

Went to get us some proper breakfast and the Sunday papers.
Be back soon.
Love,
M

His heart, which only seconds before hovered down by his ankles, was now lodged in his throat. He knew that people used love to mean all sorts of things. Some folks threw the word around like spare change. Not Joe. It had been so long since he'd even entertained the possibility of love that he was startled to see it mentioned in relation to him.

For a few months after the divorce, he'd received letters from his son signed, "Love, Joey." By the end of the year the letters stopped coming. Eventually, so did the love. They barely spoke anymore. There was a call at Christmas, one on his son's birthday. Both of which Joey managed to unskillfully avoid. *Tell him I'm not home.* Joe Serpe could not remember the last time they had shared meaningful words. Yeah, sure, it was his ex-wife's fault, but it was his fault, too. His wife may have started the amputation, but Joe finished the operation. He had cut himself out of Joey's life as much as he had been cut out of it. His stomach was in a knot over an issue he hated thinking about and all because a woman he hardly knew had written the word love in a note.

Joe rehearsed all sorts of things to say to Marla when she returned, none of which were ever going to reach his lips. Sex was always easier to share than feelings. Feelings take time to make sense and he hoped he would have the time. But when Marla came through the door, dress rehearsal came to an abrupt end. Joe sensed something had changed, something big.

"What is it?" he asked, seeing the strain in Marla's expression.

At first, she said nothing, needing time to collect herself. She put the coffees, bag of bagels, and papers down on the little kitchen peninsula that was the only table-like thing in the apartment. She took a big breath.

"I know you don't want to discuss it," she said, "but I have to ask. How did you get those video tapes?"

"Of the rapes?"

"Yes."

"Like I said last night—"

"Joe, you can tell me anything. I can always claim I was treating you and that our discussions would be considered priv—"

"Wait a second, here," Joe said, hobbling over to the kitchen. He softly placed his hand on Marla's shoulder. "What's going on? I feel like I'm in one of those movies where the world changed while I was sleeping."

"Maybe the world did, Joe." She reached over and picked up the paper. "Look!"

★ ★ ★

Bob Healy collected the paper, but only to toss in the doorway before heading off to mass. The few hours of contiguous sleep he had managed had come after sunrise. He'd shut the TV off and finally made his way up to the bedroom. Maybe it was the bed itself, he thought. Since that Saturday morning he'd rolled over in bed to find Mary's side of the sheets so cold, Bob had felt ill at ease. Sure there was the stuff with Serpe, but there was more to it. Without Mary, without the kids around, without his job, Healy felt like a stranger in his own home.

That's what he was thinking about as he drove west down Main Street toward Church Street. The radio was tuned to a local news station. He paid the anchorman little mind. Just before Church, a fireman stepped out into the road to stop traffic. Two trucks pulled out, sirens wailing. Something told Bob to pay attention to the radio. He turned the volume up full blast, but it was moot against the sirens and screaming horns. The trucks pulled past him, the din fading in the distance. He turned down the now blaring radio. Whatever he'd wanted to listen to had, like the sounds of the fire engines, come and gone.

"The Doppler Effect," Healy said to himself, slapping the steering wheel in a gesture of self-congratulation. That's what his high school science teacher had taught him, always using sirens as an example of how noise changes from when it's coming at you to when it's moving away from you. He was quite pleased with himself, waiting at the red light to turn. An electronic version of *Beethoven's Ninth* was coming from his inside jacket pocket. Last week his ring was *Pictures at an Exhibition*. Next week *Danny Boy*. Yes, *Danny Boy*, most definitely.

"Healy," he said, wedging the little phone between his ear and shoulder as he turned.

"It's George."

"Like I wouldn't recognize my little baby brother's voice."

That little baby brother line was fraternal button-pushing at its finest. George's standard comeback was a profanity-laced tirade interrupted by the occasional reminder of how much taller he was than his older brother. Bob Healy winced in preparation for George's assault. It was not forthcoming.

"You really haven't heard?" is what he said instead.

Healy was confused. "Heard what?"

"You better come over here for breakfast."

"I'm on my way to mass."

"Forget Mass, big brother, this is more important."

Healy turned left onto Indian Head Road toward Commack instead of right toward the church.

George, his wife, and their two kids had a neat colonial along Townline Road. It wasn't an especially big house, nor exceptionally pretty. But on the market it would sell for about six hundred grand. Commack had good schools and on Long Island, the quality of the school district and the value of your house were bound together like strands of DNA. George stepped out the front door the minute Bob pulled onto the blacktop driveway.

George, in his late thirties, was six-foot-three, two hundred thirty pounds, and while he didn't tower over his brother, he did make Bob feel old when they were together. George, even in his bathrobe, looked the part of the lawyer. It was something about how his brown hair was so neatly cut and parted and how his face was perpetually clean shaven. He and Bob didn't look much alike, but they did share their father's bright blue eyes.

"Where's Beth and the kids?" Bob asked.

"Church."

"So I had to miss Mass, but—"

"So you really haven't heard?"

"This again! Jesus, little brother, just tell me. What I haven't heard."

"Toussant."

"What about him?"

"They found him," George said.

"Good. It's about time."

"Not so good," George contradicted.

"Why?"

"They found him dead."

"Dead! Dead how?"

"Not breathing dead. Dead dead. That's how."

Bob was losing patience. "That's not what I—"

"I know what you meant, shithead, but I like to bust balls too."

"Great. Consider mine busted. Now what happened to Toussant?"

"He OD'd."

"On what?"

"Bullets."

★ ★ ★

One look at the headlines explained Marla's mood swing.

MURDER SUSPECT MURDERED

Joe let go of Marla's shoulder, took the paper, sat down and turned to page three. If Joe had hoped more information would allay his fears, he was sorely disappointed.

BODY FOUND NEAR LAKE RONKONKOMA
VICTIM WANTED FOR QUESTIONING BY COPS
IN HOMICIDE OF RETARDED MAN
BY KEN RIGA
Staff Writer

> *The partially frozen remains found on the Brookhaven Town shoreline of Lake Ronkonkoma by two teenagers have been tentatively identified as those of Jean Michel Toussant. Toussant, a mental health therapy aide, was sought by Suffolk County Police for questioning in the Valentine's Day homicide*

*of Cain Cohen. Cohen, twenty, whose severely beaten body
was discovered by coworkers inside the tank of a heating oil
delivery truck, was mentally retarded and resided in a group
home at which Toussant was employed.*

*Lt. Robert Didio, spokesperson for the Suffolk County
Police Department, confirmed that Mr. Toussant was a
suspect in the Cohen homicide, but refused to elaborate on
how serious a suspect. He went on to explain that pending
a full autopsy and toxicological testing, the county medical
examiner had listed gunshot wounds as the apparent cause
of death. Lt. Didio also declined to be more specific about the
caliber of weapon used or number of wounds.*

*Toussant, a naturalized American citizen born in
Port-au-Prince, Haiti, was last seen at his place of work
on February 14th after an alleged confrontation with Mr.
Cohen. No one connected with the state funded corporation
which runs the group home in Ronkonkoma could be reached
for comment.*

*The police request the public's assistance with this in-
vestigation. Anyone having information about the Cohen
homicide or the whereabouts of Mr. Toussant during the last
two weeks is asked to call the Suffolk County Police hotline
at (631)555-TIPS. (Cont'd on page 38A)*

Joe was stunned. Only twice before had he felt anything like
this: the day I.A. brought him in for questioning and September
11th, 2001. He believed in unfortunate coincidences as much as the
next guy, but for him to accept Toussant's death as being unrelated
to Cain's homicide or even Reyes' was asking more than he could
give. Something was going on that connected all three murders.
What it was, Joe could not divine. Some threads connected one of
the murders to another, but not both. For instance, the possible connection between Cain's death and Toussant's was self-evident, as was
the connection between Cain's and Reyes'. What was the connection

between Reyes' and Toussant's? And if the information Joe got from the MexSal Saints about the AFA involvement in the Reyes murder proved accurate, the picture became even murkier.

Never mind all of that, Joe had his own neck to worry about. He and Healy had kidnapped Toussant and were, by extension, implicated in the murder. Innocent of the crime though they might be, they may well have facilitated Toussant's murder. Joe wracked his brain trying to recall if he or Healy had left any obvious evidence connecting either of them directly to Toussant. The crack! Shit! Had he wiped all the vials? The plastic bag? And would the cousin now come forward? If he did, it wouldn't take a genius to connect the dots of Toussant's abduction to the fire inspection to Steve Scanlon back to him.

"Are you okay?" Marla asked.

"Okay and me are pretty far apart at the moment."

"Did you kill him?"

"I wanted to," Joe admitted.

"But you didn't."

"No."

She came around behind him and threaded her arms under his. She kissed his neck and then rested her cheek on his head. He stood up and walked her back into the living room.

"Why are you limping like that?"

"Listen, Marla, I'm gonna tell you how I got those tapes and how I developed this limp overnight. Then I'm gonna ask you to break the law. If you don't wanna do it, I'll understand. The cops will eventually work their way back to me, anyhow. And maybe it's better if you walk away now."

"I'm not going anywhere."

"But there's stuff about me when I was on the job ... Stuff about my partner you don't know about. It's ugly. The cops aren't gonna believe me and you'll get tarred by being associated with me. I can't let you—"

"I'm all grown up, Joe Serpe. Letting has nothing to do with this. So tell me how you got the tapes."

"This is a bad idea."

"No, not telling me is a bad idea. You need my help. Let me give it to you, please."

Joe told her everything. She listened, never interrupting. When he was finished, Marla loaded the three videotapes into her bag.

"I'll take good care of these until this thing blows over."

"You're withholding evidence in a murder case. That's a felony."

"I know what it is," she said, looking appropriately nervous. "I know what I'm risking."

"Why are you doing this?"

"I could say I'm falling in love with you. Which would be true and would probably scare you to death, but I suppose it's my upbringing. My folks were poster children for good intentions. They were the kind of people whose philosophy was a mishmash of misinformed Judaism, Pete Seeger lyrics and public service announcements."

"You know what they say about good intentions and the road to hell."

"I know, but I'd like to believe that there are some good intentions not meant to be used as paving stones."

"Okay, but maybe we shouldn't see each other for—"

"Forget it," she said. "I'll deal with these tapes. That's my issue. But you're not getting rid of me, Mr. Serpe, not this easily. I'll call you later."

Joe listened to her car pull away. He looked up at his ceiling and pointed his finger at God. "You better not be using her to fuck with me. That I won't forgive. That I'll—"

The phone interrupted the rest of his threat.

"It's Healy."

"I was figuring you'd call."

"You heard?"

"Read it in the paper. It could be bad for us."

"Bad for us, worse for you," Healy said.

"How's it worse for me?"

"Saw my brother George. He's in the D.A.'s office. They found a Mayday Fuel Oil, Inc. refrigerator magnet in the ice a few feet from Toussant's body."

"Fuck!"

"You didn't go back and get him after you dropped me off at home, did you?"

"No."

"Okay," Healy said, relieved, "your word's good enough for me."

"It didn't use to be."

"A lot of things didn't use to be."

"Thanks. The paper says he was shot. How many wounds? Where? What kinda gun?"

"Looks like a 9mm. Three entrance wounds, two exit. One shot in the back above the right shoulder blade. One in the back of the left leg and one in the head. Ballistics should be done in a few hours and the autopsy's going on right now."

"Drugs?" Joe asked.

"The tox screening won't be done for—"

"Not in his system."

"Oh, right, those drugs. Nope. George didn't mention them finding anything on him."

"Is there a warrant out for me?"

"Not yet, but you know the minute Hoskins or Kramer get wind of this, you're seriously fucked. You better get lawyered-up before they come for you and maybe you better warn that fireman friend of yours—what's his name, Scanlon—that trouble's coming his way, too. You want some names?"

"Nah. Unfortunately, I already know too many lawyers."

"Yeah, I guess you would."

"What about you? What are you gonna do?"

"Don't worry about me, Serpe. I can handle myself."

"Famous last words."

"Yup. I suppose we all think that. Good luck, Joe. Anything you need from me, just ask."

"Thanks."

"What'd'ya do with the tapes?"

"That's been seen to. Listen, I do need your help."

"I offered, so ask," Healy said, almost enthusiastic.

"I had a little meeting with the MexSal Saints."

Healy was incredulous. "Meeting?"

"Something like that. I'll tell you about it some other time. Anyway, they denied having anything to do with Reyes' murder."

"They would."

"Maybe, but I believed 'em. You ever hear of the Americans for America?"

"Those clowns that think Pat Buchanan is too liberal and think we should build a wall along our southern border? Yeah, I heard of them. They're the ones stirring up things in Farmingville. Why, the Saints think one of them did Reyes?"

"Makes a sick kinda sense."

"I'll check around."

"Listen, Healy, forget checking around. I got a better idea."

"Yeah, like what?"

"How good are you at picking a fight?"

"Why?" Healy asked.

"Time for a little undercover work. You up for it?"

"Probably not, but tell me anyway."

When Joe got done detailing his plan, he went back to bed to wait. He wondered how long it would take for the cops to show. He decided there was no formula for figuring out the cops or how many gang members could dance on the head of a pin.

Monday
March 1st, 2004

PETER MAXX

T he cops never came, not on Sunday, anyhow. Healy had called him a few times during the day to see if he was all right or if he'd gotten a sniff from Hoskins. Marla called too, assuring him that the tapes were in a safe place. Joe'd had to reassure her that he would be fine no matter what happened. Neither of them believed a word of it. It's a strange thing, reassurance. If we do enough of it, we can nearly trick ourselves into believing it. Nearly.

Like a condemned man reading cookbooks, Joe spent a good portion of the day skimming the real estate section of the papers. If he got through this mess, he decided, he would move. He was through with ghosts and grief. With that vow still fresh on his lips, he sat down next to the answering machine.

"Goodbye, little brother." Joe pressed the erase button. Then, the tears wiped from his eyes and his throat cleared, he pressed RECORD. "This is Joe Serpe. Leave a message and I promise to get back to you. Bye."

Joe knew it was an empty gesture. If things went as badly as they might, he wouldn't be getting back to anybody, not for a long while. But a man in his shoes could afford an empty gesture. And besides, it was time to finally let Vinny rest. Joe was not a stupid man. He knew he had used Vinny's death to camouflage the collapse of his own life. Since Cain's murder, since Marla, it had dawned on him that the camouflage had long been unnecessary, that the only one looking at the rubble was him.

Given that he was waiting for the hammer to fall, Joe didn't expect to sleep but for a few fleeting minutes. But when sleep came, it came hard and deep.

★ ★ ★

There were no dramatic dreams, no visitations, only calm blackness. When he woke in the morning, it was to the sound of his own voice. That would take some getting used to. He hoped to have the chance. He reached for the phone.

"Yeah."

"It's Healy."

"Hey, Bob," Joe said without hesitation. "Did you speak to your brother? Are they on their way?"

"They already knocked on someone else's door."

Serpe was confused. "Someone *else's* door?"

"Which you want first, the good news or the bad?"

"Since I'm not handcuffed or sitting in an interview room, I kinda figured that's the good news."

"Your boss."

"What about my boss?"

"Suffolk Homicide's got him at the Fourth."

"Frank?"

"The cops picked him up this morning at about four."

"Shit, but that can't be. Frank didn't—"

"It was his gun, Joe, his prints—"

"Whaddya mean, *his* gun? Frank doesn't—"

"Yes, he does, a 9mm Smith and Wesson registered to him. He's got a carry permit. When the cops executed their warrant on Mayday's offices, they found it. It'd been fired, three bullets missing from the clip. The refrigerator magnet had his prints on it and he's got no real alibi for Saturday night."

"Fuck!"

"It's pretty bad. You know those lawyer names you were thinking about for yourself, I'd turn that list over to your boss in a hurry."

"Can you meet me over there?" Joe asked.

"Over where?"

"At the Fourth. I can't let him do this alone."

"You'll be no help to him there, Joe. Get his wife the names of those lawyers and tell her to have him keep his mouth shut."

"But—"

"But nothing. You know I'm right. Us showing up there will just piss the cops off and make it harder on your boss. Maybe tomorrow, after he's arraigned, I can get George to get you in to see him. Not today."

"Christ, Healy, it just keeps getting worse and worse."

Healy asked the question they'd both been avoiding. "Do you think he did it?"

Joe Serpe hesitated. Experience had been a hard teacher. Frank was a tough guy, but not a violent man. Then again, if six years ago you'd've asked Joe if he would have suspected Ralphy of being a thief and a cokehead ... Joe had worked for Frank for three years, considered him a close friend, but never knew he had a gun and a carry permit. And Joe understood just how deeply Frank felt about Cain. There was a special bond between them. He'd known people to kill for less, a lot less. The bottom line was, you could never know someone well enough or closely enough to rule them out. You couldn't know yourself that well.

"I don't know," he said at last. "I wanna believe he didn't have it in him, but I guess maybe he did."

* * *

Bob Healy strolled down Horseblock Road with a purpose. He knew Joe Serpe would have been much better suited to the dog and pony show he was about to perform, but that just wasn't the way things had shaken out. Though Serpe had once been a department legend for his undercover work—they didn't call him Snake simply because of his name—it wasn't as if Healy was completely inexperienced in going this route.

Early on in his career at I.A., he'd worked a big case against a cop believed to be selling intelligence, uniforms, and radios to the Westies. Healy had set himself up as a rogue IRA man who'd come over to the states to start a new criminal enterprise. It was a way, he told the bad cop, to fund activities in the North and pocket a little change for himself. In the end, Healy had been so convincing that the bad cop introduced him to several of his underworld associates. The sting led to a truckload of indictments. The case helped make Healy's reputation. But that was two decades past and this time there would be no backup, no safety net. He would be truly on his own.

Healy was no more than five feet from the protesters when a young Hispanic man, another of the anonymous day laborers, stepped into his path. Both men went down in a heap. The protesters took notice. Even the nasty-faced man with the bullhorn turned to look.

"*Lo siento*," the Hispanic man said, getting quickly to his feet.

"Speak English," Healy barked back.

The young man offered Healy a hand to help him stand. Healy slapped it away.

"I don't need your kinda help." Healy struggled to his feet.

"*Permiso, senor. Lo sieñto.*"

"Fuck you, Pedro. Go the fuck back to Mexico or wherever it is you came from."

Fuck and fuck you were universal, requiring no translation, and the young man shoved Healy. That really got the protesters attention. At least five of them, led by Bullhorn, came to Healy's aid. But before they could reach him, Healy lifted his pant leg to show the young man the short barrel .38 strapped to his ankle.

"Come here and shove me again, ya fuckin' wetback. I'll stick this gun up your ass."

The day laborer knew when to run and took off across Horseblock, nearly getting whacked by, of all things, an oil truck. Out of the corner of his eye, Healy could see the protesters focus on his revolver.

"You all right?" asked Bullhorn in an accent that was definitely more Phoenix than Flushing.

"Yeah," Healy said, brushing off his pants. "Can you believe the balls on that guy? Government's a damn joke. You build your fence an inch too high and they're all over you with fines and penalties. These jokers here," he pointed across the street, "they come here illegally and they wanna use my tax money to build them a hiring hall. I'll tell ya, the world's upside down. I'm only glad my dad isn't alive to see it."

Bullhorn held out his right hand. "Pete Strohmeyer, East Coast organizer for America for Americans."

Healy took the hand, shook it, but regarded Strohmeyer warily. "Bob Healy," he said without enthusiasm.

"That was quite a nice little speech you just gave there, Mr. Healy."

"Ah, I'm just disgusted is all."

"We're having a recruitment meeting this evening at the VFW hall in town. Why don't you come and see what we're about?"

"Nah," Bob said, "I've never been much of a joiner."

"Now's the time to start joining, Bob. We're being invaded and we could use good men like you, men not afraid to stand up and be counted. Here." Strohmeyer handed Healy a leaflet and pamphlet. "This will explain some about the problems we face, the lies the media tell about us, and outlines our strategies for victory. But I would really like it if you could come to the meeting."

"We'll see," Healy said, flipping through the pamphlet. "Maybe."

"Excuse me, but I've got to get back to work. It was a pleasure meeting you, Bob. I hope to see you this evening."

With that, Strohmeyer led his gang of five back to their usual spot and began screaming at the day laborers across Horseblock Road. Healy smiled to himself. Serpe would have been proud.

* * *

Joe Serpe knew Healy was right, that he should stay away from the Fourth Precinct, but he was getting antsy, feeling guilty. Calling Tina, Frank's wife, had only made it worse. She'd picked up the phone, cursing, threatening, begging for the reporter to please just leave them alone. That near ripped Joe in half. It had been the same for his wife. The constant assault by the press had driven her to a nervous breakdown. They don't call it that anymore, a nervous break down, but it was a perfect description of what his wife had gone through. She was never the same after that.

It had taken a minute for Joe to calm Tina down and convince her that he wasn't a reporter. When she finally realized it *was* Joe, she broke down, sobbing loudly into the phone. Crime, he thought, had a lot of unseen victims. They always try to scare kids out of criminal activity by taking them to prison and talking to lifers. He wondered if spending some time with women like Tina and his wife wouldn't be more effective. His heart ached. And for the first time he understood that Bob Healy was right. All the good deeds he could perform would never make up for the pain he'd caused his wife.

When her sobs slowed to a manageable pace, Tina explained how she'd basically barricaded herself and the kids inside the house. She said that several news trucks had set up shop on the street and the chiming of the front doorbell was constant. Joe could hear the *bong bong bong* in the background. Nor had the phone stopped ringing, but she was afraid to take it off the hook in case Frank was calling.

Joe distracted Tina by making her write down the names, addresses and phone numbers of several lawyers. He told her to get out of the house, to go to a relative's or a motel, and that if she got word to him where they were, he'd get word to Frank. When she began to argue, Joe put his foot down.

"Tina, you'll want to listen to me about this. I lived through it. My family did, anyway. You know Frank didn't murder anyone and he'll be back sooner than later. If you want him to have a wife and family to come home to, save yourself and the kids and get away from there."

"It may already be too late," she said.

Joe ignored that, chalking it up to Tina's being distraught and exhausted.

That had been hours ago. He had tried Marla's cell, but she was working and hadn't gotten back to him. Healy was off doing whatever it was he was doing to track down leads on the Reyes murder. The only one not doing anything was Joe. Idleness never suited him.

He showered, inspecting the damage to his legs. He was walking a little easier and some of the swelling had gone down. The bruising, however, had spread out from the points of contact and had begun to resemble psychedelic finger paintings. Peter Maxx could probably have sold his legs for a bundle.

Dressed and out the door, he didn't quite make it to his car.

"Where you goin' with that limp, Snake?" Detective Lieutenant Hoskins was anxious to know.

Serpe played dumb. "What's this about?"

"Your boss, he killed the frog nigger."

Joe must have looked as disgusted as he felt.

"Come on, Snake, what's a matter? You never heard the word frog before?" Hoskins laughed at his own rapier wit. "You used to be a city cop, so don't get all squeamish on me. Get a few drinks in Ralphy and every other word out of his mouth was nigger. You gonna tell me a Brooklyn guinea like you never used the N-word?"

Apparently, God had chosen Monday March 1st, 2004 as the day for Joe Serpe to be confronted with the worst aspects of his past life. First it was Tina dredging up what he had made his own wife and son suffer through. Now this.

"You're not here to discuss the Rainbow Coalition, or Ralphy or whether the greasers in my neighborhood whispered nigger in the schoolyard. And where's Kramer, anyway?"

"Kramer, maybe he's home polishing his yarmulke. How the fuck should I know? This is a little unofficial visit, anyways."

"Unofficial? To what do I owe the pleasure?"

Hoskins got up close to Serpe. "Listen, cunt, no one's here to step between us now. The Heeb ain't here and neither is that other cunt, Healy. So it's just you and me, boyo."

"What about it?"

"How fucking stupid do you think I am, Snake?"

"Got an hour?"

"That's right, have a laugh, but I know things. Maybe your boss—"

"Ex-boss," Serpe corrected.

"Whatever. Maybe he did kill the nigger. The evidence sure points that way. Personally, I don't give a shit—as far as I could tell, he needed killing. But Frank Randazzo didn't find Toussant on his own, not unless they teach skip-tracing in truck drivers' school. Do they teach you that there, Snake?"

"I didn't go to school."

"Yeah you did, the school of the streets. The best kinda school. The kinda school where you learn to track people down who ain't interested in being found. So, you gonna let Frankie boy twist in the wind like you let Ralphy twist or, for once in your miserable fucking life, are you gonna stand up and take the rap?"

"What are you talking about?"

"Okay, Serpe. Just like I thought. You're still a cowardly cunt. Just remember I gave you a chance to do the right thing here. I'm gonna nail your ass to the wall. Remember that." Hoskins turned to walk away.

"Hey Hoskins," Joe snapped at him.

"What?"

"I want you to remember something, too."

"I'm listening."

"The time's gonna come when this shit will all be cleared up. And when that happens, I want you to call your dentist."

"What the fuck you on about now? Why should I call my dentist?"

"Because if you talk to me like that again, I'm gonna kick your teeth out through your ass. Remember that!"

Joe turned, walked back inside his apartment and slammed his door shut.

Monday Evening
March 1st, 2004

A SCRATCH, A BLEMISH, A SMALL CUT

Healy showed up. There was never any doubt that he would. But as he approached the VFW hall, a frail looking woman in her late sixties walked up to him. She handed him a slip of paper with an address on it.

"What's this?"

"I recognize you from this morning," she said. "You're the one that got into a shoving match with the wetback."

"That was me."

She pointed at the slip of paper. "It's a precaution against the media. They try to come to our meetings all the time, distort our point of view. You go on over to that address. You'll be okay."

"Thanks."

Ten minutes later and two villages away, Bob Healy found himself outside a run-down tavern on a dead end street. It was an old fashioned bar built out of the first floor of a house. The flickering neons in the front window were collectors items, touting beers like Ballentine Ale and Rheingold. The wood sign in the parking lot had made a lot of termites happy for a long time. The place was not called the Dew Drop Inn, but it should have been. It's actual name, Jerry's Joint, was such a disappointment.

In any case, the parking lot was full and cars lined both sides of the curb, halfway up the street. There was a burly, linebacker type at the door collecting the strips of paper the woman had handed out at the VFW hall.

"Paper," he barked at Healy.

Bob patted down his pockets. "Left it in the car."

"Go get it!"

"I'll be right back." He started for the car.

"Wait!" Pete Strohmeyer called out. "Come on back, Bob."

Healy turned around to see Strohmeyer standing next to the linebacker.

"He's okay, son," Strohmeyer vouched. "Let him in."

"Thanks."

"Thank you. See you inside, Bob."

Jerry's Joint harkened back to old Suffolk County, before it had been transformed from potato and sod farms to golf courses and vinyl-sided McMansions. There was a dart board, a pool table, and enough taxidermy on the walls to please the most ardent hunter. There were black and white pictures of roadside produce stands, men on fishing docks astride their catches of the day, clean-shaven men in military dress. The bar itself was strictly 40s and 50s: Bakelite and Formica. The stools were chrome and red vinyl.

The pool table had been shoved to one side and a few rows of folding chairs had been neatly arranged in front of a rostrum. A red, white and blue banner hung on the wall behind the rostrum. *DON'T TREAD ON ME* formed the top half of a circle in the middle of the banner. *AMERICA FOR AMERICANS* formed the lower half of the circle. At the center of the circle was a silhouette of the flag being raised at Iwo Jima.

But this wasn't a clan rally. No crosses were burning. No one was foaming at the mouth, no one was chanting racist slogans. There was no shouting at all, or even much drinking, as far as Healy could tell. What Healy saw was a room full of people not unlike himself: white, middle-class, and confused. They were worried, unprepared for the changes in their corner of the world. When these people had purchased their homes ten, twenty, thirty years ago, they couldn't have imagined a scenario where a forgettable little hamlet in central Suffolk County would become the focus of national attention.

He didn't sense hate in the room, but fear. He understood that fear was like heated metal, something that in the hands of a skilled smithy could be molded or cast into almost any shape. Given the right conditions, fear and hate weren't so far apart.

He found a seat in the last row of folding chairs. There was a pamphlet on the seat just like the one Strohmeyer had given him that morning. Healy picked it up, shoved it in his pocket. Almost before he was fully settled, a woman sat down next to him. She was a handsome woman, with unpretentious gray hair that fell to her shoulders. Healy had always admired women who didn't try to hide themselves. She had clear blue eyes and a proudly lined, unmade-up face, a pert nose and cushy lips. God, he thought, how long had it been since he even noticed another woman's features?

"Hi, I'm Barbara," she said, nervously offering her hand to Healy. "Christ, I don't even know what I'm doing here."

He took her hand. "Bob Healy."

"A pleasure."

"What did you mean about not knowing why—"

"Because I'm sympathetic to these day laborers, but I'm worried about my house. My husband died eight months ago and—"

"Sorry."

"Thank you. But he didn't leave any insurance and the house is basically all I've got."

"Do you work?"

"Home Depot as a cashier. It's okay, I guess, but I've got a girl in college and we've borrowed against the house. If the property values plunge, I'm screwed."

Healy could hear the strain in her voice. He imagined Barbara was like most of the other folks in Jerry's Joint, embarrassed. They were here because they didn't know where else to go. It's easy to judge people, put labels on them, but labels are often wrong. Now he almost felt guilty for his charade.

"How about you?" Barbara asked.

"What about me?"

"Why are you here?"

"I guess the short answer is because I had a run in with one of the Mexicans this morning and I was invited to come. The real answer is that since my wife died, I've been kind of adrift, worried about the same kinds of things you are."

"Sorry about your wife. What happened?"

"Pancreatic cancer."

"My Jimmy had a stroke."

Oddly, they smiled, both realizing that neither could have imagined having a conversation remotely like this only a year ago.

"Listen to us," Bob said.

But that's where their conversation stopped. A rotund man stepped up to the rostrum and called everyone to order. The bar quieted down as people filled in the empty seats. Behind the fat man and in front of the banner stood Pete Strohmeyer and the man he'd called son. Now that the linebacker was standing in the light, Healy could see just how menacing he really looked. Everything about him was square, from his head to shoulders to chin. He had those blank eyes, both penetrating and empty all at once. Healy could also see that his left arm was bandaged up pretty good, so that white gauze swallowed up his hand, wrist, and half his forearm. If the linebacker's arm was in that bad of condition, Healy thought, he'd hate to see what the other guy looked like.

The fat man started with some prepared remarks about the sad state of affairs in their community. While on the one hand they were being overrun by illegal immigrants, they had been systematically abandoned by the police, the I.N.S., the politicians—every branch of government on every level. Throughout this entire ordeal, he continued, there had only been one group that had been steadfast in its support of the locals. Only one group that had helped them organize, mount resistance, and protest. Only one group who had shown them a way not to be helpless, given them hope. Naturally, that group was America for Americans.

Pete Strohmeyer stepped up to the lectern, thanking everyone for their attendance and for the fat man's kind words. He was in his element, his face fairly glowing. Strohmeyer spoke not only with an elegance and ease, but with fire and focus.

"You have been abandoned. You have been sold out. Your worth has been minimized, the value of your lives and property degraded. You have been labeled, manipulated, used, chewed up, and dismissed. Why? What did any of you ever do except work hard, raise families, follow the law, pay your taxes and stand with your hands to your hearts during the Pledge of Allegiance? What sin did you commit other than to want to preserve your small piece of the American dream? Even that dream is a lie, because they've taken the promise that is the birthright of everyone born in this country and sold it for a plate of rice and beans to people who want only to take from this country and not give back, people who don't appreciate its values, people who want to suck dry the vitality of our nation and then spit on us.

"Well, folks, to borrow the sentiment from a famous movie, I'm mad as hell and I'm not going to take it anymore. I don't take it anymore. I've done something about it. About five years ago I helped found an organization that is a levee against the tide, that is the lone sane voice in the din of lies. That organization is America for Americans. Let me tell you a little something about how we started, why we started, and what we want to do for and with you.

"First off, we need to get something straight. What you've got here in your town on Long Island is a scratch, a blemish, a small cut. My son and me are from the once great state of Arizona. And let me tell you something about Arizona. The problem we have there is no blemish. It's a cancer, a festering infection, a gaping sore. We have been invaded, swept up in a brown tide of people who come to Arizona to steal our jobs, deal drugs to our children, piss on our flag, and send their illegally made funds back home.

"But like you, we were abandoned. Our politicians talked out of both sides of their mouths. One of them even suggested we facilitate the illegal crossings by having regular bus service. It was too dangerous, she said, letting these poor people have to be smuggled in by unscrupulous scavengers. Well, that was the last straw. Some of my friends and I decided to fight back. We lobbied, protested, patrolled the borders on our own. We got rid of backstabbing politicians who would have used our tax money to help these unclean, uneducated, undeserving criminals steal our dream. This is how we did it … "

Strohmeyer went on like this for about a half-hour, railing against the government, the media, the brown tide, the Border Patrol, the INS, even the Catholic church for giving the illegals shelter and places to organize. As his talk progressed, his speech became more feverish, more full of half-truths, stereotypes, false statistics, and distortions. But he never strayed too far afield, always picking at the fresh scab of the audience's fears and confusion. Near the end of the speech, Strohmeyer introduced his son, Pete Jr. Though not nearly the speaker his father was, his size commanded people's attention.

The son echoed the father's themes, recounting horror stories from his schooldays in southern Arizona. He assured us that as bad the invasion was for adults, it was worse for kids. He told tales of rape, robbery, special treatment for the kids of illegals at the expense of the regular students. His key theme, however, was the establishment of neighborhood patrols. He said that America for Americans had just recently started up car and foot patrols in the area and that the rise in vandalism and violence would not be tolerated.

"We can't patrol borders here," he said, "but we can take back the streets." He was careful not to criticize the cops, but said they could only react to crime, not prevent it. Unfortunately for Healy, his moment in the sun was at hand. The linebacker repeated the story of this morning's confrontation as was told to him by his father. Healy was asked to stand. He got a big round of applause. Barbara, Bob noticed, was not clapping. That done, the son asked for volunteers to join the patrols. Several men in the crowd moved forward and signed their names. Healy went too. When he turned back around, Barbara was gone.

The men signed up. The hate was passed. Money was raised. Hands were shaken and backs were slapped. The bar began to empty out. As Bob made to leave, he was stopped by Pete Jr.

"Can I buy you a beer?"

"Sure."

"Two Buds," the younger Strohmeyer ordered.

"Sorry about not letting you in before. My father is kind of strict about following the rules."

"No sweat. My old man was the same way."

"Father tells me you carry a .38."

"A .38. Sometimes a Glock. Sometimes both."

"Are you a cop?"

"Used to be—NYPD detective." Healy knew it was best to lie as little as possible. "So when do we start on the patrols?"

"Tomorrow night, I guess. I'll have to check with my father."

"How'd you hurt the hand?"

"Punched a wall," Junior said without hesitation. "I got a little drunk a while ago, got into a fight with this girl I've been seeing up here and I slammed it into her bedroom wall. Busted and cut it up pretty good. Went to the hospital and had it looked at and—"

"Hey, son," the elder Strohmeyer interrupted. "We don't want to bore Mr. Healy with the details of your temper."

"Sorry, dad. Did you know Mr. Healy was a cop?"

"Really?"

Bob tried spinning this to his advantage. "NYPD detective, Internal Affairs. My job was like what you're doing here. I spent my career exposing traitors, people who sold their own brothers out for a quick buck."

If Healy thought that was going to elicit a warm response from Strohmeyer, he was wrong. A "How interesting" was all he got.

"I'll say goodnight, then," Healy said, shaking the hands of the father and the son.

When he got outside, Barbara walked up to him.

"Have you been waiting out here all this time for me?" he asked.

She ignored his question. "That's how it starts, you know?"

"How what starts?"

"Group hate. The lies and fear. That's how it always starts."

"So that stuff you told me inside about your husband dying, it was all—"

"—the truth. I really am worried about my property value and how I'm gonna get my girl started right in the world, but I won't associate with people like that Strohmeyer. I couldn't look myself in the face. Some of my neighbors joined up and I thought I'd come see for myself what these people were really like. Now I get that my fears about them were well founded."

"So why tell me?"

"Because," she said, "you seem like a nice guy, and a gentleman."

"Thank you. I—"

"Never mind. I'm just being silly. You've got the right to do what you want. I'm sorry."

Disappointed, Healy felt moved to comfort her. "You're not being silly. And you've got nothing to apologize for."

"I hope you can say the same for yourself, Bob. There's some kinds of dirt that rubs off on you and you can never get the stain out. Good night."

"Let me walk you to your car."

"No, that's all right. My car's right over there."

Bob Healy watched her pull away, making a mental note of her tag number, but he wouldn't track her down, not yet. Even if he were prepared to explain the real reason for his being at the meeting, there was something else for which he was unprepared. In the wake of his attraction to Barbara came a flood of guilt. Until he dealt with his guilt, he'd be no good to anyone, especially himself.

Tuesday
March 2nd, 2004

TIMOTHY LEARY

Joe had already spoken with Bob Healy, if only briefly. They didn't discuss Healy's visit to Jerry's Joint. Neither man was in a particularly talkative frame of mind. Serpe was too preoccupied with Frank's plight to ask about every detail concerning Healy's handling of the Reyes matter. Besides, he trusted that Healy would tell him if there was anything worth telling. For his part, Healy couldn't get Barbara off his mind, or the guilt that came with her.

Bob did have some information for Joe, most of it bad. Frank had lawyered up, but hadn't chosen to be represented by any of the criminal attorneys Joe had suggested to Tina. He'd been arraigned at the Cohalan Court Complex in Central Islip. At the arraignment, Frank pled not guilty and was denied bail. He was remanded to the Suffolk County Jail in Riverhead. The one positive note was that George Healy had arranged for Joe to visit with Frank in a more private setting at the jailhouse than was usually permitted.

"Don't get too excited," Bob Healy had warned Joe. "George told the D.A. you're going there to try and convince Frank to plead out."

★ ★ ★

Frank, handcuffed to the table, was already seated when Joe came into the room escorted by a sheriff's deputy. He looked terrible—pale, gaunt, unshaven. He was dressed in his own clothes, including jeans and a western style shirt with the Mayday logo embroidered on the left breast. Joe had one just like it. It didn't escape his notice that Frank's belt and shoelaces were missing. If it was possible for a room to be simultaneously sterile and grungy, then this room was. Everything about the place was hard: the steel, the edges, even the air. The stink of the pine-scented cleaner burned the lining of Joe's nostrils. Still, just being there made Joe want to shower.

In our daily lives, Joe thought, we're used to concessions made for aesthetics. No such compromises are necessary in modern jails or prisons. Function, function, function; that's the driving force.

Joe remembered a street corner dealer caught up in a neighborhood sweep, begging him and Ralphy to let him go. The guy offered to roll over on his own mother, he'd do anything to not go back to Rikers again. When asked for a reason, the guy said he couldn't stand the ugliness of the place, that he'd kill himself. Joe wondered whatever became of that guy.

The deputy went over the rules, said they had up to a half an hour, and that he'd be just outside the door. Joe thanked him. Frank was mum.

"What are you doin' here, Joe?" Frank asked as soon as the door clicked shut.

"What do you think I'm doing here? I'm here to help."

"Go away, Joe. You can't help me."

"Frank, you pretty much saved my life and I'm not about to turn my back on you."

"I'm not askin' for any favors. You don't owe me any. So just get lost."

"Sorry, buddy. I'm not a deserter."

"I bet your ex-partner's wife wouldn't see it that way."

Joe stayed calm. He got that Frank was trying to get rid of him any way he could.

"What about Tina and the kids?"

Frank looked nauseous. "They're taken care of no matter what happens to me."

"Don't be an idiot, Frank. There's no taking care of this kinda shit. They're gonna be scarred by this forever. Money won't make this right. Nothing will. I know. So if you didn't kill Toussant, stop this crap now while you can salvage things."

"Fuck you, Joe. Get the fuck out!"

The deputy knocked on the door. "Everything all right in there?"

"Just five more minutes," Joe shouted before Frank could answer. Then he got back to the business at hand. "Okay, Frank. You did it and I can't help you. You wanna get rid of me?"

"Yeah."

"Convince me. Tell me where you found Toussant, how you got him to the beach, why you were so stupid as to leave a refrigerator magnet behind and your gun in the office. You convince me and I'm outta here. You might as well practice now, because if you cop to a plea, you're gonna have do elocution before the judge."

Frank shifted uneasily in his metal chair.

"Come on, Frank. Just tell me where you found Toussant and I'll get outta your hair."

"He was hiding out in … He was hiding out in Wyandanch."

"Yeah, and how did you find him there?"

"You said you'd get out if I told—"

"Just tell me how you found him."

"I went looking for him there."

"You're full a shit. I know it and you know it."

"Deputy!" Frank screamed. "Deputy, get me outta here, now!"

"Listen, Frank, I don't know what you're hiding, but it isn't worth it. You're gonna ruin a lot of people's lives. Let me help—"

"All right, that's it! Party's over," the deputy barked, pushing in the door. He pointed at Joe. "You, outside now."

"Think about what I said." Joe said in parting.

"Leave it be, Joe, please. I'm beggin' ya."

"Now, fucko!" the deputy insisted, slapping his hand down on Joe's shoulder.

* * *

Healy had called Serpe five times since they'd spoken earlier and had gotten nothing except familiar with his new phone message. On the fifth try he simply hung up. Now not only was he waiting for Joe's call, but for George's as well. Last night's bout of insomnia had been a productive one. His mind constantly drifted back to the sight of the younger Strohmeyer's battered hand.

You didn't have to be a retired detective to know that stabbing someone to death can be a dangerous proposition for both parties involved. The person wielding the knife is often cut in the process. The more stab wounds, the greater the chance that the attacker will be injured. He had called George right after getting off the phone with Serpe. George wasn't happy.

"Are you nuts? You want me to ask the lab to retest all the blood samples at the Reyes murder scene to check for a second contributor. This isn't even my case, for fuck sakes! What are you playing at here, big brother?"

"It's not playing."

"And it's not police work either. In case you've forgotten, you're retired. And this is Suffolk, not Kings County. You've got no standing here."

"But this could clear more than one case," Bob said. "Couldn't hurt to put a few feathers in your own cap."

"My cap's just fine the way it is, bro. Besides, neither this, Toussant or that retarded guy's case has anything to do with me. The D.A.'s going to start wondering why I've got my fingers up everyone else's ass."

"Because you're ambitious, little baby brother."

"Fuck you, dickhead."

That was more like it, Bob thought. That was the George he knew.

"Try and get them to test the samples," Bob urged. "Like Uncle Mick used to say, 'I got a feelin' in me gut.'"

"That was gas. Uncle Mickey was a drunk."

There was no arguing that.

★ ★ ★

The snow was falling at a pretty steady clip as Joe drove away from the jail complex and headed toward the Long Island Expressway. It was one of the great contradictions of the island that this far east the L.I.E. was anything but the world's biggest parking lot. The only time it got real heavy out this way was when most of Manhattan moved to the Hamptons for the summer. Then, on Friday nights heading east and on Sunday nights heading west, the expressway was as ridiculously crowded as those sections closer to the city.

Joe pulled onto the expressway completely unchallenged by other traffic. There were a few red taillights visible in front of him, but they were almost a full exit ahead. Accustomed as he was to driving in this weather, Serpe enjoyed the solitude and peacefulness it afforded him. It was one of the things he liked most about driving the tugboat, his time alone. So with the Moody Blues proclaiming Timothy Leary's death and Joe feeling he had the world to himself, he moved into the center lane.

He tried to think of who Frank was protecting. He had to be covering for someone. Short of actually having executed Toussant, it was the only explanation for Frank's self-destructive bent. Clearly, Frank was scared and not for himself. It couldn't be Tina and the kids, he thought. You'd really have to take liberties with the word protection to consider the hell Frank was putting them through a good thing. No, it had to be—

Bang!

Joe's car fish-tailed wildly. He fought hard to steady the car, his heart pounding, adrenaline pumping. A blow out? He didn't think so. He had the car just back under control when—

Bang!

This time he felt it coming, caught a streak of black in his side view mirror. A Lincoln Navigator with deeply-tinted windows slammed into his rear passenger side quarter panel, causing the fish-tailing to start all over again. Christ, had he been that far lost in his own thoughts that he was unaware of another vehicle so close to him? You had to love these assholes in their fucking SUV's. Just because the damned thing had four-wheel drive and weighed more than a tank, didn't mean you could drive it like one.

Joe righted the ship once more. He slowed to allow room for the Navigator's driver to regain control of his vehicle and pull to the shoulder. But Serpe had misread the situation. The Navigator hadn't accidentally slid into him. As Joe slowed, the Navigator swung out right and turned sharply back left, its nose smacking hard into the rear wheel well of the Accord. There was no controlling the car now. It spun out, turning circles on the slippery road surface before riding onto the grass that divided the east and westbound lanes. Oddly, that seemed to help Joe get the car back under his command.

He hit the gas, shot off the grass back up onto the roadway, and got it up to eighty-five, but the Navigator was a brute and was back at his side within seconds. Joe's only hope was to try to buy some time until he got to an exit or to a more crowded area of the expressway where the Navigator's actions would be restricted by the presence of other vehicles. Problem was, any delaying tactics he might use were nearly as dangerous as the Navigator. The road surface was so slick that he couldn't afford to push the speed much more, nor could he bob and weave. He waited. When he saw the Navigator swing out wide right once again, preparing to go for his wheel well, he slammed on his brakes.

Unfortunately, the car did not stop. Instead it skidded uncontrollably, but all was not lost. Because the Accord's rear end swung left just as the Navigator gored it, the big Lincoln's hit was off target, barely clipping the Honda. Now it was the Navigator that was out of control, spinning, nearly tipping over on its side, sliding into the grass. When Joe came out of his skid, he raced to the approaching exit. He sped off the road, around one curve and then another. The big Lincoln was nowhere in sight, but Joe was paying too much attention to what was not behind him at the cost of missing what lay ahead. The Honda hopped the curb and slammed into a clump of trees.

Bang!

This time it was the air bag. But because of the angle at which the car had jumped the curb, Joe's head snapped sideways and thumped against the door glass. At first he just felt sort of disconnected, more an observer of what was going on than a participant. Then came the pain. It didn't last long. Blackness fell down on him, and he had no weapons to fight it.

★ ★ ★

Healy had gotten a call, but not from Serpe. It was Strohmeyer Jr., calling on the cell to let him know where to meet tonight. Healy had been purposefully vague about his address and had made sure to give out only his cell number as the exchange wasn't traceable to a particular town. He was under no illusion that he'd be able to hide the fact that he didn't live anywhere near Farmingville or Ronkonkoma. He had already worked out a cover story to tell if need be. In any case, he didn't figure the AFA was real choosy about where their recruits came from. He was white, had half a brain, and carried a gun. What else did they need?

The house phone rang.

"Healy," he said.

There was an unnatural silence on the other end. Healy thought he could hear labored breathing and some sort of movement.

"Hello," he shouted.

"Healy?"

"Serpe, is that you? Are you drunk?"

"Healy," the voice repeated.

"Where are you, Joe?"

"I'm not sure. I smacked up my brother's car."

"Are you okay?"

"My head's all foggy and I'm bleeding a little. Come and get me."

"Where are you?"

"I remember leaving the Suffolk County Jail and it was snowing pretty bad. Frank's scared. He's protecting somebody, but I don't think it's—"

"Okay, Joe, let's stay on point here. Try to remember where you are."

"I guess I'm near the L.I.E."

"That's something," Healy said. "You were headed west on the L.I.E. from Riverhead. We can work with that. How bad are you bleeding?"

"Not bad. I got a bad headache and—"

Healy thought he heard Joe puking up his guts. "Should I call the cops?"

"Just come get me."

* * *

After he hung up with Healy, Joe tried Marla's number and got her machine. This is the message he left: "It's me. I love you. Don't be mad." He snapped the phone shut, knelt over, and emptied out the remainder of his breakfast and lunch.

* * *

An hour after putting down his house phone, Bob Healy pulled up to what was left of Vinny Serpe's 2000 Honda Accord. He couldn't believe what bad shape the car was in for what looked to be a low speed run-in was some scrub pines. When he clicked his flashlight on, Bob noticed streaks of black paint all across the crushed passenger side of the Honda. Well, that explained it, Healy thought. There had been an impact with a black vehicle that launched Serpe's Honda over the curb. If there were skid marks, they were obscured by the snow and there was no black car in sight.

"Come on, Joe," Healy said, pulling Serpe out of the driver's seat. The stink of vomit was intense.

"Bob?" Joe asked, voice thick, his eyes glassy and unfocused.

"Yeah, it's me. Let me have a look at your cut."

It was hard enough to see anything through Joe's thick hair, and the darkness wasn't helping any. The flashlight wasn't of much use either as the blood had dried and caked up.

"Okay, I'm taking you to the ER at Stony Brook. I don't think you're bleeding anymore, but I think you've got a concussion."

"I'm all right."

"You probably will be, but you're not now. Come on."

Healy walked Joe back to his car and help fold him into the front seat. He reached over him and put his shoulder belt on.

"Stay here. I've got to make some calls and get your car picked up."

When he got back into the car, Joe seemed agitated.

"Frank's protecting someone!"

"Yeah, you said that before."

"I did? When? I don't remember."

"Try and keep calm, Joe. You got a nasty knock."

"What happened to me?"

"You had a car accident."

"I know that."

"But do you remember the actual accident itself? You don't re-member a black car hitting you?" Healy asked.

"A black car? I remember leaving the jail and then … There's like a jumble of stuff that doesn't make any sense. What's this about a black car?"

"You got black paint all over the passenger side of your car."

Suddenly, Joe was agitated once again. "Call Marla! Did you call Marla?"

"Marla?"

"A woman."

"I figured that one out, but who is she, someone you're dating?"

"Dating, yeah."

"What's her number?" Healy asked.

Joe handed Healy his cell phone and passed out.

★ ★ ★

When he came to, he was on a gurney being wheeled into an examining room. The lights hurt his eyes and he felt the world spinning. When he shut his eyes and the gurney came to a full stop, the spinning of the planet stopped as well. He could hear people speaking, thought he recognized Healy's voice, Marla's too, and a stranger's. All he wanted was to be unconscious.

"Mr. Serpe. Mr. Serpe," the strange voice called to him. "That's it Mr. Serpe. Can you please sit up. Good. Good. Take it slowly. Slow."

When he opened his eyes, he could make out Marla's face, Healy's and the stranger's, a doctor, Joe guessed. But Joe had that disconnected feeling again, like he was locked away in a bunker in his own head watching himself watching. He could feel one eyelid being pulled back, his eye forced to follow a beam of light. Then the same routine was followed with his other eye. He was poked and prodded for a good ten minutes and then sent to X-ray.

★ ★ ★

"Is he all right, doc?" Healy asked. "His memory keeps going in and out."

"Well, he's got a concussion, but I suppose that's no revelation to you. I'm just having x-rays taken as a precaution. I don't really think he's got a skull fracture. The cut is relatively minor. His memory ... Let's just say it's not uncommon for there to be some measure of memory loss with this type of head trauma. His brain got thumped up against his skull pretty hard. He's a little disoriented, but it's nothing that rest shouldn't take care of. I'll prescribe some stuff for the pain and I'll schedule him to either come back for a follow up visit with me or another physician."

"As he heals, will any of his memory return?"

"I've got a very simple answer to a very complicated question. I don't know. The brain isn't like any other organ. He might regain some, but the closer you get to the actual impact, the less likely he is to recover those memories. This isn't like TV or the movies. You don't get whacked on the side of your head and wake up perfectly oriented and remembering everything clearly." The doctor regarded Healy with suspicion. "Why are a few minutes of memory loss so important? It says here that Mr. Serpe received his injuries in a routine traffic accident."

"Exactly," Healy said. "He smacked his car into some trees and it's probably not important. I was just wondering if maybe another car was involved that might have left the scene. That's all."

The doctor seemed satisfied with that explanation and excused himself, saying he'd check up on Joe when he came back from X-ray. Marla, who had sat quietly as Healy questioned the doctor, approached Bob. They had shared only a few words before Joe was brought in to be examined.

"I never got a chance to thank you for calling me," she said.

"No problem. He asked me to call before he conked out."

"Are you a friend of Joe's?"

Healy laughed. "I've got a very simple answer to a complex question. I don't know what I am to Joe."

Now *she* laughed. "I guess that makes two of us. How do you guys know each other?"

"We were both city cops once."

"Were you a detective like Joe?"

"Yes and no."

"What does that mean?"

"I was a detective, but not one like Joe."

Marla opened her mouth to ask another question, but Healy cut her off.

"Listen, can you handle it from here? I've got somewhere I really have to be."

"Sure. And thanks again, Mr. Healy."

"Bob."

"Bob," she repeated, smiling. "I don't know Joe very well, but I know him well enough to say you must mean something to him for him to call you first."

"Thank you, Marla." He offered her his hand. "Joe's lucky to have you."

She took his hand. "I think I'm lucky to have him."

"I think you are, too."

* * *

They met in front of Jerry's Joint. Strohmeyer the Younger suggested they take his car the first few nights out so he could show Bob the routes he and his teams of vigilantes took. Healy agreed without complaint. Bob had already done enough driving for one day and his car smelled a little like vomit, courtesy of Joe Serpe.

They were into Farmingville within ten minutes. As he drove, Strohmeyer Jr., parroting his father, explained that their patrols served several purposes, only one of which was to bolster the citizenry's—read that, white citizenry's—morale, to set an example of how they could stand up for themselves. The other goals of these patrols were symbolized by what Pete Jr. called the three Ps: Protection.

Preemption. Prevention. It was all very lofty stuff that meant nothing. Healy didn't really expect the kid to admit that the actual purpose of these patrols was probably provocation and violence.

He took a very circuitous route through town and into Ronkonkoma and back again. As he went, Pete Jr. pointed out what he called "trouble spots" to Healy. These were places known to be frequented by the "rice and bean" crowd. The trouble spots ranged in nature from bars and restaurants to churches and clinics.

Strohmeyer Jr. went on to say that at least three cars, two men in each, were out at any one time and that they patrolled the streets from sunset till about two in the morning. The AFA's goal was to have at least eight cars on the streets and to extend the patrols until the groups for the shape-ups began forming at around six AM. Healy barely spoke, waiting for the right opportunity to begin broaching the subject of Reyes' murder. Something he figured he'd have to do in small increments over the course of several nights.

"You'll have to get a Nextel phone," the kid said. "This way we're all on one network and can communicate from car to car. We can help you with the cost of that. It's one of the things we raise money for."

"Great," Bob said. "You don't really expect much trouble on a night like this."

"No, sir. The brown tide recedes in the cold and snow."

Healy felt like he had his opening. "So when do you get your most action?"

The kid may have been built like a linebacker and not been very eloquent, but he was no fool either.

"Action? Look, Bob, like I said before, action is not what we're about. We're about–"

"I'm sorry, Pete."

"That's okay. My father warned me when we first started these patrols that some people would join in the hope of getting into fights. There's a lot of pent up anger in this town and it only hurts our cause when people act stupidly."

"I never used my weapon in anger in twenty years on the job. I guess I was a little careless in how I worded what I was saying before," Healy explained.

"My father didn't figure you were a hothead."

"How's the hand? Looks painful."

"I can handle pain."

"Learn that playing football?"

A prideful smile lit up Pete Jr.'s face. "Four years at Arizona."

"Go Wildcats. You play linebacker?"

"Standup defensive end, but special teams mostly."

"Special teams, yeah, that would explain learning to deal with pain."

That did the trick. The younger Strohmeyer was glad to meet a New Yorker who knew college football. They discussed the bowl games and the unfairness of the BCS ratings. They talked about the draft and how little money professional football players made compared to baseball and basketball players.

"It's not right," Bob said.

"No, and none of the money except your signing bonus is guaranteed."

The kid seemed all right, Healy thought. His head seemed to be screwed on straight and he was not unsympathetic toward nor unaware of the plight of the less fortunate.

"The black guys really get a bad deal," Pete Jr. complained. "When they're recruited they get promised a pro career, but they usually just get chewed up and spit out without really getting an education. I think if a college recruits you, they should either fund your education no matter how long it takes or compensate you, even if you get hurt or cut from the squad. Maybe then the recruiters would be more up front."

It was not an unreasonable point of view. But Healy knew better than to make judgements based on simply liking a guy. Christ, he'd always liked and respected Joe Serpe, but he never let that effect the way he built his case against him or his partner. He remembered that he had once had a fierce argument with his dad about the trust-worthiness of a neighborhood kid. His dad warned him off the kid. Bob argued that the kid was really nice and he was always respectful of his elders.

"Yeah," his dad said, "and the English cocksuckers that tried to tear the guts out of Ireland loved their children. Didn't make them good neighbors."

Bob tried to take advantage of the newly established bond between him and the boy.

"So I get that we're out here trying to protect, preempt and prevent, but there've been two murders around here recently."

"The retarded man was killed in a dark oil yard. What can we do about that? Besides, I don't think we even patrol down that far. We don't. I'm sure we don't. The Reyes guy … Hey, if these wetbacks want to kill each other, they're going to kill each other. Believe me, Bob, you've got no idea what it's like in southern Arizona. You don't want to get into the middle of that shit."

"No, I suppose not. Watch it!" Healy screamed.

Strohmeyer Jr. still had his game reflexes and jerked the wheel just in time to avoid the man stumbling out in front of his car. He slammed on his brakes and was out of the car before Bob had even unlatched his seatbelt. Healy couldn't believe they'd missed him. If manner of dress was any indicator, the guy lying face down in the slush was a day laborer. He sported the standard uniform of a hooded sweatshirt, denim jacket, dirty jeans and work boots.

Here it was, Healy thought, a test.

"Hey, Bob, help me turn this guy over."

Healy knelt down opposite Pete Jr.

"Okay, slowly. I'll stabilize his neck. If he's badly injured we don't want to make it worse. On the count of three. One. Two. Three."

They rolled him gently over onto his back. His face was puffy and bruised. He was bleeding from his nose, his mouth and cuts on his cheek and above the eyes. His breath stank of alcohol.

"Bar fight," Strohmeyer Jr. said.

Healy agreed.

Then Pete Jr. started asking questions of the injured man in remarkably fluent Spanish. As the man's eyes were almost swollen shut, it was difficult to see if he was as surprised by this as Healy. The laborer's answers were slurred and, from the puzzlement on Pete's face Healy surmised, incoherent.

"He's Mexican and his name's Hector. That's about all I got. Come on, Bob, let's get him into the back of the car and call the cops."

When they got him in the car and Strohmeyer had called it in, Healy was curious as to why he had called the cops.

"This is just the kind of stuff we want in the papers, Bob. The media hates us, but my father says that doesn't mean we can't use them. You yourself brought up the murders. Before these guys got here, how many murders do you think there were around here in a given year? How much gang activity? How many bar fights on a snowy Tuesday night? Like my father says, it just proves we are right. The people on this island will be overrun. The more coverage, the better. Just one thing, when the cops get here don't mention that we are out on patrol. That's the rule. We don't want the cops thinking we did this."

So far this kid was failing all the tests. He wasn't a screed spewing, halfwit, hate monger. He really seemed to think things through. His only blind spot appeared to be his father's teachings, which he accepted without question. He wouldn't be the first. He had been gentle and respectful of the guy now bleeding all over his backseat. Healy couldn't help but root for the kid.

But if he was wrong about Pete Jr., where did that leave him? Where did it leave Serpe? Maybe he and Joe had been too quick to trust the word of some shithead gang leader. The truth was that the only two people with any viable connection to Cain Cohen's homicide were themselves dead. There wasn't a lot here to be encouraged about. Or maybe, Healy thought, staring at Peter Strohmeyer Jr., there was.

A cop showed in about five minutes. Officer Martinez, a handsome twenty-something cop with a white smile and neat mustache, seemed almost happy to have something to do.

"Pretty quiet tonight?" Healy asked.

"This weather, shit. It's dead out here, not even many fender benders. It's a night for staying home, for getting under the covers with someone to keep you warm. You know what I'm saying?"

One look at Hector and the cop called an ambulance. He didn't even bother trying to question him. Bob and Pete Jr. gave their stories, the ambulance came, and they said goodnight to the cop. When the cop left and the patrol started up again, something had changed.

"See the blood there on the backseat, Bob? That blood there is the problem. You get all these men, they come to our country. They have one purpose in coming—to make money and send it back to the sewers they came from. They're not like your ancestors or mine. They don't want to be Americans. They don't bring their families. They don't bring their women. They're lonely with a lot of time on their hands. It's not natural. They get shitfaced, get in fights. They take our jobs and some of them, the slick ones, the ones with a little English, they're ... They're the real dangerous ones."

Healy couldn't believe it. It was as if someone had thrown a switch in the kid's head. Not only had his demeanor and his language changed, but he had gotten louder, angrier. This was more of what Healy had expected. Something the cop had said must have set him off. Maybe not, maybe it was the cop himself. It was both, Healy decided. Officer Martinez had commented about getting under the covers with someone to keep you warm.

A woman! What else? Now it started to make some sense. Healy couldn't afford to let young Strohmeyer regain his equilibrium.

"Yeah," Bob agreed. "I'm happy that my daughter's grown up and moved off the island. I don't think I could have stomached her bringing Hector over for Thanksgiving dinner. If my Mary wasn't dead already, that would've killed her for sure."

Pete Jr. didn't answer immediately. His silence had nothing to do with careful contemplation of his response. No, his fingers got so tight on the steering wheel that all the blood went out of them. It was easy to see where the blood in the kid's fingers had gone as his face turned an angry shade of red. He started driving a little faster, his steering became more erratic. Still, he said nothing. Healy turned up the heat.

"When Colleen, that's my daughter, was a freshman at C.W. Post, she had a roommate, nice girl named Ava. Ava was from the Midwest somewheres, Ohio maybe. Anyway, Collie used to bring her over to the house for holidays when she couldn't afford to go back home. Ava began dating this really good guy, Brad. Athletic, smart, respectful; a man not unlike you, a man with a plan. We had him over to the house, too. Frankly, I wished he was dating *my* daughter.

"Then in sophomore year, things changed. Collie was home for spring break. She and her boyfriend were going on a double date with Ava. Mary and me just assumed it was gonna be Ava and Brad. We got some surprise when the car pulled up in front of the house. It was like one of those weird old Chevies with a sparkly green paint job that sat like six inches off the ground. What do they call those things?"

"Out west we call them lowriders," Strohmeyer said through clenched teeth.

"That's it. That's right. So, Ava and this little guy come bouncing out of the car. He doesn't shake my hand, asks for a beer, and screams at my daughter to hurry up."

"Did you throw the little cocksucker out of your house?"

"Didn't have to. One look at this guy and Colleen's boyfriend says they're running late and that they'll meet them at the restaurant."

"What happened to your daughter's friend?"

"The guy knocked her up and abandoned her. After that, we kind of lost track of Ava. I can't help but wonder about her sometimes."

Peter Strohmeyer Jr. slammed his good hand against the dashboard. "Fuck, that's what I told Cathy was going to happen to her, but she won't listen to me, Bob. She won't even talk to me anymore."

"You wanna tell me about it?"

"I can't. My father says a man deals with his troubles by himself."

"Hey, Pete, no disrespect to your father, but I'm a dad, too. I've made a lot of bad decisions and given my kids some awful advice. Fathers don't know as much as you think. And besides, you're your own man now. Don't you think there are some things you can make your own decisions about?"

He hesitated. "I guess you're right."

"I'm listening."

And listen he did.

It wasn't a very remarkable story. Pete Jr. had met Cathy at a bar in Selden. She was pretty, bright, and worldly, more worldly than the girls he knew back in Arizona. She had grown up in Manhattan and was in her first year at Touro Law School. To keep her expenses at a minimum, she was living with an aunt in Ronkonkoma and working as a bartender on the weekends. To hear Peter tell it, Cathy was the one. The feeling wasn't exactly mutual. She liked him well enough. The sex had been unbelievable—though he admitted to not having had a whole lot of previous experience. Healy recalled the first time he had mistaken sex for love and how deeply it had hurt. But sympathy was something he couldn't afford to offer at the moment.

"So what happened?"

"She told me she didn't want to date me anymore, that it was okay for us to hang out sometimes, even for us to fuck once in a while if we both felt like it."

"What did you say?"

"What could I say? I didn't want to lose her. And I guess I understood where she was coming from. I think she wanted—"

"Okay, Pete, she's the best thing since Paris Hilton, but it sounds to me like you're gonna start making excuses for her."

"Sorry."

"No apologies necessary, but something else musta happened."

"I followed her. You get pretty good at it, doing this patrolling and all. And my father taught me how to be a good hunter."

Strohmeyer Jr. explained that he spent days following her around and that he was pretty convinced their breakup wasn't about another man. Then, on Valentine's Day, he decided he'd try a grand gesture. He waited in the bar parking lot for the end of her shift, two dozen boxed red roses on the seat next to him, and an engagement ring in his jacket pocket. But when Cathy came out of the bar she was holding hands with this bar back, Garcia. They went to her car. He watched them makeout, watched her go down on him.

Healy thought the kid would explode. Apparently, that's exactly what he had done. Strohmeyer yanked Garcia, his pants still unzipped, out of the car and proceeded to knock him around the parking lot. A crowd started forming and Cathy barely stopped him from killing the guy. Healy asked if that was how he had really hurt his hand.

"No. I went to her aunt's house in Ronkonkoma few nights later to try and explain, to apologize."

Healy felt he was almost there. Just another little push …

"Apologize! What did you have to apologize for?"

"I still love her."

"Yeah, you still love her and some Mexican's dicking her up the ass."

Strohmeyer jerked the steering wheel hard right, the car bouncing off the curb. When it came to rest, he stuffed the transmission into park.

"You must have been pretty furious when she told you to get out, that she never wanted to see you again," Healy kept at him.

"I wanted to kill her."

"But you didn't kill her. You were out of your mind when you got back into your car. What did you do then Pete? You went hunting, didn't you? Hunting for the first wetback you could find."

"Get out, Bob!"

"What did you do when you found him, Pete?"

"Get out now!"

"You beat him up bad, but you couldn't stop yourself."

"Get the fuck out!" Strohmeyer screamed, grabbing Healy by the throat. His grip was solid steel.

Healy, always blessed with arms too long for his body, chopped his left fist down into Pete's groin. That took the wind out of Pete's sails, enough so that Healy could free himself of the kid's grip. Healy pushed his back against the passenger door, but didn't get out nor did he go for his .38.

"Sorry, kid," Healy apologized. "I just think you should get it off your chest."

"I can't," he said, some of the color draining back into his face. "I just can't."

Experience had taught Healy when to push and when to stop pushing. He decided he wasn't going to get anymore out of Strohmeyer Jr. tonight.

He extended his right hand. "Okay, I understand. Maybe you will have to deal with it yourself. Let's forget about it and finish up the shift. Tomorrow night, we won't even discuss it. But if you ever do want to talk about it, I'm up for it."

Pete took Bob's hand. "I'm sorry too. It's just that when I think about Cathy, I get a little … "

"Trust me, kid. We've all been there."

They spent the next two hours together in near silence. Officer Martinez was right, it was a night for staying home and getting under the covers with someone warm. There's nothing like dark, empty streets to remind a man of his loneliness.

Wednesday
March 3rd , 2004

JUST THE FALLEN

There are phrases we hear all the time that we accept without bothering to consider. How many times, Joe Serpe wondered as he opened his eyes to a new day of excruciating pain, had he heard it said that someone was kept in the hospital overnight for observation? He had an image in his mind of having woken in the middle of the night.

Nurse, what are you doing?

Observing you, of course.

Joe might even have laughed had the clamp crushing his skull loosened just a notch. Still, as bad as the pain was, his thoughts were a lot clearer today than … Christ, how long had he been in the hospital? He pressed the call button.

A bored looking nurse dressed in scrubs came into the room.

"How's the headache, Mr. Serpe?" she asked, neglecting to pronounce the 'e' at the end of Serpe.

"Serp-ee," Joe corrected. "And the headache feels like a curse."

"Well, you're more coherent than you were last night. That's good. I'll get you something for the headache." She checked her watch. "The doctor should be making his rounds within the hour. Would you like me to get your sister? She's sleeping out in the lounge."

He wasn't quite as coherent as the nurse thought, because the last time Joe checked he didn't have a sister. Maybe concussions are like bad Star Trek episodes, only with more pain and fewer commercials.

"Mr. Serpe ... Your sister?"

"Sure, send her in."

Marla looked awful and wonderful. He sat up in bed. It wasn't quite as dizzying and painful as he expected, but it wasn't a joy either. Marla sat down next to him, running her hands over his head, silent tears streaming down her checks. She kissed him in a most unfamilial manner.

"Here, Mr. Serpe, take one of these and—" the nurse stopped mid-sentence. At least she no longer looked so bored.

He took the capsule and swallowed without water. The nurse left, shaking her head.

Joe held Marla close. "Sis, if I'd only known you were such a good kisser ... "

"They weren't going to let me stay or give me any information, so I told them I was your sister. How's your head?"

"Hurts. How long have I been in here?"

"Bob Healy brought you in last night. You weren't making much sense."

"What happened to me?"

"You don't remember?"

"I know I went to visit Frank at the Suffolk County Jail. It was snowing and I think I remember getting on the L.I.E., but things are sort of a jumble after that."

"You had a car accident just off exit 70. That's where Bob found you."

"My brother's car, shit! What—"

"Bob took care of it. It's at his friend's body shop. He called before to see how you were doing. He wants you to call him if you're up to it."

"Good, yeah, I have to tell him that Frank's—"

"—protecting someone. Joe, you told him. He knows."

"God, I musta been in bad shape yesterday, huh?"

"You scared the shit out of me."

"I wasn't trying."

"Do you remember leaving me a phone message?"

He just smiled. Marla rested her head on his shoulder.

★ ★ ★

"Are you nuts?" George Healy shouted at his brother. "First you got me sticking my nose in every case since Judge Crater's disappearance and now you want me to ask the cops to search all their records for yesterday's accident reports and abandoned cars. It snowed yesterday, if you hadn't noticed. You have any idea how many accident reports there are going to be?"

"Just the L.I.E."

"Just the L.I.E. what?"

"Between exits 72 and the Suffolk/Nassau border. So it would probably be a Highway Patrol report."

"Do me a favor, Bob. Go to the dictionary and look up the meaning of the word 'retirement.'"

★ ★ ★

As Joe had asked, Marla went back to his apartment to feed Mulligan and to pick out some clothing for him that didn't smell of vomit or number two home heating oil. She understood that much of his request. She was far less certain about why Joe wanted the big picture of him and Frank standing under the Mayday Fuel Oil, Inc. sign. Removing the picture from the dresser, Marla noticed another picture. In it, Joe, his hair all black, face clean-shaven, held a young boy in his lap. The boy had Joe's face, a Yankees cap on his head, and an oversized first baseman's mitt on his right hand. She replaced the picture and, as instructed, reached into the rear of his sock drawer.

She felt the edges of a small box and got it out. Curious as she was, Marla didn't open it. She packed all of this stuff neatly into Joe's gym bag, rubbed Mulligan's cheek and locked the door behind her. When she pulled out of the driveway, Marla was too lost in her own thoughts to see the black Navigator trailing her down the block.

* * *

The three of them sat in the booth of the Venus Diner. Joe, his head finally feeling a little better, sat next to Marla. Healy, just having finished detailing his first night on patrol with Pete Jr., sat across from them.

"So, you think he did Reyes?" Joe asked, sipping his coffee.

"The Strohmeyer kid did something to somebody. That I'm sure of. Was it Reyes? I don't know, but the time line fits. I'll push him a little harder tonight."

Joe didn't seem terribly pleased. "Even if he did Reyes, that leaves us with no connection to Cain."

"Maybe, maybe not," was as close to encouraging as Healy would get.

"And if this kid killed Reyes, there's nothing to tie it to Toussant's murder."

Healy countered. "Not for nothing, Joe, but who says there has to be a connection?"

"I say. I feel it in my gut."

"I said that to my brother and he told me it was gas."

Marla laughed. "Can I steal that line?"

"Be my guest," Healy said. "So, you guys going back to your apartment?"

"Not what I had in mind. There's stuff that needs to be done this afternoon."

"Like what?"

"Marla's going home to get some sleep," Joe said. "She didn't get much last night."

"You're the one that needs to rest," Marla argued, a yawn betraying her.

"I'll rest tonight when Bob's out with this Strohmeyer kid. In the meantime, him and me, we've got somewhere to go."

"Where's that?" Healy asked.

"A motel."

"A motel, huh?" Healy puzzled.

"Maybe more than one."

Even Marla was curious. "Why motels?"

"I may not remember much about yesterday, but I know Frank. He's scared. There's a reason he's taking the fall for somebody here."

"Blackmail. You think he's being blackmailed!" Healy said.

"I do. What's the best way you know to blackmail a married man?"

"Sex," Marla chimed in.

"Exactly. And when I spoke to his wife, she was weird about their marriage."

Healy was skeptical. "It's a stretch."

"Let's go find out."

★ ★ ★

Located on the south service road of Sunrise Highway in Bayshore, the Blue Fountain Motor Inn was a monument to three hour rentals and questionable taste. Not that it showed much of itself to the outside world. It was the kind of place that you'd drive by without noticing unless you knew where it was or were specifically looking for it. Even so, you might miss the place. It had a small, poorly lit sign and narrow driveway. Pull into that driveway and you were greeted by a too-large, cast concrete fountain painted in sun-bleached royal blue. From the looks of the fountain, it hadn't pumped a drop of water since Reagan's last term. In the summer, the rain water that collected in its five basins was probably the breeding ground for half the mosquito population on Long Island.

The Blue Fountain was the fourteenth such venue Joe Serpe and Bob Healy had visited since leaving Marla at the diner and making a brief stop to make copies at the local Staples. Joe's headache, which had come and gone in waves, was cresting again and Healy was getting discouraged.

"Your idea makes some sense, Joe, but you might be wrong."

"I know Frank," he said, dry-swallowing another pain pill.

"Okay, but this is the last stop today. It's getting late and I've got to meet Strohmeyer in a few hours."

"Last stop. Whose turn?"

"Yours."

They got out of the car and strode into the office. The name of the motel didn't matter. Whether it was the Blue Fountain or the Spinnaker or the Lighthouse, these places were all pretty much the same—long rows of low slung concrete boxes with beds, bathrooms, and porno channels. The offices were interchangeable as well. The one at the Blue Fountain was no exception. It featured more bulletproof glass than a small bank. There were signs posted all over the place explaining everything from acceptable means of payment to how to use the hot tubs. It kind of reminded Joe of the Suffolk County Jail, only less inviting.

"Hey!" Joe rapped on the glass, holding up the replica of his old detective's shield that Marla had retrieved from his dresser.

The sloe-eyed, middle-aged man at the desk was so intimidated he nearly fell asleep. He did put his magazine down as a small concession to Joe and Bob's presence.

"Can I chelp you, officers," the desk clerk asked in a vaguely Russian accent.

"Detectives!" Serpe corrected.

"Vatever. You are long vay from chome, no? You are New York City police."

"A long way from home," Serpe mocked. "Look who's talking. Where you from, Moscow?"

"Kazakstan."

"Thanks for the geography lesson. You ever see this guy here?" Serpe asked, sliding a copy of Frank's picture through a slot in the partition.

He didn't bother looking. "No."

"Look at the picture, comrade!" Healy barked.

He looked this time. Healy thought he saw a faint, fleeting glimmer of recognition in the clerk's eyes, but he couldn't be sure. It was just a flash.

"No." He slid the picture back out.

"You're sure?" Joe said.

"Many people come to motel. Ve look at their money not their faces. They return key, don't steal towels, is all ve care."

"How many other people work the desk?"

The clerk had enough talking for the time being and held up two fingers.

"Okay, I'm gonna leave this picture with you to show the other clerks," Joe said, jotting down his cell phone number on the back of Frank's photo. He slid it back through the partition. "Anyone remembers anything, have them give me a call. You mind if we look around, talk to the housekeepers?"

"Go, but don't bother the guests."

"Thanks."

They walked down the four rows of rooms. Only ten had cars out front. They found the housekeeper, a fat, sixty year old woman from Guatemala eating in one of the vacant rooms. She was no help, spoke more Russian than English, and she didn't recognize Frank from Frank Sinatra.

As they walked back to Healy's car, Joe hesitated in front of one the rooms. Healy was worried Serpe might be getting sick again.

"What's up? You okay?"

"Yeah, my head's feeling a little better, but that's not it. Forget it. I thought I had something, but it's gone. I guess my head's gonna take some time to unscramble."

They continued on, leaving behind the black SUV parked in front of room 217.

Back in Healy's car and heading to Serpe's apartment, they got down to discussing their favorite desk clerk from Kazakstan.

"So?"

"I think he's full a shit," Healy said. "I thought he recognized Frank."

"Me too."

"So, okay, let's see what we got. Frank's cheating on his wife. Maybe he's getting blackmailed, maybe he's not. Toussant's murdered, if not by Frank, then by his gun. He's willing to take a murder rap to protect someone, but you don't think it's his wife."

"You sound skeptical," Joe said.

"Sorry, Joe, but it doesn't hang together. It seems like there's two, maybe three completely separate things going on here and I don't see how you can tie them up in any way that makes sense."

"I know."

"You may not wanna hear what I have to say next," Healy warned.

"Never stopped you before."

"Bottom line?"

"Bottom line."

"You don't need any wild theories, magic bullets, or anything else to make sense of it."

"Then what do I need?" Joe asked.

"To believe Frank did it."

★ ★ ★

Joe crashed: too tired to think, almost too tired to breathe. There is a dimension of the womb in the surrender to exhaustion. He surrendered, falling into bed and letting the warmth and comfort of his weariness wash over him, pull him under and consume him. But only one sleep lasts forever and tonight was not the occasion for his. No, tonight he would be spit out, returned to finish what he had started.

When he opened his eyes he noticed the answering machine light flashing, flashing. He checked the clock. It was 9:27. His headache, though not completely gone, was now of human proportion. He almost smiled. He'd had sinus headaches worse than this. He had lived through those.

He pressed play.

You have two messages. First message:

It was a woman. Marla? Not Marla, Tina. She was crying, but not just crying. It was worse than crying. She was choking. Fighting herself, forcing herself to speak, to try to speak. He could make out her saying Joe. She didn't seem to be able to get beyond his name. *Click.*

Second message:

Same as the first, but Tina was winning the battle. If not winning, then fighting herself to a standstill. "Joe," she said more clearly now. "Frank tried to … " That was as far as she got for ten seconds or so, choking up again. "He tried to hang himself. In jail, he tried to hang himself. They airlifted him to Stony Brook." *Click.*

Joe grabbed his keys and ran out to the driveway. Twenty seconds later, he was back inside dialing a car service.

* * *

Pete Jr.'s demeanor was more like the night they first met at Jerry's Joint. Healy remembered a department shrink once using the term "flat affect." Well, that seemed to pretty much sum up the face Strohmeyer Jr. was showing the world this evening. It was more than just his expression, or lack thereof. He barely spoke to Bob. And for two hours they drove the streets of Farmingville and Ronkonkoma in the kind of silence long-married couples grow accustomed to.

"I'm sorry about last night, kid," Healy said in hopes of getting the ball rolling.

Another half-hour passed before Pete Jr. made a sound. The silence and his own fatigue had lulled Healy into a kind of stupor. That, and the fact that he wasn't as familiar with the streets in this part of Suffolk as Serpe might be, were responsible for him not noticing the kid had strayed off course.

They had turned north off Horseblock, up a huge hill and down the other side. Eventually they came to a wide, well lit boulevard Healy guessed was Middle Country Road, but further east than he tended to travel. The kid doused the headlights and let the car drift to the curb. He killed the engine. If there was something special to see, Healy was missing it.

"That's the Blind Pig," Pete Jr. said, pointing across the street.

If that was supposed to mean something, once again Healy failed to recognize its significance. Because of last night and his long day of checking out motels with Joe Serpe, he already felt off and slow-witted.

"I love her, Bob. I try not to, but when I try it just gets worse."

Now Healy caught on. They were parked across the street from the bar where Cathy worked. Junior was obsessed with her. Bob had been in the same place once upon a time. Many years ago, he had stood across the street from an old girlfriend's house, watching, praying, planning. Most men had been there. Men are fragile things. Women are the more resilient of the species. Men are brittle. Separate a man's shoulder in a touch football game and he'll continue to play until he can no longer breathe. Tell him goodbye and he breaks.

"I know how that is," Healy said. "I know exactly how that is."

"I want her back so bad it makes me crazy."

Improvising, Bob chose not to push, not by himself, anyway. He would let someone else do it for him.

"You wanna go have a drink? It's on me."

Pete Jr. hesitated.

"No, I couldn't stand to have her look at me the way she did that last time."

"You can't hide forever. I've tried it."

"But—"

"Don't worry, Pete. If you want, I'll talk to her for you."

Strohmeyer's face lit up. Healy had uttered the magic words. Rescue fantasies never die, they just grow less ambitious with time. At Pete Jr.'s age, the dream of someone to set things right was still a powerful one. And with a father like his, the dream would be downright intoxicating.

"If I could only make her understand."

"Well, let's give it a shot."

Once again Pete Jr. was out of the car before Healy had unbuckled his seatbelt.

★ ★ ★

Currently, Joe Serpe didn't feel anything but sorry for Tina Randazzo. If he gave it any thought, he didn't suppose he liked her very much. He had met her only twice in the three years he had worked for Frank. It wasn't like on the force where there were parties with other cops and their spouses. The oil business was different. There was a purposeful separation between the job and family. It was a bit of a wild west business that attracted all sorts of fallen angels, and just the fallen. The oil yard was no place for a woman like Tina.

Tina was the high school prize, a unanimous selection to the All Star Wet Dream Team. She had done a lot of print ad modeling, put herself through the State University of New York at Binghamton, and was all set to turn the fashion world on its ass. Apparently, someone neglected to tell the fashion world. When the jobs dried up, lack of funds forced her to move back to her parents' house in Babylon. It killed her to do it and she was determined to get out. Frank—roughly handsome, driven, successful—seemed as good a way out as any.

Frank had confided to Joe that Tina felt she had married beneath her station and that she wasn't shy about letting him know it. That was just the type of thing to hurt Frank, a savvy, street-smart guy who'd barely squeaked by in high school and who'd lived by his wits. For years Joe Serpe listened to Frank pour his heart out about their marriage, but never offered advice. Who was he to give marriage counseling?

The curse of beauty is that when it shows cracks, the cracks show wide and deep. Tina proved the point. Her imperial thinness had turned against her.

"Joe. God, Joe." She embraced him for a long time. He could feel her tears on his neck.

He pushed her back gently to arms length. "Tell me what happened."

"They found him in his cell, hanging from a bed sheet."

"What do the doctors say?"

"I don't know. They won't tell me anything. They're only talking to the cops."

He guided her over to a vinyl couch in the lounge.

"The kids all right?" he asked.

"I sent them down to stay with my parents in North Carolina."

"Okay. That was smart."

"You went to see Frank yesterday," she said. "He told me."

"Yeah, when I left him I got into a car accident and spent the last night in here."

"Are you—"

"I've got a concussion. I'm okay."

"I'm glad," she said automatically.

"Listen Tina, I don't think Frank did what he's accused of, but I get the sense that something else is going on here. First off, Frank would barely talk to me yesterday, said he didn't want my help, and kept trying to get rid of me. And the other day, when you and I spoke and I mentioned salvaging the marriage, you said something like you didn't think there was anything worth saving."

Tina was silent. She hung her head, grasping the top of her Coach bag with both hands as if it were a lifeline. It was a familiar scene in precinct interview rooms. It was that last gasp at holding out, that second before the suspect decides to spill his guts or give up his accomplices. Joe knew that sometimes they needed a little help when deciding. So he helped.

"I think Frank was being blackmailed."

Tina's hands relaxed. She unclasped the bag, reached in and removed a clear plastic case. She held it out to Joe.

"It's a DVD. I got it in the mail a few weeks ago."

"What is it?"

"I don't want to talk about it. Take it home and watch it."

"You sure?"

"We didn't—don't have a great marriage, Joe. A lot of that is my fault. But I really did—do love him. I just hope I get a chance to tell him."

Joe took the case, sliding it into his jacket pocket. Then he held Tina's hand. A malicious voice cut through the silence.

"Ain't this a pretty picture? What's a matter, Snake, you can't wait? If you two want a room, I think that can be arranged."

Before Joe could react, Tina shot off the sofa and was swinging wildly at Hoskins' face. He was quick to take a step back, but not before she had landed a clean left hook. The diamond of her engagement ring left a nice gash under the detective's right eye. It took both Joe and Kramer to pull her away.

* * *

Healy almost hated to see the expectant smile on the kid's face. The smile didn't last long. As soon as they stepped through the door into the noisy pub, the bouncer spotted Strohmeyer Jr. and headed towards him. None of this was lost on Pete. It hadn't escaped Healy's notice either.

"Go get us a table, Pete. I'll handle this guy. Do you know his name?"

"Everybody calls him Ox."

"Okay, go get us that seat."

Obediently, Pete slipped off to find them a booth.

As the bouncer approached, Healy understood why they called him Ox. He was a squat, thick man whose bald head, neck and shoulders were all of a piece. The guy was like a warehouse on legs.

"Your friend's not welcome here," Ox said, no aggression in his voice.

"Look, Ox, he doesn't want any trouble. We're here to have one drink and—"

"Listen, mister, I got no problem if you wanna stay, but *he's* gotta go." This time, Ox put a little muscle into his words.

"Okay, just let me go over and get him. Like I said, he doesn't want trouble."

"Go get him."

Healy, disappointed that this wasn't going as he hoped, about-faced and went to find the kid. He had wanted to get a beer or two into the kid, get him talking. He thought that seeing Cathy might knock him off balance. As he went, Bob looked at the bar. He figured the brunette working the sticks to be Cathy.

She was attractive enough in a modern sort of way, thin and muscular. She had a pierced navel and tattoos. Maybe it was an age thing, but Healy liked women with curves, not cuts and angles. Though only in his late forties, he had grown up in an era when only women's ears were pierced and the only people with tattoos were bikers and your drunk uncle who had fought on Guadalcanal.

She might not be his cup of tea, but Healy appreciated her style behind the bar. She was in control, flirting just enough with all the schmos to give them hope they had a chance with her, but not so much that they'd walk away crushed when she turned them down. Her tip basket was probably quite full.

Pete Jr. had exercised good judgement in selecting a corner booth far from the bar that kept the pool table between them and Cathy's line of sight. Bob slid in next to the kid and opened his mouth to speak, but Strohmeyer cut him off.

"She's beautiful, isn't she?" he said, getting all starry-eyed.

No. "Yeah, Pete, she's great. Listen, Ox says we've got to go."

"In a minute, Bob. I just want to look at her for—"

"Pete, we don't have a minute. We really got to—Shit!"

Ox was coming in their direction, his placid demeanor replaced by angry red knots of skin and bent lips that barely looked human. But it wasn't Ox they had to worry about.

Thud!

The dull sound of a liquor bottle smacking against the kid's skull caught Healy completely off guard. He turned just in time to see Cathy spit at the stunned Strohmeyer, who was now falling onto Bob's shoulder.

"You son of a bitch!" she screamed at him. "I'll kill you!" Cathy made to swing the bottle again, but Ox grabbed her arm before it started on its downward arc.

"Get him outta here!" the bouncer demanded, locking Cathy up with one arm.

Healy didn't need to be told twice. He latched onto the kid, who, though not unconscious, was definitely not all there. It took every ounce of Healy's strength to get the kid across the street and back into the car. He pulled the keys out of Pete's pocket, started the engine, and headed west down Middle Country.

"Where you going, Bob?" the kid asked in an other-worldy voice.

"To get some ice. Cathy whacked you one pretty good. I don't think you're bleeding, but I wanna keep the swelling down."

"No."

"No what?"

"Turn left here," Pete said, his voice still strange. "I want to show you something."

Healy was torn. He might not get Strohmeyer this vulnerable again. On the other hand, he didn't want to risk having the kid die on him. Healy was forced to admit to himself that in spite of it all, even the cruel things the kid had said the previous night, he kind of liked Pete. That when it comes to women, all men are idiots. It's just that when you're younger, it's harder to hide your stupidity. He found himself hoping he was wrong about the kid and Reyes.

"Let me get you some ice first. Then you can show me whatever you want."

"Turn left, Bob, please."

* * *

Marla was frightened by how much she needed to hear from Joe. She was even more frightened by how she felt when he finally called.

"How's your head?"

"Still there. I've got a headache, but I guess that's gonna be par for the course for a while."

"What's up?"

"Can you come and get me?" he asked.

"I'll be over in—"

"I'm not at my apartment. I'm at University Hospital."

Her heart was pounding. "I thought you said—"

"I'm fine. It's Frank. He tried killing himself tonight."

"My god! Is he all right?"

"They think he'll live," Joe said.

"I'll be there in half an hour."

"Do you have a DVD player?"

"What?"

"A DVD player, do you—"

"Yeah. Why?"

"That depends on what we see on screen."

* * *

In spite of the late hour and the nearly empty roads, it had taken them twenty minutes to get there. Some of that was attributable to the darkness and Healy's unfamiliarity with this part of Long Island. It galled Bob that this kid from southern Arizona knew the island better than him. Although Bob had lived in Suffolk County for decades, he still considered himself a Brooklynite. Point to almost any spot on a map of New York City and he could tell you how to get there by road, bus, or subway. Point to a spot on Long Island east of the Smithaven Mall, and he needed directions.

Strohmeyer had seemed to regain his wits about ten minutes into the drive, but continued to refuse Healy's offers of first aid. No, the kid was determined to get here. Wherever here was.

What here was, however, was pretty obvious. They had turned off a twisty, one-lane asphalt strip about two hundred yards back and pulled onto a gravel road. Pete had told Bob to park in a small dirt clearing in the midst of some tall pine woods. It was silent except for the sound of the engine and their breathing. Healy imagined that on a breezy summer night, this would be a beautiful spot for lovers who were short on motel cash. It was certainly a better choice than the Blue Fountain.

Pete Jr. reached over and killed the engine, grabbed the keys, and, as was his habit, got out of the car first. He walked around to the trunk, unlatched it, got a flashlight and a shovel. Healy wasn't liking this, not one little bit. It was eerily reminiscent of the kind of place he and Joe Serpe had taken Toussant. But when Strohmeyer handed him the shovel, it eased Healy's nerves some. Without a word, Pete just started walking into the woods, never turning on the flashlight. Fortunately, Healy could hear the kid's footsteps on the mat of fallen pine needles and see his breath in the cold air, because as they got further into the woods it got darker and darker still.

Strohmeyer's feet fell silent. Healy hurried to catch up. Ahead of him, a flashlight snapped on. A cone of light began slicing wide gashes in the blackness, the wounds sealing themselves as the back edge of the light passed through. Pete seemed to be searching for a specific spot, focusing the beam on an increasingly smaller area of the forest floor. By the time Healy stepped up to the kid, Strohmeyer had completely steadied the beam. It shone on a raised patch of earth covered with needles and branches between two big pines. You didn't have to be a cop to figure out what was buried under there.

"Cathy showed me this place."

"I figured."

"It's the first place we ever did it. You think she takes Garcia here?"

"I don't know, Pete. Why?"

"I left her a present. The ground was so hard, Bob," Pete said, no emotion in his voice.

"Who is it?" Healy asked, careful to keep his own emotions in check.

"Just some illegal I gave a lift to."

"Did he have a name?"

"Must have, but I didn't know it. Does it matter? It was probably Jose. That's how I think of him, as Jose. He had three thousand bucks in cash on him, but no ID."

"Three thousand—"

"Yes sir. You see, the illegals can't risk bank accounts and they usually live together in large groups. So they can't just leave their money laying around the house. These guys even sleep with it on them and carry the cash with them all the time. That is, until they can wire it home."

"Did you kill him for the money?"

"No, but I took it. He didn't need it anymore."

"Why are you telling me this, Pete?"

"Because I can't live with it. I can't sleep or anything without Cathy. And I want her to know. I want her to know she's the reason."

"Did you kill him here?"

"Yes, with that shovel. He was pretty drunk and easy to handle. I beat him pretty good. He didn't have much of a face left when I buried him."

"Did it feel good?"

"Great."

"Didn't get Cathy back, did it?"

"No."

Healy dropped the shovel on purpose. When he knelt down to retrieve it, he removed his .38 from the ankle holster and held it down by his side.

"You know I'm going to have to call the cops."

"I know, Bob. It's okay. I just want this to be over with. I want Cathy to know."

Healy didn't have the heart to tell the kid this was a long way from being over. The minute he called the cops, it would just be beginning.

"Does your father know?"

"He does now," Pete Strohmeyer Sr. said, stepping silently out of the woods, a flashlight in one hand and a nine millimeter in the other.

* * *

Joe Serpe was no prude and he had seen his share of porn, but it was another thing altogether watching his friend's star turn. The DVD featured Frank Randazzo, several stage props, and not quite a cast of thousands.

It was perverse, but Serpe was glad Marla was there to watch the video with him. If Joe were alone, he might have clicked the DVD off once it confirmed his belief that Frank was being blackmailed.

Marla convinced him that it was important to watch the whole thing through to the end. She was right, of course. As difficult as it was for him to watch, Joe understood that he couldn't afford to miss anything that might help salvage Frank's life.

As the video progressed, different things came to light. First they noticed that the DVD lacked a soundtrack. Whether this was a purposeful omission or simply a function of sloppy dubbing was impossible to know. Within ten minutes it also became obvious this was not a disc of one encounter, but a compilation of many encounters—a highlight reel, so to speak. As the camera was stationary and the perspective remained constant, it was pretty clear that the camera was hidden and that Frank had no clue he was being taped. Given the stationary nature of the camera and the fact that the top quilt on the bed was always the same, it was a good bet that these trysts not only took place in the same motel, but in the same room. Although Joe couldn't recall what the bedcovers looked like at the Blue Fountain, he was pretty confident that's where this had been taped.

The woman in the video had an exotic, almost Asian face and was built not unlike Tina, but with a competent boob job and ink black hair. Both Joe and Marla agreed that she was in her early twenties, twenty-five at the outside. Their encounters had a sort of natural progression. At first there was a sweet discomfort, almost a shyness between them. There was a lot of kissing and stroking. By encounter number four, the kissing was gone and Frank was in her mouth even before his clothes were off. By encounter six, they had run through every position in the known universe and each had gone every place there was to go. By their eighth meeting, the woman had introduced toys, a leather riding crop, and handcuffs into the mix. Initially, Frank seemed very ill at ease, but eventually got into the spirit of things.

Meeting nine featured a third player. She was blond, curvy, tattooed, pierced, and even younger than Frank's regular. Whereas the black-haired woman's vibe didn't scream "prostitute," Serpe had been a cop too long not to immediately recognize the blond for a working girl. Whether she was a part of the bigger picture or had just been hired by the other woman for the day was difficult to tell, at least initially. Then she did something that gave not only herself away, but the other woman as well.

"Look at that," Marla yelled, hitting the pause button. "She just looked right at the camera."

Marla was right. Throughout the DVD to this point, the black-haired woman had displayed amazing restraint by never once peering up to where the camera was hidden. She was so disciplined you could almost believe she didn't know it was there. Then Blondie slipped.

In a chair half a yard from the bed, only Frank's bare legs were in the frame. Blondie was on her back, legs spread, arms fully extended, her hands grabbing fistfuls of black hair. Though there was no sound, Blondie's mouth was wide open in canned ecstacy, giving the performance of a lifetime as Frank's girl went down on her. Then, without prompting, she turned her head to the right and stared directly into the camera, even squinting. Apparently, the black-haired woman noticed and slid up Blondie's body. She pulled her hair roughly as she positioned her perfectly waxed self over Blondie's mouth. As she did, she unconsciously gazed over her left shoulder at the camera. It was all over in a matter of seconds.

Joe felt he was still missing something, that there was a detail up on the screen that part of him knew was there, but that he just couldn't grasp. His eyes were killing him and his headache was getting worse.

"Shut it off," he said.

"But it's not finished. We should watch the—"

"I know, but I need to rest. My head's killing me."

Marla shut off the DVD, got Joe some water for his pills, and brought him a cold cloth. He fought sleep, but not for very long. When she was sure Joe was asleep, Marla restarted the DVD.

★ ★ ★

Strohmeyer Sr. didn't mince words.

"Drop the gun and start digging."

Healy did as he was told. Pete Jr. was right about the ground. It was frozen hard and blisters rubbed up on Bob's palms almost immediately.

"Not there, asshole! Over there, by the other hump."

Healy, leaving his .38 on the dark forest floor, trudged over to where the first man was crudely buried.

"Dad, don't do—"

"You disappoint me, son. You put everything I've worked for at risk. But I'll mend it. I always do."

"I didn't know what to do. Cathy … I was so—"

The father shook his head. "If you had only listened to me, boy, and not taken up with that trash. I told you nothing good would come of it."

Nothing had. The kid fell silent.

Healy was making very little progress, barely scratching the surface of the frozen earth. He hadn't said anything in the hope, slim as it was, that the son could persuade his father to stop the killing. It was now pretty clear that wasn't going to happen.

"You know you're not going to get away with this."

Strohmeyer Sr. laughed. "Talk about cliches. I expected more of you, Mr. Healy."

"Seems everyone's a disappointment to you."

The father quickly lost his sense of humor, pulling the nine millimeter's trigger. The bullet pinged off the shovel blade, knocking it out of Healy's increasingly raw hands.

"I am an expert shot and quite the hunter. How else do you think I managed to creep up on you out here?"

"Frankly, I don't give a shit, Strohmeyer. I don't know how they treat cop killers in Arizona, but they don't take too kindly to it here."

"I'll tell you what I know about cops, Healy. Whether they're from Sedona or Smithtown, cops hate Internal Affairs. There's not a cop who will shed a single tear over your obituary. To other cops, men like you are pariahs. They will no more mourn your death than the death of a sewer rat. That's if they ever find you out here."

Healy hated to admit, even to himself, that Strohmeyer was not far wrong. Although Internal Affairs personnel were no longer treated like the enemy within, they still weren't the most popular kids on the block and never would be. Of all people, the only cop who would care about his murder would be Joe Serpe. Now it was Healy who, in spite of everything, was smiling. God, he thought, really did have a rich sense of irony.

Healy's smile unnerved Pete Sr. "What are you smiling at?"

"You wouldn't understand."

He fired a second shot. This one ripped a chunk off the heel of Healy's right shoe. "Dig faster."

Healy ignored him.

"Why'd you follow us tonight?"

"I followed you last night, too. Let us say I was suspicious of you since that night at Jerry's. Something wasn't quite right about you. Then I thought back to the incident on Horseblock Road and how it was just too perfect. I also did some checking up on you. You live in Kings Park, nowhere near Farmingville. That, in and of itself, wouldn't necessarily bother me. We get believers from all over Long Island. But when I debriefed my son about last night and he told me that you seemed more interested in him than in the cause … "

Healy's hands were bleeding now and he decided the time had come to do something more than dig his own grave. He dropped the shovel.

"Pick it up and start digging," the father barked.

"No."

"I am going to kill you, Healy."

"You okay with that, Pete?" Healy asked the almost forgotten member of the funeral party. "I understand why you killed Jose, here, but me? Are you comfortable with this?"

"Shut up!"

Strohmeyer Sr. uncorked another round, this one taking flesh with it.

"Fuck!" Healy doubled over, grabbing his left ear, but he couldn't afford to stop now.

"I never did anything to you, kid. You're having a hard enough time living with the murder you committed already. How you gonna live with this?"

Pete Sr. lined up the killing shot.

"Dad!" the son screamed.

Both Healy and the father turned slightly. Things had changed. Now not only was the son holding a flashlight in one hand, but a nine millimeter of his own in the other.

"Drop it, Dad, please."

"Son, you're not supposed to be armed."

"I wasn't supposed to be a lot of things. I know I have been a terrible disappointment to you and I am sorry."

"Son—"

"Please, Dad. I can't let you do this. I won't!"

But Peter Strohmeyer Sr. was a stubborn man, a man who thought he always knew the right course. He swung his hands back into firing position.

Bang!

Never in the history of time had a fraction of a second lasted so long. The pain in Healy's ear vanished. He squeezed his eyes shut and sucked in his breath as he waited for the impact. He knew what to expect. He would be knocked back some, then there would a burning, searing pain. If it hit bone and flattened, the bullet would slow down, gouging out piles of flesh as it went. Or if he were lucky it might be a thru and thru, passing in and out before he could let out his breath. But he knew good fortune was not likely to be on his side. Strohmeyer Sr. was not the type of man to fire once and be done. He would finish Healy up with a headshot just to make sure.

Someone was screaming. It wasn't Healy. Bob exhaled, opened his eyes. Peter Sr. was rolling on the pine needles, his left hand grabbing his right wrist, blood oozing out between the fingers. Healy ran to the father, kicked his automatic into the woods and grabbed the flashlight. He retrieved his .38.

"I'm sorry for all of this, Mr. Healy," the kid said. "I just want Cathy to see how much she means to me."

"It's okay, Pete," Healy tried to calm him. "Sometimes things get out of hand and we can't control them. The jury will understand. Let me call the cops and get an ambulance for your dad."

Peter Strohmeyer Jr. turned the flashlight up so that it illuminated his face from the chin up. "I am the jury."

"Take it easy, Pete, I'll see the cops treat you okay."

"Mr. Healy, is it true that when cops kill themselves they use only one bullet in the chamber so that if their kids find them, the children can't hurt themselves?"

"Son!" the father shouted. "Stop this now and hand over your weapon to Healy."

"Kid, don't do anything stu—"

Tears were streaming over Pete Jr's face. "Just answer me, please," he begged.

"Yes, Pete, that's how they do it."

"Thank you, Mr. Healy."

Before Bob Healy could react, the kid placed the muzzle of the nine millimeter to the underside of his chin, halfway to his Adams apple and blew a hole threw the top of his skull. The night grew even darker, but would never be quite so silent.

* * *

Serpe's eyes fluttered open. His head didn't feel half bad. Marla had curled herself up in his arms. It felt so natural, her there, almost a part of him. But even new love can't stand in the way of a man's bladder. Gently, he slid out from beneath her and answered nature's call. When he got back, he checked the clock. It was nearly four in the morning, Marla hadn't stirred, and he didn't feel much like sleep. He knew he would go back to watching the DVD eventually, but not yet. He paced around her apartment, went into the kitchen, poured himself some orange juice. When he closed the refrigerator, something got his attention. He found himself staring at the Chinese takeout menu Marla had magnetized to the fridge door.

"Fuck!"

He ran to the TV and switched it on, got the DVD remote, hit play. The silent version of Frank's greatest hits started playing once again. Joe was helpless with remotes and couldn't stomach the thought of watching the whole thing again just to get to the part where Blondie makes her debut.

"Marla," he whispered, kissed her cheek. "Please get up."

"What time is it?

"It's time to get up."

She sat up, rubbing sleep out of her eyes. "What's wrong?"

"Nothing, I just need your help with the clicker."

She sneered, but dutifully took the remote from him. "What?"

He explained about needing to advance through the DVD until Blondie showed up. Within two minutes, Marla had advanced the video to the point Joe wanted and handed the clicker back to him. He hit play. On screen, the two woman were going down on each other, black hair on top. Then they reversed positions.

"There!" Joe said. "Freeze it!"

"There what? All I see is her fat ass."

"Not her ass. What's *on* her ass."

"A tattoo? What about it?"

"Can you make out what the tattoo is?" he asked.

"Writing."

"Yeah, but it's not English, is it?"

Marla got up close to the screen. "No, I think it's Cyrillic."

"Like Russian?"

"Like Russian," she agreed. "I could probably get it translated for you by someone in my family. We're Russian Jews on my mother's side."

"What, are you going to bring this video to an old age home? You'd kill half the residents. What would you say: 'Hey, anybody know what the Russian on the chubby hooker's ass means?'"

"What am I going to do with you, Joe Serpe?" she wondered, leaning over and kissing his cheek. She got up and went into the bedroom. When she came out, she held a sketch pad and a charcoal pencil.

★ ★ ★

The cops didn't have as much trouble finding the spot as Healy anticipated. Within ten minutes of the first blue and white's arrival, it seemed like half the official vehicles in the county were there. The first cop had a little difficulty grasping what he had walked into and, upon reflection, Healy understood why. Even in New York City, cops don't usually show up at crime scenes that involve a homicide, a suicide, and two other victims with gunshot wounds.

Healy was forced to repeat his version of the evening's events so many times to so many people that the story started taking on a life of its own. He felt as if he were repeating folklore and not detailing things to which he had actually been a party. With each telling, the things he described got further and further away. At least the EMT didn't seem particularly interested in anything other than bandaging his earlobe and raw hands.

Thursday
March 4th, 2004

IDIOTS AND THE DEAD

arla had never been to a motel so early in the morning, nor had she ever blown off work two days running. She wasn't quite certain which dubious accomplishment she was most proud of. At the moment she was leaning toward the former, because she had the added honor of being the one to rent the room while Joe kept his head below dashboard level in the front seat of her car. He wasn't willing to risk being spotted.

"Room 113," Marla said, tossing the key on his lap.

"Great, my lucky number. Can I use your cell phone? I want to check in with Healy and see how last night went."

"I knew I forgot something. Where's yours?"

"When I got Tina's message about Frank, I ran out of my house. Then when the car service came, I just forgot it. I guess I was still a little discombobulated."

"Whatever happened, I'm sure it can wait."

Marla had actually never been more wrong about anything in her life, but because Healy's excitement had happened so early in the morning it didn't make *Newsday* or any of the city papers. And because Joe wanted to make absolutely certain Marla understood exactly what he was up to, they hadn't listened to the car radio on the way over to the motel.

"Describe the desk clerk," Joe said.

"A tired looking bottle blond in her late forties. She was pretty once, but hasn't come to grips with the aging process. She's the type of woman who thinks that another inch of makeup will undo in a moment what it took cigarettes and gravity decades to create. I guess I shouldn't be too critical. My mother wears so much makeup you swear you could peel it off in one piece like a latex clown mask."

Joe shook his head. "Did she have an accent?"

"Accent?"

"What did she sound like?"

"Like blinis and borscht," Marla joked.

"Is that supposed to mean something to me?"

"She sounds like Natasha from Rocky and Bullwinkle."

"Now *that's* an answer, I think."

The moment they walked into Room 113, Joe's suspicions were confirmed. No two motels could possibly purchase the same hideous orange top quilts. This was definitely the place where Frank had made his porn debut and all the sequels. Now to find the right room.

"Okay, time to go hunting for a chambermaid," Joe said as they slipped out of the room. "You're sure your Spanish is good enough to make yourself understood?"

"How many times are you going to ask me that?"

"Sorry."

There were very few cars parked in front of the four rows of rooms. That they hadn't spotted the maid's cart in the first three rows was of no worry to Joe. They had the room for three hours and he was sure he and Marla could figure out something to do to kill the time until they went looking again.

"Over there, at the end!" Marla shouted, and then realized she had been too loud. "Sorry."

When Serpe peered into Room 420, he recognized the woman he and Healy had spoken to the previous afternoon. She was drinking coffee from a Styrofoam cup and eating the last bite of an egg sandwich. At first, she didn't seem to remember Joe. When she did recall his face, she didn't exactly leap up and give him a big kiss. No one likes you when you are a cop and that doesn't change when you're only pretending to be one. He didn't waste time and got Marla involved.

"Her name is Maria," Marla said, smiling. "And she says she has a green card."

"I don't care if she's got a pair of jacks. Just describe the two women to her and ask if she's seen them around. If she tells you she's never seen the black-haired one, she's full of shit."

Joe had used that phrase on purpose. It was another one of those lines that usually didn't require translation.

"The blond, Maria says, she doesn't know. The one with the black hair … Maybe."

Joe again decided not to waste time. He knew that maybe meant 'more money, please.' He took out the roll of cash he had stored in his pocket just for this purpose. He snapped off a ten. Maria sneered as if he had insulted her honor. He added a twenty. Maria seemed less hurt, but still wasn't having any. When he added a second twenty, she licked her lips. When she went for the money, Joe yanked it back. Now she just looked angry.

"Tell her the money is hers, but I want to hear everything she knows about the black-haired woman, including what room she always takes her men to."

Although Serpe understood only enough Spanish to facilitate oil deliveries, he could read the disdain on the chambermaid's chubby brown face.

"She calls herself Tatiyana. Maria says she's a real bitch, but that the motel management treats her like royalty, almost like they're frightened of her. She always gets Room 217. That's all she knows."

The chambermaid held out her hand. Joe gave her the fifty bucks as promised. She stuffed the money in the pocket of her silly pink polyester uniform without bothering to thank him. But instead of taking offense, Joe peeled a fifty dollar bill off the roll and waved it at Maria. There was no translation necessary now. Without prompting, Maria began pushing her cart towards room 217.

* * *

Even though his moms hated it, living so close to Kennedy airport was a ceaseless source of excitement to Jamal Maybry. Walking to school was the best part of his day. Always out of the house early so he could take a detour through the off-airport cargo area, Jamal enjoyed the rush of the big jets swooping low over his head. In his opinion, the whine of the engines, the suck of the backwash, the smell of spent kerosene were the greatest things a boy could experience. He never tired of it, some days cutting school just to stand at the edge of the runway for hours on end.

Today, however, he had to get to school. They were giving one of those grade level achievement tests and he knew his moms wouldn't stand for his missing it. So when the JetBlue A320 whooshed past and its tail disappeared over the border fence, Jamal took his special shortcut through the abandoned lots.

He guessed he was in too much of a hurry when he stumbled over some ratty-assed roll of carpet. They dumped all kinds of shit in these lots.

"Damn!"

He stood up, brushed himself off, kicked the carpet roll in anger. But something wasn't right. When his foot connected, it felt like the stupid thing was filled with jello or some shit. He bent over and gave the carpet a push.

Fighting both the urge to scream and vomit, Jamal ran towards his house.

The chubby blond girl landed flat on her back. The shadow of an inbound Delta 767 passed directly overhead, her fixed blue eyes too dead to notice.

* * *

Bob Healy slid the coffee cup across the table to his brother. George took a sip.

"Jesus Christ!" He ran to the sink and spit it out. "The milk's curdled."

"Is it? I'm sorry."

"And look at this place. It's a mess."

"I know," Bob confessed. "It's not only the emotional things you lose when your wife dies."

"At least get a cleaning lady in once a week."

"Okay, George."

"So like I was saying before you tried to poison me, the lab's going to do that second set of tests on all the blood samples from the Reyes crime scene. You're sure the Strohmeyer kid did him, right?"

Bob hesitated. "Well, no. I think maybe he did. But I'm not sure. Last night before he … In his state of mind he might've done anything that would have gotten Cathy's attention."

"Cathy?"

"Forget it."

George pulled his attache case onto the table, opened it up, removed a manilla folder.

"Here are those police reports you wanted."

"What reports?"

"The Highway Patrol logs for the L.I.E. from—"

"Oh, right. Sorry. Thanks, little brother."

"That's it from me, though, bro. Go back to being retired before you get something more vital shot off than the bottom eighth inch of your fucking earlobe."

"Maybe I'll take up painting."

"Very funny. Remember how well that worked out for Van Gogh." George stood, leaned over, and kissed his brother on top of the head. "Go find somebody to love."

It wasn't a half-bad idea, Bob thought. Besides, he'd never been much of an artist. He went to the phone and tried Serpe's numbers again.

* * *

Maria parked her cleaning wagon directly between Rooms 217 and 218. She checked over both shoulders one last time to make certain neither the desk clerk nor the motel manager was around. She slid her passkey into the lock, gave it a twist, and shuttled Marla and Joe inside. Maria held up her right hand to indicate they had five minutes. Joe nodded his head that he understood. Maria closed the door behind her. They waited. They heard her knock on 218. No answer. They listened to her step inside and close the door behind her.

Joe turned to Marla. "Get on the bed."

"What? "

"Come on, I need to see the angle so I can figure out where the camera would be."

Joe straddled Marla as Tatiyana had straddled blondie and he looked back over his left shoulder. It didn't take more than thirty seconds to find where the camera had been. There was a television in the upper right hand corner of the room held in place by a metal bracket. Just beneath the bracket was a fresh patch of joint compound about three inches in diameter. The camera had been removed. This wasn't a good sign. People were covering their tracks.

Truthfully, Joe had very little to go on besides the DVD, a wall patch, and his suspicions. Neither the wall patch nor the DVD proved a thing by themselves. With Frank still unconscious, Joe couldn't even prove blackmail. As things stood now, the only thing Joe had viable proof of was that Frank had cheated on Tina with at least two women and that he might even have enjoyed having it filmed.

"Let's go," he said to Marla.

Joe put his hand on the door paddle, but he heard the sound of clickety-clackety heels coming their way.

"It's the desk clerk," Marla whispered, peering through a slit in the brown and orange drapes.

Joe turned to Marla, his index finger across his lips.

The heels stopped right outside their door.

"Vere are you, you fat bitch? Maria, *vena ca!*"

She pounded on the door of 217. Stopped. Pounded again. Stopped. She stepped to the right, pounded on the door of 218.

"Maria! Maria!"

Joe looked over at Marla, saw her shaking. Caught her eye and mouthed, "We will be okay." She smiled. Her smile convinced no one, least of all herself.

Maria wasn't answering the door at 218. Now they heard the jingle of keys and the heels moving back to their door. A key slid in the lock, turned, the paddle pushed down …

"*Lo siento, lo siento,* Ilana," Maria was breathless in her apology and began reeling off rapid fire Spanish.

Joe caught the word *bano*, Spanish for bathroom, several times.

Though it was nearly impossible to understand Ilana's perversion of Russian and Spanish, it was pretty obvious she wasn't pleased with Maria.

Joe gave Marla the thumbs up and waved his palms at her to stay calm. The wheels of the cleaning cart squealed as Maria pushed it away. Ilana's heels smacked the pavement, moving off in the opposite direction.

Letting another minute pass, they stepped out into what was turning into a sunny, if chilly, March morning. Neither the chambermaid nor the desk clerk were anywhere in sight. They walked back to their original room quickly, but not at a run. Marla was still shaking when they closed the door behind them.

★ ★ ★

Detective Jones opened his mouth to speak, but his partner, Detective O'Brien, put up his palms, then pointed straight up at the underbelly of the United 747 passing over head. They had quickly grown weary of screaming above the noise and then having to repeat themselves anyway once the jets passed.

"I wanna show you something," Jones said, his hair blowing in the jets backwash. "Over here."

They ducked under the tape back to where the dead girl's body waited to be bagged.

"What, you notice something?" O'Brien asked.

"Yeah." They knelt down over the corpse. "Let's roll her over. Ready? One. Two. Three. See that tattoo?"

"Yeah, and so … "

"She was probably Russian. Maybe a pro or at least into S&M."

"Who are you, Sherlock fuckin' Holmes?"

"The tattoo means slave in Russian."

"And a schmuck from the Bronx knows this how?"

"Spent four years in the bag in the Six-One Precinct."

"Brighton Beach. Russia in Brooklyn."

"Correct. Now let's get outta here. These jets are giving me a fucking headache."

* * *

As they rode back to Marla's apartment, Joe tried waiting her out. Silent and ashen, she seemed completely spooked by what had gone on back at the Blue Fountain. Serpe could have kicked himself. He had let the job ruin his marriage. Now his single-mindedness about Frank and Cain had let him get someone involved in things she had no business being mixed up in. He resolved not to let her get in any deeper and was about to say so.

"How did you do it, Joe? All those years on the street, how could you not be scared?"

"Only idiots and the dead aren't scared. I was scared all the time. The trick is not showing it. If the trick was not being scared, no one would ever step outside their house."

"How do you learn not to act frightened?"

"You just do, but you don't have to worry about it. You're out of it now," he said.

"Where are we going, Joe? My apartment's that way."

"We're going to rent a car. You need to have your life back."

"I don't want it back, not the way it used to be."

"Take it back, just for a few days. For me."

★ ★ ★

Three weeks ago it took Bob Healy several minutes to recognize Joe Serpe. Now all he could do was worry about the guy. He couldn't seem to get a hold of him and couldn't believe Joe hadn't somehow heard about last night. Healy resolved to try both of Serpe's numbers one last time and to keep himself occupied until he finally heard back from the man. He looked around and decided George was right about a lot of things. The house *was* a complete mess. Healy picked up the police report logs and began thumbing through them.

★ ★ ★

He didn't like having Marla use her credit card to rent the car for him, but he had little choice. Plastic is a luxury men with bad credit histories can't afford. The divorce and the legal fees from his troubles had ruined Joe financially. He was better now, having been named Vinny's sole beneficiary and working a job that paid him a nice chunk of change in cash, but until Marla he hadn't felt the need to reestablish himself.

The plan was to drive back to his apartment, shower, and try to set up a meeting with Tina. Those plans changed as he tried pushing back the front door. It stuck and then moved back, but not as easily as it should have.

Mulligan was dead. Some sick fuck had slit the cat open down the middle and turned him inside out, leaving him just inside the door so there was no chance Serpe would miss him. On the wall, in the cat's blood, were written the words: "LEAVE IT ALONE" and a phone number, *Marla's* phone number. Nothing else in the apartment was disturbed.

He fought back his tears, dialing Marla's number frantically. He became almost sick at the thought of not getting through to her.

"Hello," she said.

"It's me."

"What's the matter? Your voice is—"

"Get out of your apartment. Stay with family and make sure you're not alone at night."

"Joe, what—"

"Do it now!" he screamed at her. "Just fucking do it and don't argue. Keep your cell on you and call me when you settle on a place."

He slammed the phone down. Joe got a bag and wrapped Mulligan in it. He borrowed a pick and shovel from his landlord's shed and dug a grave. After tamping down the frozen dirt over the last remnant of his old life, he knelt by the grave and let out years of uncried tears. Just as Cain's death had let him live again, it had taken the slaughter of an old tomcat to make him realize just how much he had lost.

It was only when he came out of the shower that he noticed the messages.

* * *

Using location, time frame, and paint color, Healy had narrowed it down to three possibilities. Two, really. Of course there was a chance that none of these vehicles were responsible for the damage to Serpe's car or for the streaks of black paint left behind. There was a good chance that the car or truck had just taken off, never to be seen again.

The least likely candidate was the 2002 black Corvette stopped for excessive speed in bad weather conditions. The time was right: about 1:45 PM. The location was right: between exits 72 and 71 on the westbound L.I.E., but there was no notation about damage on the car.

The other two candidates seemed far more promising. About ten minutes after he stopped the Corvette, the same cop approached a 2004 black Lincoln Navigator that was pulled to the far right shoulder of the westbound L.I.E. just east of exit 70. The officer noted severe body damage to the front driver's side of the vehicle. When he asked the vehicle's operator if he needed assistance, the driver refused, saying he had pulled over to make a call.

The third and, in Healy's opinion, the most likely candidate was an old black step van that was written up for several violations including, but not limited to, operating an uninsured vehicle and the operation of a motor vehicle with a suspended license. The body of the van was badly damaged and the driver was arrested for an outstanding warrant. This guy had probably lost control in the snow, smacked into Serpe, and run.

Healy was just copying down the info when the phone rang.

★ ★ ★

Joe Serpe had never talked to anyone on his block. Christ, he barely spoke to the landlord. But he knew someone had to have seen something, so he started knocking on doors. Many of the people who recognized him as that quiet guy from across the street, invited him in for coffee. As he went from house to house, Joe realized that God was not responsible for his invisibility. Over the last four years, he had made himself disappear. Unfortunately, his new good neighbor policy wasn't netting him much information. No one had seen anything unusual. As he walked back across the street, he saw Healy's car parked in the driveway, Healy unloading paint cans from his car.

As Healy primed the wall to cover the writing, Serpe scrubbed Mulligan's blood off the linoleum tiles. Both men were deep in thought: Joe trying to make sense of what Healy had told him about the Strohmeyer kid's suicide and the possibility that his gut feeling was dead wrong, that there was no connection between Cain's murder and those of Reyes and Toussant. Healy was straining to see what possible connection there could be between Frank Randazzo's adultery and the three murders. Both of them were making much more headway with the physical tasks at hand. The bloody graffiti was now completely hidden and the cat's blood had been scrubbed away, along with years of neglected grime.

Neither Serpe nor Healy had any doubts about the warning written in Mulligan's blood. Someone, probably the blackmailer, wasn't happy with Joe sticking his nose into Frank's business. And now that Marla had been threatened, if indirectly, Serpe wasn't sure it was worth his continued involvement. Frank had made his choices and was paying for them. Tina would land on her feet. Women like Tina always did. Besides, Joe had lost enough. It was time for someone else to feed the beast. Soon the time would come when both men would have to admit defeat and get back to their lives.

Healy decided he would take the first step in that direction.

"Joe," he said, using a rubber mallet to close the primer can. "There's something I've been meaning to tell you since that Saturday you delivered oil to my house. It's about the case we made on you and your partner."

"It's ancient history, Healy, I don't wanna—"

"Okay, even if you don't want to hear it, I need to say it."

"I owe you that much. Go ahead."

"The original investigation—"

There was a knock on the door.

"Hello," Joe called out, rinsing the mop in the sink.

"Joe, Mr. Serpe," she said, sticking only her head inside.

Joe didn't know her name, but recognized her as someone who lived on the other side of the street.

"Come on in."

Joe wiped his hands on a towel and rushed to greet his neighbor. He held out his hand and introduced himself.

"My name's Pat," she said, taking his hand, "Pat Dahl. I live at number eighty-two, the brown ranch across the way there."

"Nice to meet you, Pat. This is my friend, Bob Healy. He's helping paint the place."

Healy nodded, smiled.

"So, what is it I can do for you, Pat?"

"My husband, Carl—you spoke to him today. The bald man with the—"

"Oh, yeah. Nice guy. Used to work sanitation in the city, right?"

"That's my Carl. Anyway, he says you told him someone was coming here to show you a car, but that you couldn't be home and you'd lost the man's number."

"I know it was dumb of me, but I really need a newer car."

"Oh, Joe," she said as if they'd been friends for years, "believe me, you wouldn't have wanted that thing. It was creased and dented all along one side."

"Really?"

"Trust me, I saw him pulling out of your driveway at about nine o'clock. That's when I go to the gym."

"Just so we can be sure it was the car I was thinking of, can you describe it to me?"

"I'm sorry, Joe, I wouldn't know one car from another. It was big and black. I guess it kind of looked like Jack Cantor's car. He lives at number ninety-six."

"Thank you very much for the heads-up, Pat. I don't need someone else's lemon. It was a pleasure meeting you. And say hello to Carl for me."

"Don't be a stranger," she said, and closed the door behind her.

Neither Healy nor Serpe needed to say it. They gave Pat thirty seconds to get back across the street before they took a walk down to number ninety-six.

Jack Cantor's car was a dark blue Lincoln SUV, but a smaller model—the Aviator, not a Navigator. If Healy was hoping the sight of it would somehow spark Joe's memory, he was wrong. The events of that Tuesday afternoon would be lost to Serpe forever. Healy, on the other hand, hadn't suffered a concussion. He didn't actually need Joe's memory, because he had the benefit of someone else's.

"Let's get back to your apartment, Joe. There's a police report I need to show you."

Friday
March 5th, 2004

BRIGHTON BEACH AVENUE

J oe met Tina in the waiting room.

The firm of Bayles, Cohen & Mann was located on Main Street in Babylon Village. They were a fairly diverse and successful firm for one located in such a lovely section of nowhere. Long Island is full of quaint little south shore towns with narrow streets, marinas and big brass clocks. But not many law school students daydream about passing the bar to set up practice in Babylon Village.

Bayles, Cohen & Mann did their share of ambulance chasing, real estate closings, divorce work, and criminal defense. They did, however, have one particular specialty. They were known as the lawyers to the home heating oil industry. So it was no surprise that Frank sought their services when he established Mayday Fuel Oil, Inc. It didn't hurt that Tina's father, a local insurance broker, had played golf with Steven Mann every Saturday for twelve years before moving to the Carolinas.

"How is Frank?" Joe asked.

"Better," she said. "He's breathing on his own now and the doctors think there's a chance he won't come out of it too badly damaged. They just don't know how long the oxygen was cut off from his brain. If he's going to spend the rest of his life in jail, what does it matter if he gets better?"

"That's what we're doing here, Tina, to try and make sure that doesn't happen."

"You watched the DVD?"

"I did."

Tina faced the floor, her face red with embarrassment, her hands once again squeezing the top of her bag.

"Men do stupid things sometimes. Things that don't make any sense to anyone but them. Then when they think about it, it doesn't even make sense to them."

Tina didn't want to go there. "How's *your* head, Joe?"

"It's much better. I'm still having headaches, but less and less severe all the time. So, did you check your bank accounts?"

"All the ones I know about."

"And?"

"Nothing. There haven't been any sizeable withdrawals for months. It's just the same boring stuff—the mortgage, utilities, food shopping, small ATM withdrawals, the kids' karate classes. Just stuff like that."

"How about deposits? Were the deposits smaller than usual?"

"No. Are you sure he was being blackmailed?"

"Yeah, Tina, I'm pretty sure. I don't know if this will make you feel any better, but Frank didn't know he was being videotaped and the women with him did."

"Do you know the expression cold comfort?"

"Mrs. Randazzo, Mr. Serpe." The secretary got their attention. "Mr. Mann will see you now."

★ ★ ★

Bob Healy pinched the phone between his ear and neck, waiting for Rodriguez to get back on the line. Skip Rodriguez, basically a sweet guy with a mean streak, had been Healy's last partner at I.A.B. He and Bob worked well enough together, but as the years passed, Skip's sweetness soured and the mean streak grew. He was good at his job, only just a little too cold-hearted for Healy's taste. Healy had thought about calling George and decided against it. He wasn't up for his little brother's lecture on the joys of retirement. And though he could've bullshitted George about why he needed to have him run a plate, there was some info Skip could give him that George could not.

As he listened for Skip to pick up, Healy thumbed through *Newsday*. Maybe, he thought, Serpe was right not to pay too much attention to the papers. There was very little new in the news, just a chronicle of old sins committed by a different cast of characters. The headline on a story on page 8 caught his attention, but Rodriguez got back on the line.

"I ran the tag like you asked," the detective said. "2004, Black Lincoln Navigator registered to Black Sea Energy, Inc., 2243 Brighton Beach Avenue, Brooklyn."

"That's the Six-One Precinct, right?"

"Right. What's this all about, partner?"

"You got anyone in the Six-One owes you a favor?"

"Are you kidding me? With all that Russian mob money floating around boardwalk, there's always someone jammed up at the Six-One or the Six-O in Coney Island. Why?"

"Because maybe I'd like to have a private conversation with somebody."

There was silence on the other end of the line. Healy could hear Rodriguez's wheels turning. Skip would want to know what was in it for him and was figuring out how to ask the question without offending his old partner. Bob saved him the trouble.

"If there's a case in it, Skip," Healy said, "it's all yours, but you've gotta throw me a bone here."

"I'll get back to you."

When Healy resumed his reading, he nearly turned the page before remembering the headline.

WOMAN'S BODY FOUND IN JFK LOT

There was nothing extraordinary about the story. Bodies had been dumped in the marshes and vacant lots surrounding Kennedy airport since before it was called Kennedy. What got Healy's attention was the police theory about the murdered woman having been a prostitute. The police also speculated that the unidentified woman might have been Russian or from some area of the former Soviet Union. When he saw the police artist's rendering of a tattoo found on an unspecified area of the woman's body, Healy was no longer just interested. He was downright fascinated.

★ ★ ★

Marla scribbled away, catching up on paperwork that had gone neglected even before she'd blown off the last two days. She'd always found that throwing herself into her work was a good coping mechanism. Joe had frightened her. It seemed to her that was his intent, yet he refused to discuss it with her even after she called to tell him she had done what he asked. He made her promise over and over again that she would go straight to her folks' house after work and would not go out alone at night.

Ken Bergman, the home manager, knocked and walked in without waiting to be invited. Marla didn't have the energy to lecture him about proper etiquette. And truth be told, she was kind of glad to see Kenny. She knew what he wanted, what he always wanted from her. It was the subtext of all their interactions. He had never made a secret of his crush on Marla. They had even dated a few times early on, but it hadn't turned out well. For Ken it had been magic; not so for Marla. He'd tried everything to win her affection.

Marla subscribed to the notion of immediate attraction. She needed no more proof than that first few seconds she had stood in Ken's office next to Joe Serpe. And if she hadn't surrendered to Kenny's charms before Joe, she wasn't going to succumb now. Lately, Ken had sort of settled into following Marla around the home like a lovesick puppy. Oddly enough, he was just the type of man she had always envisioned herself marrying someday, even if she had never been enthusiastic about it.

"How are you feeling?"

She was puzzled. "What?"

"You've never missed two days in a—"

"That. Oh, much better. Thanks for asking."

"You know I would have been happy to nurse you back to health," he said.

"Very cute, Kenny. Give it a rest, okay?"

"Seriously, Marla, I would do anything for you."

Now she was losing patience. "Ken! If you came into my office to—"

"Okay, okay, I surrender … for now. There really is something we need to discuss. Everyone's handled Cain's murder pretty well except Donna. She's been acting out and making herself a real problem for everyone, including the other residents. She's been reprimanded at her job several times. I think it's time for you to intervene."

"Of course, but why didn't you come to me sooner about this?"

"Well, I knew how close she and Cain were and I suspected it would be harder for her to come to terms with his death. But now we've reached the point where her behavior is too detrimental to ignore. And frankly, Marla, you've seemed a bit preoccupied lately."

There was no arguing that.

"Is she in-house today, Ken?"

"That she is."

"I'll set something up with her as soon as I wade through some of this paperwork. That work for you?"

"You're the shrink. I'm just the juggler. Let me know how it turns out."

★ ★ ★

Steven Mann was what Joe expected—affable but guarded, well-groomed and sharp. His office too held few surprises for Joe. There was the college degree from NYU, the law degree from Michigan, the framed letters from clients, the photos with politcos and sports figures, golf trophies, and model yachts. Mann took control of the conversation. He was used to it, comfortable with control. If you stripped away the niceties and the careful language, this is what he wanted to know of Tina:

1. *How the fuck is your dad's golf game?*
2. *Is your husband, the fucking murderer, going to survive?*
3. *Who the fuck is this clown with you?*
4. *What the fuck are you doing here wasting my time?*
5. *You're still pretty hot. If your husband dies, how would you like to fuck?*

Joe was no fool. Although he had been shown the door in disgrace, Serpe still had a nose for trouble, an ear for bullshit, and could read between the lines. He also knew when to talk and when to keep his mouth shut. During the preliminaries, he kept quiet and watched.

"So, Tina, what is it that I can do for you?" Mann asked.

"I think maybe Joe would be better qualified to explain all that. I'm going to step outside for a few minutes. There are some aspects of this I'd rather not witness." She stood, smoothed her skirt and placed a hand on Joe's shoulder. "Come get me when … " She let it hang.

Joe waited for the office door to click shut before tossing the DVD on the lawyer's desk.

"What's this?"

"Blackmail. That a DVD player under the TV?"

"Yes."

"Put it in."

They watched only about five minutes worth, just enough for the lawyer to get the gist of it. Joe explained about the DVD being sent to Tina, about how he had checked out the motel, about his visit to Frank in jail and about how someone had apparently tried to run him off the road. Then he described the message written on his apartment wall in Mulligan's blood.

"It's deplorable, all of it, but I don't see what I can do to help," Mann said.

Joe went and got Tina.

"Well, it all adds up to blackmail, but so far Tina can't find any unusual bank activity in any of their accounts. That leaves the business."

"Not necessarily," the lawyer countered. "Frank could have some accounts you don't know exist."

Tina spoke up. "No. Frank and I don't have the greatest marriage, but I know in my heart that he wouldn't keep money away from his family. It's just not something he would do."

"Tina ... Need I remind you what is currently in my office DVD player? I'm certain there are many things you believed Frank incapable of, but ... "

Joe didn't like the way this was going. Mann was trying to turn the conversation away from where they needed it to go.

"Okay, maybe you're right, Mr. Mann. Maybe Frank kept a slush fund or something. But you could help us eliminate the business as a possible source of money for the blackmailers. If he—"

"I don't mean to cut you off, Joe," Mann said, cutting Joe off, "but why come to me? Why not go to Frank's accountant? I'm sure he would—"

"Not to cut you off, Mr. Mann, but the accountant won't talk to Tina about the business."

"That's right," Tina said. "I called him yesterday and he said he wouldn't discuss any aspect of the business with me."

"Tina, it hurts me to have to say this to you, but I'm afraid I'm going to have to give you the same answer. You have no legal standing when it comes to Mayday Fuel Oil, Inc. Now, if Frank should, god forbid, be convicted or if he should not recover from his injuries, then—"

Joe was out of his seat. "Are you nuts? This woman's husband is facing second degree murder charges, he's tried to hang himself in jail, it's pretty clear he was being blackmailed, and you're gonna stand on some legal technicality?"

"I don't think I like your tone, Mr. Serpe."

"You don't?" Joe asked, grabbing one of the intricate model yachts that decorated the office. "Well, I don't like a lot more than your tone."

Snap! Joe cracked off the mizzen mast of the model ship.

"What are you—"

Snap! Another mast fell prey to Joe's strong hands.

"Listen, asshole, let's forget about Frank for a second here. Apparently, someone tried to kill me, my cat's been slaughtered and my girlfriend's been threatened. So, I'm not in the mood for legalese and bullshit," Joe said, sending the model crashing to the floor and grabbing a big golf trophy. "Club championship, I'm very impressed."

"Tina … Please!" the lawyer implored.

"You should be ashamed of yourself, Steven. I wonder if the state bar would be interested in the story of a lawyer who promised to get a minor her big start in modeling if she would only suck his–"

"That was once, almost twenty years ago, and I was very drunk," Mann argued half-heartedly. "How many times do you want me to apologize for that? And I did make calls on your behalf."

Tina was a bulldog. "What about the business, Steven?"

"All right," the lawyer surrendered. "All right, but if you had just waited a few days this would have all been moot."

The lawyer buzzed his secretary and asked her to bring in the Mayday file. Joe put the golf trophy back in its niche and took his seat. As the secretary entered the office, she gazed at the smashed model in the middle floor to which no one seemed to be paying the slightest bit of attention.

"Leave it, Lois. We'll see to it later. The file, please."

She laid it on his desk and left, shaking her head as she went. Mann opened the file, grouped certain papers together, skipped others. When he was satisfied that he had things just so, he spoke.

"Frankly, Tina, I can see how it might appear to you that Frank was being blackmailed. For all I know, he was. However, the business would not appear to be the source of funds for extortion payoffs."

"Why's that?" Joe asked.

Mann turned the document of sale so that Tina could clearly see it. "Because the business no longer exists."

* * *

Marla remembered being in therapy herself and how her therapist would sometimes ask her to give voice to her tapping fingers or toes. "What we do," her therapist would say, "is often more revealing than what we say." Marla never forgot those words, always making a point to note not only what the residents said, but what they did, how they moved. There is nothing less valid about physical expression than verbal expression. This was especially true of the population she treated, which could sometimes be almost completely non-verbal.

Donna slouched in the seat, twirling her hair, not making eye contact with Marla. Usually, her face was like a billboard, an uncomplicated message for all the world to see. It was one of the things about doing therapy with this population that Marla so enjoyed. Most people wasted so much of their energies building complexities, masks and defenses meant to hide the truth of their natures from the world and themselves. Getting to the residents' feelings was often not a problem for Marla. At times, their feelings were all they had. But there was a real downside to this proposition. With Cain, for example, his feelings were almost too raw, too much at the surface. Impulse control was frequently the issue that would bring people to her office.

"So, Donna, I hear you've been having some trouble lately. You want to talk about it with me?"

"I miss Cain."

There it was, that immediacy and honesty, but it wasn't lost on Marla that the Downs' girl still couldn't or wouldn't make eye contact.

"I miss him too. He was one of the most special people I ever met."

"He was more special to me."

"You're right. I think he was closer to you than anybody in the world. It's very hard for any of us to lose—"

"He loved Frank more. He wanted to be like Frank."

"Donna, I can't speak for Cain, but maybe I would say that he felt one kind of love for Frank and one kind for you. Maybe the way you feel differently about Ken and about me."

"I don't love Ken or you."

Point well taken.

"All right," Marla said. "It hurts very much to lose someone we love, but I think it's supposed to hurt. It's a way for people to understand how much the dead person meant to us. We all understand how much pain you're in, even the people at McDonalds know."

"You don't know!" Donna shouted, looking right at Marla for the first time. "I'm mad at him."

"You're mad at Cain? Are you mad at him because he died?"

"That's stupid. He didn't want to die."

"So why are you mad?"

"The secrets he made me promise not to tell nobody."

★ ★ ★

Tina stared at the documents in disbelief, but she was certain that was Frank's signature on all the paperwork. Steven Mann, she thought, might be a lecherous old bastard, but he would never have been party to anything too shady. He made a few bucks from his dealings with Frank, but that was nothing in comparison to what he and his partners netted from the bigger, full service companies that pumped more oil in one month than Mayday had pumped in all the years it had been in business. Those big oil companies swallowed up their smaller competitors all the time. It was more cost efficient for them to buy out their competitors' customers than to fight for them. "Are you sure this is right?" Joe asked. "He sold out to Black Gold Fuel, Inc., Steve Scanlon's company?"

"That's right. Mr. Scanlon and his lawyers sat with Frank and myself in the conference room right next door to this office. Why, does that surprise you?"

"You bet your ass I'm surprised," Joe said. "Frank never mentioned selling out to me. And Steve Scanlon never mentioned he was interested in buying. Besides, Scanlon runs a much smaller operation than Mayday. Wonder where his money came from?"

"Well, Mr. Serpe, the secrecy does make sense. Maybe Frank was reluctant to tell you because he might have thought you'd be worried for your job. And Mr. Scanlon might have kept it quiet so to avoid a competitive bid. As to where he got his money … "

Bullshit! "I guess that makes sense."

"When was this sale completed?" Tina wondered.

"Just before Frank was … About ten days ago."

Joe thought he had found his answer. "And the proceeds of the sale went–"

"Sorry to disappoint you, Mr. Serpe, but Frank didn't sell the company for cash to pay off blackmailers. If anything, it was quite the opposite."

"What does that mean, exactly?" Tina was curious to know.

"About half the proceeds have been used to fully fund the kids' college tuition accounts and to establish a trust fund for each child. Another quarter was used to satisfy the remaining mortgage on the house, time share, cars and to pay off any outstanding debts you may have had. And any day now, Tina, you should be receiving a bank check for the remainder of the funds, less our fees. You've been well provided for."

Tina lapsed into a stunned silence.

"Was it a fair price?" Joe asked.

"More than fair. Now if there's nothing else … "

"Just one more question."

"Yes, Mr. Serpe, I live to serve," the lawyer moaned.

"What was the name of the law firm that represented Steve Scanlon during the negotiations?"

"Watson, Medford, O'Donnell & Stahl. Lois will give you their contact info on the way out."

"They a big firm?"

"Very."

"Too big for a two-truck operation like Black Gold Fuel?"

The lawyer kept his cool, but doubt turned down the corners of his mouth.

"I couldn't say. My duty is to serve *my* client's interests. If you have questions for Mr. Scanlon, I suggest you ask him."

Mann stood to usher them out of his office. The question and answer period was now officially at end. To Tina he offered yet another apology for his past indiscretion and expressed the requisite sympathy for her plight. To Joe he offered nothing but an expression of relief at seeing him go. As he left the office, Joe reached back, knocking the golf trophy out of its niche.

★ ★ ★

"What's the name?"

"Schwartz, Detective David Schwartz," Rodriguez said.

"What a surprise, a guy named David Schwartz in Brooklyn."

"Yeah, it's kinda like finding a donkey named Sean O'Brien in Galway."

"Or a spic named Juan Rodriguez in the South Bronx."

"Very funny, Healy."

"So this Schwartz guy jammed up or what?"

"Nah. I did you a solid, for old times sake."

"You wouldn't do a favor for your own mother, Skip."

"I did plenty for yours."

"Did she thank you, at least?"

"I couldn't tell, her mouth was always full."

Healy was glad to let his old partner rip him, even at his late mother's expense. It was an aspect of the job he really missed, the sort of strange comradery and affection expressed through the exchange of insults. Oddly enough, the only times he'd felt comfortable since Mary's death were the rare opportunities he had to talk to Skip and the times he spent with Joe Serpe.

"So, this Schwartz, what's his deal?"

"They tell me he's the bomb. You want to know something about the Russians, he's your boy."

"Thanks, Skip. I owe you."

"You bet your ass you owe me. Remember who you call if there's a case here."

"How could I forget?"

★ ★ ★

"These secrets, Donna, what are they about?"

"Cain made me promise not to tell."

"That's very loyal of you, because I can tell how hard it's been for you to keep them. You were a good friend to Cain. The best friend."

"He loved Frank more."

"But how about you, Donna? How did you feel about Cain?"

Donna flushed red, turning away. That was answer enough.

"There are some promises we keep forever," Marla said. "There are some we can tell when people die."

"But Cain didn't tell me what kind of promise."

"When people tell us secrets, it means they trust us."

"I know that."

"It also means they trust us enough to know when to tell."

"I guess."

"If it would help find the people who hurt Cain, then you should tell."

"What if it was about Frank doing bad things?" Donna asked. "Cain didn't tell anybody but me, because he didn't want to get Frank in trouble."

Silent alarms went off in Marla's head. Confidentiality rules were very murky when it came to the mentally impaired. As important as Joe had become to her and as much as she wanted to help solve Cain's murder, she would not sacrifice her career. She loved her work and the people with whom she worked. On the other hand, she didn't want to waste days begging written permission from Donna's legal guardian.

"Do you remember Joe from the oil company?"

"I'm mad at him."

"Why?"

"Because he hurt Cain's feelings. He made Frank take him off his truck."

"I know that Joe feels bad about that, Donna. He—"

"He's a liar."

"Joe?"

"He promised to protect Cain from Mr. French."

"Sometimes people make promises they want to keep and can't. You know that Joe used to be a policeman, right?"

"Cain told everybody. It made me crazy how much he told me that."

"Joe wants to find out who hurt Cain. I'm helping him and another policeman is helping him. You could help too."

"I could?"

"I know you could."

"How?'

"By holding onto Cain's secrets for just a little while longer."

Friday Evening
March 5th, 2004

TRUCKS CAME

The Down's girl refused to look at Joe. She was angry, that much he could tell. It was truly written on her red face. There was, however, a paradoxical stiffness in her slouched posture. He remembered back to Cain's funeral, to the abject purity of the girl's grief, how she had chided Cain's parents. Clearly, he had done something wrong, but what, exactly? Marla had been very vague on the phone, saying only that it was important for the three of them to speak. Of course, nobody was speaking.

"Donna, you know I'm Italian," Joe said. "Italians, when we're mad at each other, we scream and yell. It's scary, but it's good too because we get it out."

Out of the corner of his eye, he caught the smile flash across Marla's face.

"I'm not Italian," Donna said.

"But you're mad at me. I can see that. Don't scream if you don't want to, but at least you should tell me what I did wrong."

"You lied. You said you would protect Cain."

Joe was stunned. That sticks and stones rhyme was bullshit. Words *could* harm you. They just had. In a rush, it all came back to him, the reason he had stepped back into the fire. Cain was dead.

"I'm mad at me too, Donna. Sometimes I think that if Cain was on the truck with me that day, he would still be alive."

"You hurt his feelings when you made him get off the truck."

"I know. I also know that why I did that had more to do about me than him."

"I don't understand."

"I'm not sure I do either. But I do know I owe it to Cain to—"

"He loved working on the truck with you."

Joe smiled. "I owe it to Cain to find out who did this to him. Is there something you know that could help?"

The Down's girl looked directly at Marla.

"Remember what we talked about before," Marla said. "Cain trusted you with the secrets, so only you can decide if telling is right."

It didn't take long to decide. Right and wrong were very clear things in her mind. Joe envied her that.

"Cain would sneak out at night sometimes," she said. "He would go to the oil place. He loved it there best in the world. He would sit in the trucks and pretend to drive."

"How do you know he would pretend to drive?" Joe asked.

Donna's eyes got wide. Her ruddy skin whitened. Her hands started to shake. Worst of all, she stopped talking. Joe had reacted without thinking. He had asked precisely the wrong question.

"Donna, no one is going to get in trouble for this," Marla assured her. "The only thing Joe is interested in is finding out who hurt Cain. If you are going to tell, you have to tell everything."

"You went with him sometimes, didn't you?" Joe said.

The Down's girl stared at the floor. "Yeah. Cain knew a way to walk in the shadows past the cameras at the home. He was smart like that."

"He must have loved you a lot to share that with you."

Donna beamed. "He did. He even showed me his secret hiding spot in the oil place where no one could see him. Then he said I couldn't go with him no more."

"Why?"

"Because some trucks came and we had to hide in the secret place."

"Trucks, what kind of trucks, Donna?" Joe was curious.

"Trucks. Big trucks. I don't know."

"Did they have tanks? Were they tank trucks like in the oil place?"

"Uh huh. One was long and shiny like foil stuff."

"There were other trucks also?"

"Two," she said, holding up a like number of fingers.

"Were they smaller than the big foil truck? Were they like the kind of truck Cain used to go in with me?"

"I guess."

"Did they have words or pictures on the side?"

"The little trucks had a picture on them, like a triangle."

Marla fished a crayon and a piece of paper out of her desk. "Can you draw the picture for Joe?"

"I think so."

As Donna struggled to recreate the picture on the side of the oil truck, Joe stared over at Marla. She wasn't beautiful. She looked exhausted, but at that moment he wouldn't have traded her for anyone in the world. Angela, his ex, was a knockout—sable hair, rich brown eyes, perfect olive skin. But even at the altar, Joe had doubts. He hadn't so much fallen in love with his ex-wife as he had fallen into expectation. They were the right age. They came from the same background, the same neighborhood. Joe had a steady job and gave her the security she always craved. It was more like a completed checklist than love. When he looked at Marla, Joe wasn't thinking about checklists.

"I think that's good," Donna announced, sliding the paper to Joe.

"It's perfect, Donna," he said, sliding it, in turn, to Marla.

"Do you recognize it?"

"It's an oil well. It's the logo for Black Gold Fuel, Inc."

"Will that help?" Donna asked.

"I think it helps a lot."

"Can I go back to my room now?"

"Donna," Marla interrupted. "What about Frank?"

"Frank?" Joe was confused.

"Cain made me promise never to tell about the trucks, because he said Frank could get in trouble."

"Was Frank there that night the trucks came to the oil place?" Joe asked.

"No. Other men were there."

"What other men?"

"They talked funny," Donna said.

"Did they *all* talk funny?"

"No, just the men that got out of the real big truck."

Joe slid Donna's logo picture back in front of her. "The men that drove these trucks, the ones with this painted on the tanks, did they talk funny?"

"No. Can't I go back to my room now?" she practically begged Marla.

"I know this is hard," Joe said. "It's hard to break a trust and tell secrets. Maybe I couldn't protect Cain, but maybe you can help me protect Frank. We both know how much Cain loved Frank. Will you help me?"

"Okay."

"Did Cain tell you why he was afraid Frank would get in trouble even though he wasn't there that night in the oil place?"

"He said the men were doing illegal pumping stuff. I don't remember the words."

"Truck transfers?" Joe asked.

"Yeah, maybe. Can I go to my room now, Marla?"

"Soon."

Joe continued. "Did Cain say anything else, Donna?"

"He said that Frank could get in trouble cause they were doing the bad pumping in his oil yard."

"Did Cain tell you the names of the drivers of the bad trucks?"

"I don't remember them no more."

"Steve, maybe?" Joe tried.

Donna's round face lit up. "Steve, yeah. That was one. I remember now. The other name was a funny name."

"Cain said he knew both drivers?"

"I already told you that."

"Sorry. This other driver, it's okay if you don't remember his name. Can you remember what Cain said about him or what he looked like?"

"Big. He was very big."

"Bigger than me?"

"A lot bigger." Donna stretched her arm up toward the ceiling.

"Did Cain say anything about him?"

"Cain didn't like him. He was mean to Cain."

"Fuck!"

"Marla, Joe said a bad word! Joe said a bad word!"

Marla kept out of it.

"I'm sorry, Donna. Forgive me."

"It's okay." She smiled impishly. "Cain said bad words sometimes. He said you and Frank taught him good."

Joe felt his face reddening.

"Do you think you know this other man?" Marla asked.

"Dixie."

"That's the name Cain said. That's the name!" Donna drummed both palms against Marla's desk in celebration.

"You did great, Donna," Joe said. "Thank you. Someday, maybe, if I come by and take you and Marla to the oil place, do you think you can show me Cain's secret hiding place?"

"Can I sit in the truck and pretend?"

"Sure."

"Marla, can I go back to my room now?"

"Go ahead. Tomorrow we can talk about how telling the secrets felt, okay?"

"Okay."

Donna didn't hesitate. She trundled out of the office without looking back.

★ ★ ★

Tatiyana blew a crimson red kiss at the mirror in room 217. She hated losing her steady gig. Frank had been her only work for months. It was easy work and it paid very well. She had even grown fond of Frank. So fond that she hated involving that fat blond pig with her tattoos and sloppy pussy, but it hadn't been her choice. Her employers had grown impatient with her. Now it was back to the old grind, entertaining potential business partners and visitors from home. There was the knock at the door. Oddly, Tatiyana felt nervous. Now she smiled at her reflection. What was there to be nervous about? She had been letting anonymous men shove their cocks in her for food and money since she was a thirteen year old girl.

"One moment," she said, letting out her breath slowly.

He was a big man with filthy hands and that sick smile certain johns have. She never saw that smile on Frank's face. Frank never looked at her like a lab specimen. Then again, Frank didn't know until the very end that she was a whore. But even after he saw the tapes, he simply looked wounded. To most of the men who "visited" her, Tatiyana was a sort of freebie, something to use in anyway they chose. Those were the ones who smiled that smile.

Tatiyana opened her mouth to welcome him in. He wasn't interested in welcomes, grabbing her by the hair and pushing her back into the room. He used his free hand to slam the door behind him. When she tried to speak again, he twisted her hair harder.

"Suck my cock, bitch!"

She did, just in the hope that he would let go of her hair. He did not, but relaxed his grip enough so that the pain was gone. When he was hard, he tightened his grip on her hair once again, dragging her to the bed. Finally, he let go of her hair.

"Bend over and let me see your cunt!"

She did. He ripped her underwear apart as if it were made of tissue paper and then rammed himself inside her. It hurt, but she could tell it wouldn't last long, not with how he was pounding against her ass. Then he let out a snort and a sorry groan. He was done. He fell down on the bed next to her. She didn't hesitate, quickly running into the bathroom.

Before stepping into the shower, she stared at herself in the bathroom mirror. She suddenly looked very old and tired for twenty-six. She had parted ways with God at the age of twelve, but found herself praying for him to let her find a way out of the game.

As she stepped out of the shower, a heavy fist slammed into her nose, snapping the cartilage into several pieces. Reflexively, Tatiyana put her hands up to her face as she collapsed backward, her warm blood pouring down her chin. The back of her head smacked hard against the shower wall, cracking the vinyl lining. Tears and blood had blinded her so that she could not see her executioner's face, but she could feel his calloused hands flipping her onto her stomach. She flailed at him. He swatted her arms away and placed his knee on her spine, cupping his hands under her chin. First, her windpipe collapsed as he snapped her head back. Then her spine cracked.

In that split second before she lost consciousness forever, Tatiyana thought God had finally answered her prayers. She was out of the game.

Saturday
March 6th, 2004

CANADIAN PENNIES

ob Healy moved around the house picking up six months worth of newspapers, TV Guides, magazines, etc. George was right about the house being a mess, and papers were an easy place to start, but Bob's sudden cleaning had more to do with nervous energy than anything else. Joe Serpe was on the way over. Finally, after three weeks, they had some concrete pieces to the puzzle, something more than guesses on which to hang their hats. Then the phone rang and some of the puzzle pieces began to change shape.

"Hey big brother." It was George.

"If you're calling me, it's not good news," Bob said.

"Good and bad."

"Christ, not again."

"You want to read about it in the papers tomorrow or hear about it now?"

"Okay, George."

"Good news first. The results are in from the second tests on the blood splatter samples from the Reyes murder scene. Your hunch was right on. They found a second contributor in one of the blood samples."

"What's the bad news?"

"It wasn't the Strohmeyer kid."

"I knew it," Healy said.

"Hey, don't get weepy on me, big brother. It's not like the kid was Mother Theresa. He did beat some poor drunk Mexican to death with a shovel."

"I know. It just confuses the issue. So who is—"

"So far, he's a John Doe," George said.

"That's just great."

"Well, maybe John Doe's not the right name. Maybe Ivan Doesky would be more accurate. Seems the second contributor was of Slavic descent."

"Russian?"

"Could be. Why?"

"What, I can't be curious?"

"For the last few weeks whenever you get curious, I get headaches. So what is it?"

"Maybe nothing."

"The flip side of maybe nothing is maybe something."

"Shit, little brother, the doorbell's ringing. I gotta go."

Click.

Bob Healy was lying about the doorbell, but just as he put the phone back in its cradle Joe Serpe knocked on the front door.

They sat at the kitchen table, Joe Serpe doing most of the talking.

"Here's what I think happened," he said. "Steve Scanlon has a source for black market oil and he was using Frank's yard to do illegal truck transfers from a nine thousand gallon tanker to his trucks. That's what Cain and Donna saw that night."

"Why use Frank's yard and not his own?"

"Size, for one thing. You couldn't possibly maneuver a tanker and two trucks in Scanlon's yard. It's small to begin with and he shares it with other companies. Frank's yard is big enough to accommodate a tanker and two smaller trucks. Besides, it's got a layer of crushed concrete which would stand up to all that weight in bad weather."

"How'd he get access to the yard?" Healy asked.

"That's easy—Dixie. We all had keys to the yard in case Frank was sick, wanted a day off, or if we had to work the odd Sunday. Dixie resented the fact that Frank wouldn't put him on his own truck full time and he probably jumped at the chance to make extra cash and stick it to Frank at the same time."

"It's a long way from screwing your boss to murder. Black market oil, is it really worth killing over?"

"Let's say the rack price of oil—"

"Rack price?"

"That's how much an oil company pays wholesale at the loading terminal," Joe explained. "Okay, so let's say the rack price is a buck a gallon and you're charging your customers a buck twenty-nine-nine per gallon at two hundred gallons, that's almost sixty bucks gross a stop. You got three trucks out averaging twenty stops a truck, that's thirty-six hundred bucks a day. Multiply that by six days a week. That's over twenty-one grand a week. And that's legitimate.

"Now let's say I can buy oil at fifty or sixty cents a gallon and I'm still charging my customers a buck twenty-nine-nine a gallon at two hundred gallons. So even if it's a warm winter, you can make out like a bandit if you're buying way below rack. Plus, think of how much cash you can launder given the price difference between rack oil and black market. Is it worth killing for? You do the math. I've known crackheads to kill for a roll of Canadian pennies."

Healy was still skeptical. "So if this is such a great scam, why hasn't anyone done this before?"

"They have, but a steady supply of black market oil is almost impossible to come by. Oil is one of the most regulated businesses on the planet. From the time it's pumped out of the ground, every gallon of it's got to be accounted for. Frank used to have to be able to account for every gallon he loaded and pumped. The shipping and pipeline companies, the refineries, the companies that pump the oil all have to account for every gallon they pump. Oil companies get audited all the time and you have to have bills of lading to cover every drop of oil you deliver. That's how people get caught. Even if you can get oil on the black market, you can't get legit bills of lading."

"So you think Scanlon has a way to get black market oil *and* bills of lading?"

"Yes and no."

Healy was confused. "Yes and no what?"

"I think Scanlon is fronting for someone else. I think Black Gold Fuel was a trial balloon, a test to see if the system was workable. When his partners saw the system worked, they tried to have Scanlon buy Frank out. When he wouldn't sell, they tried blackmailing him into it. When he still wouldn't sell, that's when the shit hit the fan and things got out of control."

"If the system worked, why not go in big?" Healy asked.

"No, these guys are too smart. They want to stay below the radar screen. Once they get noticed, they're dead. My guess is they plan to follow a model of starting very, very small and buying out slightly bigger sized companies. Instead of having one big operation that makes a nice fat juicy target for the feds, they'll have five or six small operations that will pump just as many gallons, but won't get noticed. We're talking millions and millions of dollars a year here."

"I'm sold, Joe. Wait a second."

Bob Healy got up from the table and retrieved some papers from the kitchen counter and sat back down. First, he showed Serpe the newspaper article about the dead woman found at JFK.

"Holy shit! That's the blond from the blackmail video. That's her tattoo. Slave, huh?"

"Wait, it gets better," Healy said, sliding a handwritten note in front of Serpe. "Look who the black Lincoln Navigator is registered to."

"Black Sea Energy."

"Yeah, I think we just found Steve Scanlon's silent partner. But I wonder how some city fireman got hooked up with these guys?"

"Leave that to me," Serpe said.

"There's more."

"There's more?"

"Reyes."

"What about him?"

"George called me just before you got here," Healy said. "And they did find someone else's blood in the splatter samples at the murder scene, but they weren't Pete Jr.'s. They're from a John Doe of Slavic descent."

"From Mr. Kazakstan and Ilana at the Blue Fountain, to Tatiyana, to the dead whore, to Reyes' murder, to Black Sea Energy on Brighton Beach Avenue, this shit screams Russian mob."

"So, should we bring it to the—"

Serpe slammed his hand on the table. "No! Not yet. You ever work a task force with the feds?"

"One."

"Did they take all the credit?" Serpe asked.

"There was no credit to take. We didn't make the case."

"Who got the blame?"

"We did. I guess I see your point," Healy admitted.

"Well, take my word for it, the feds'll fuck everything up. They can't help themselves, because even if their intentions are good, their priorities are always different than yours. Their focus is always the big picture. The second they'd get a hold of this, they'd make a deal with Scanlon to flip on his partners and we'd never find out what happened to Cain, the Reyes kid, or to Frank. And those are things I need to know."

"But—"

"But nothing, Bob," Joe said, waving the article about the dead prostitute in Healy's face. "Look, these guys are already starting to cover their tracks. This chick is dead. My bet is Tatiyana will be soon—if she isn't already. They probably had a hand in what's going on with Frank and they tried to run me off the road and they killed my cat. If they get even a whiff that this is anything more than two washed-up ex-cops stumbling around in the dark, they'll slash and burn any ties they have to this. No, we have to move ahead the way we've been going. It's coming to a head, anyway. You go talk to that Schwartz guy today and I'll try and find out how Scanlon went from retired fireman to oil magnate in three easy steps."

"All right," Healy said. "I'm willing to give it another few days, but that's it. At some point, we're going to need the cavalry."

"Agreed."

Healy excused himself, went upstairs and came back down in less than five minutes. He had a bag in his hand.

"Take this," he said, handing it to Serpe. "I bought it for my son years ago when I hoped he might take the test to get on the job. He didn't want any part of it or the job."

Serpe knew what it was before he took it out of the bag.

"You know I'm not licensed to carry anymore."

"I know better than anybody. Just take it and be careful. There's a box of cartridges in there too."

"Thanks, Healy," he said placing the Glock back in the bag and tucking it under his arm. "I'll return it when this shit is over with."

"Keep it. If anyone catches you with it, I'll just say you stole the damn thing."

"Fuck you." But Serpe was laughing when he said it.

Healy was laughing, too, as he shook Joe Serpe's hand. "Let's talk tonight and see where we are, okay?"

"You got it. Good luck."

"Yeah, same to you."

* * *

Joe Serpe pulled onto the service road along Sunrise Highway in Bayshore. He wasn't sure what he expected to find at the Blue Fountain Motel. Somewhere in the back of his mind he guessed he hoped he'd have the good fortune to find Tatiyana working her special brand of video magic in room 217. He'd pay for her time and explain to her about what had happened to the blond. Then he'd offer to protect her in exchange for her help. But he knew it was far more likely she was already dead. And when he saw the barricades in front of the motel's driveway, he just knew whatever slim hopes he had of finding Tatiyana alive were gone.

There was a black kid posted by the barricade, pacing back and forth in the freezing cold. As soon as he rolled down his window, Serpe got a sense of what had gone on. The smell of smoke and burned plastic still hung heavy in the air.

"They closed. Open back up Monday."

"Fire?" Joe said to the kid.

"Man, you figure dat shit out all by youself?"

"Anybody hurt?"

"Nah, not too much damage neitha. Only a coupla rooms."

"Let me guess, rooms 216, 217, and 218, right?"

Now the kid stared at Joe with big eyes. "How you know dat shit?"

"They're my lucky numbers, kid."

As he pulled down Sunrise Highway, he dialed information on his cell phone. He needed to chat with Captain Kelly, Vinny's old commanding officer.

* * *

Bob Healy was as guilty of stereotyping as the next guy. He had envisioned David Schwartz as a Hasid with a shield. But the man who stood up from the booth at the Sheepshead Bay Diner and offered his hand to Healy looked a lot like Mr. Clean. Schwartz stood a good six foot three with football pad shoulders and a thirty inch waist. He had a shaved head and a neat, reddish moustache. His jaw was square, his neck was thick, but he had a kind smile and gentle blue eyes.

"Detective Healy?" Schwartz asked as a matter of courtesy.

"You can give me my hand back now, Schwartz. Jesus, how did you ever find baseball gloves that fit?"

"Didn't use one. Caught the ball with my teeth."

They both had a laugh at that as they settled into their seats. Schwartz flagged down the waitress and Healy ordered coffee. The waitress rolled her eyes at him. "Cops!" she whispered to herself.

"So Skip Rodriguez tells me you need some information," Schwartz said after the waitress delivered the coffee.

"Yeah, I'm helping out a friend that got into some shit and now he's nipple deep in it. Another few days and it'll be over his head."

"I take it this shit your buddy stepped in has something to do with the Russians, or Skip wouldn't have called me. That much I can figure on my own, but if you want my help, you're gonna have to—"

"Black Sea Energy," Healy blurted out.

Schwartz didn't say a word, not immediately. The corners of his mouth and eyes, however, took a decided upturn.

"This friend of yours, he own a gas station?" the detective wondered.

"Close. He's in the home heating oil business out in Suffolk County. How'd you know?"

"Black Sea Energy used to own a shitload of gas stations throughout the New York Metropolitan area. Now they basically do trucking and hauling and own a petroleum terminal."

"They dirty?"

"Nope. If anything, they're too fucking clean. They're owned by two Ukranian Jews who emigrated here in the late 70s."

"Connected?"

"It's hard to tell. You've gotta understand, the Russian mob is organized crime, but it isn't organized like the Mafia or the drug cartels. There really isn't even a *mob*, per se, but a sort of loose conglomeration of different organizations. There's no Carlo Gambino sitting at the head of the table or Pablo Escobar handing down orders from on high in Colombia. Although in this area many of the players are Jews, they're not all Jews by a longshot. Many are from the former Soviet Republics like Georgia, the Ukraine, Kazakstan—places like that.

"Under the old Soviet system, the black market was a way of life. Everybody was involved in it one way or the other. Government officials were involved at every level, either looking the other way or getting their cut. Plus, it's kind of difficult to get reliable police records from the Soviet era. Their justice system was so politicized, it's difficult to know, even if we can obtain the files, whether they've been tainted, rewritten, faked …

"So you see, when two guys show up here in Brighton Beach one day and start opening up gas stations, it's difficult to know exactly where their money came from. It's not necessarily dirty money. Look, when my grandparents came over, they were part of a group that pooled monies from people from their old villages and made loans to start new businesses. That's how the Pakistanis and Koreans do it now. It's how the Turks and Arabs buy gas stations."

"But sometimes the money is dirty," Healy said.

"Oh yeah. A load of it is dirty rubles getting scrubbed into nice clean dollar bills. The reason there's always been suspicions about Black Sea is that one of the biggest scams the Russians used to pull was tax fraud on gasoline. Somehow, Black Sea Energy was never caught," said Schwartz.

"There were suspicions?"

"Always, but that was really before my time. Most of the tax fraud stuff was over with by the late 80s. They've moved on."

"Who are the two guys who own Black Sea?"

"Sergei Borofsky and Misha Levenshtein. Levenshtein pretty much runs the business these days. He still lives in the area, over in this hideously gaudy house in Manhattan Beach, off Oriental Boulevard. Borofsky's in sort of semi-retirement out in your neck of the woods. I think he lives in some town called Seatuckit or something like that."

"Setauket," Healy corrected. "Pretty fancy addresses over there."

"Really? Yeah, our intelligence says he's helping his kids with their businesses."

"Do you know what kind of businesses his kids are—"

"Limo services, motels … I think his daughter might own a few gentlemen's clubs and I know one of the sons owns a string of gyms. Any of this helping you?"

Abso-fuckin'-lutely! "Maybe, but probably not."

"You're good. You're really good," Schwartz said. "Skip warned me about you."

"What are you—"

"Come on, Healy. I may be built like a house, but I still got a *Yiddisha kup.*"

"A what?"

"A Jewish head. It means I'm not half as dumb as I look or you think I am. So, you wanna just tell me what's going on here?"

* * *

Firehouses are some of the cleanest places in the city of New York. Firefighters, much more so than cops, take extreme pride in their equipment, but Joe Serpe suspected that lurking beneath the surface was a darker, more powerful motive than simple human pride. Though it was true that vigilant maintenance of their equipment might someday help save their lives, there seemed to Joe to be an almost Lady Macbeth-like aspect to firefighters' obsession with sparkling equipment. It was as if by scrubbing out the soot and washing away the stench of smoke, they could remove any reminders of the dangers they faced and the cruel facts of mortality.

Joe was shocked by the power of his reaction as he strolled through the open doors of the firehouse at 2929 West 8th Street in Coney Island. He had not set foot in a firehouse since before September 11th, 2001. It was the day Vinny got his permanent assignment at Engine Company 226 way over on the other side of Brooklyn. Those were very dark days for Joe, coming as they did, just after his expulsion from the force and during the disintegration of his marriage. Yet, for Vinny's sake, he had made the effort. He hadn't spent more than half an hour at the firehouse that day, staying just long enough to deliver the beers and six foot hero sandwiches he had brought to honor his brother. He couldn't remember Vinny ever being that happy.

"Can I help you?" a woman asked as she slopped soap on a red truck. She was about thirty. She had a flat, plain face, short brown hair and an athletic build.

"Maybe you can. My name's Joe Serpe. Captain Kelly from—"

"Serpe," she repeated. "Any relation to Vincent?"

"Vinny was my little brother."

"Mary Keegan." She wiped her right hand against her uniform and held it out to Joe. "I went through the academy with Vincent. We had to put up with a lot of the same shit from the other assholes. I was real sorry to hear about your brother. He was a gentleman."

"Thank you, Mary. He was all of that."

"You're the cop, right?"

"In another life, yeah. Now I just drive an oil truck."

"Anything I can do for you, Joe, I will."

"I'm thinking of buying into an oil delivery business out in Suffolk County with a retired fireman. This was the last house he worked and I was wondering if anyone is still around who knew him. It's a big investment and I don't know him that well."

"Hey, I completely understand. What's his name?"

"Steve Scanlon."

Mary Keegan frowned like she'd bitten into a rancid tomato. Subtlety didn't seem to be her specialty. Joe liked that.

"Nice face, Mary. I guess you aren't Scanlon's biggest fan."

"That obvious, huh?" She didn't wait for an answer. "I got posted here about a year before Scanlon retired. So you could say I knew him a little bit. Don't get me wrong—Steve was a good fireman, great driver. The thing about it is, the prick still owes me a hundred bucks. I think when he left, he was into everyone in the house for a few grand. I didn't go to his retirement party, but my guess is that anyone who did wrapped his gift in IOUs."

"Maybe it was a rough divorce or something. Times get tough when you get divorced. I can tell you all about that."

"Hey, if that was it, Joe, no one woulda said a word about it. We've all been through our own share of personal crap. His thing was gambling. I mean, we bet on all sorts of shit in the house. It helps kill the down time, but he was what my dad used to call a degenerate fucking gambler."

"I know the type. So, you wouldn't recommend going into business with him?"

Keegan hemmed and hawed. "Normally, I wouldn't say, but you being Vincent's brother and everything … No, Joe, I wouldn't touch it."

"He must have had a local bookie."

"I wouldn't know about that, but c'mon, I'll introduce you around. There are a few guys still here who worked with him."

It seemed everyone in the house above the age of thirty had a Steve Scanlon story featuring either the lies he used to borrow money and/or the excuses he made for not making good on his debts. Lending Scanlon money had even become part of the house's rookie hazing ritual. Ray Santucci, a lieutenant, related the details to Joe.

"What a pisser," Santucci said. "We used to tell the probies that they were better off lending dough to Scanlon than putting it in the bank. We'd tell them he was golden, that when Scanlon paid you back it was always quick and with a shitload of interest. The best part was watching the probies try and collect. A real fuckin' pisser, I tell ya. Of course, we never let them lend him too much bread. We didn't wanna have to make good on it ourselves. Then he went too far and we had to put an end to his shit."

"What happened?"

"The lending was one thing. After the first time, it was like let the buyer beware. If he didn't pay you back, well, you knew you were an asshole for trusting him in the first place. But we have a code in the house, in the department; you never steal from a brother."

"He stole from you?" Serpe asked.

"Not from me directly, no. But he used to collect our weekly football bets for a Russian bookie over in Brighton Beach. We're fire fighters, what the fuck do we know about football, right? So we lost all the time. Then one week this probie—Flannery I think his name was—hit it big on the Jets giving points and got the over. He was due, like, fifteen hundred bucks, but Scanlon's not paying up. He was just fulla excuses for two weeks. Flannery was going nuts, threatening to take it to the union and to the department even though we explained that as a probie, he'd be the one to get shit-canned."

"So?"

"So me and a few of the more senior guys decided to have a little talk with Stevie boy," Santucci growled. "Turns out the prick never turned in the betting sheets and used our money to make his own bets, but we made sure Flannery got his money."

"Sounds like a much beloved man."

"Don't get me wrong, he was a solid fireman. You wouldn't mind him having your back walking into a fire. But with money … You get my meaning?"

"Got it. This Russian bookie, you remember his name?" Joe was curious.

"Bookies don't exactly advertise and Scanlon never shared shit like that with us, but it shouldn't be too hard to find the guy. Go to the corner and make a left, walk a few blocks down to Brighton Beach Avenue and make a right. Only problem is, you gotta find someone that speaks English."

After a round of goodbyes and thank yous, Joe Serpe walked out of the firehouse. He had his answers. Most men's souls are for sale, some at higher prices than others. Gamblers' souls come cheaply. You'll find them on the discount rack between crackheads and tweakers.

Back in his car, Joe Serpe took Lieutenant Santucci's suggestion … sort of. He made a U turn on West 8th, turned left onto Surf Avenue and then made a right under the elevated subway onto Brighton Beach Avenue.

* * *

Bob Healy sat in his car across the street from 2243 Brighton Beach Avenue. He wasn't exactly sure what he expected to see. There was a flurry of activity on the avenue, many people passing back and forth beneath the perpetual dusk of the El, but no one seemed to enter the refurbished building that housed Black Sea Energy, Inc. Like all the other buildings along the way, 2243 was what used to be known as a taxpayer. There was a storefront at street level and a two-story brick building above. Healy had grown up in the third floor apartment of a taxpayer in Red Hook.

Unlike the buildings to either side of it, 2243 had a beautiful, if completely incongruous, green-tinted glass block and green-flecked granite entryway. The pitted and painted-over brick face of the surrounding taxpayers was not evident on the Black Sea building. Its upper floors had been resurfaced with a smooth coating of beige-colored concrete. Green-flecked granite inlays shaped like tanker trucks were embedded in the concrete. The old apartment windows had been replaced with deeply smoked rectangular glass panels that stretched nearly the entire width of the building. The structure was made to look even more out of place by the fact that at street level it was flanked by a butcher shop and a fruit stand.

One thing Healy did see was the shiny new, black Lincoln Navigator parked right out front of 2243. He noticed too that the parking meter was expired and that the scooter cop on ticket patrol completely ignored the violation. Corruption, the ex-detective thought, rarely starts big. Many of the cops he'd busted had started down the slippery slope by doing just the sort of thing the scooter cop had just done. Maybe if the damn city paid cops a living wage, they might not be tempted to compromise their futures for a bottle of vodka and a few hundred bucks at Christmas.

During the five or six seconds Healy looked away from the Black Sea Energy Building in order to scribble down the Lincoln's tag number, things took a decided turn toward the surreal. Because when he picked his head back up, Healy saw Joe Serpe strolling across Brighton Beach Avenue and through the front doors of 2243 Brighton Beach Avenue.

* * *

During his career on the cops, Joe Serpe was perhaps best known for the wild chances he took. No one believed more strongly that the best defense was an aggressive, attacking offense. He was never a fly on the wall. He wanted to push the buttons, to take the first swing. He had almost forgotten what it was like, the rush of being first in. But like an alcoholic sober for years, Serpe was drunk with his first sip. Even as he strode through the doors at Black Sea Energy, he was buzzed.

Joe had decided the time had come to shake the tree and see what fell out. He knew he was right. Cain, Reyes, even Toussant, all their murders pointed him in this direction. He could feel it, could taste it. He was so close to getting to the bottom of things, but just as close to losing it all. He had to take his shot before conceding that Healy was right, that the time had come to step back and turn things over to the law.

The interiors of the Black Sea Energy Building continued the themes established on its facade. The lobby floor was made up of six by six tiles of the green-flecked granite. Three walls were covered by one continuous mural in the style of Diego Rivera. From Joe's left, behind him to his right, the mural featured every aspect of the petroleum business: Arab men working in oil fields, hard hats at a refinery, a mighty tanker crossing a deep blue ocean, pipelines, storage tanks, trucks at the rack, gas stations, an oil truck making a delivery to a snow covered house as a happy family looked on. The mural began at the edge of a wall of green-tinted glass cubes and ended at the opposite edge of the same glass wall. There was a small sliding glass portal and a thick glass door cut into the cube wall.

Joe stepped up to the portal. A heavyset woman with big black hair sat at a black mica desk, answering phones and pecking at the keyboard of a PC. He was surprised to hear her accent, which was decidedly more Bay Ridge than Belarus. Serpe listened, not wanting to attract the receptionist's attention until he at least figured out why he thought this was a good plan of action.

"Black Sea Energy, how may I direct your cawl? Please hold."

"Black Sea Energy, how may I direct your cawl? Mista Levenshtein isn't taking cawls right now. Do you wish to leave a message?"

Joe Serpe's heart was beating out of his chest. He was thinking about what Healy had said about redemption, that all the good deeds he could do would never undo his past mistakes. He knew Christ would forgive him. Maybe he already had. Christ wasn't the issue. Joe Serpe needed to forgive himself and there would be no forgiveness if he didn't find the people who had murdered Cain.

He rapped on the glass with the replica detective's shield he had made the year before his troubles began. The receptionist looked surprised as Joe pressed the blue and gold shield against the glass. She actually got up and strolled to the window. Though heavy, she had a pleasing shape and moved with unexpected grace.

"Can I help you?"

"Tell Mr. Levenshtein I'd like a few minutes of his time."

"Name?"

"Detective Serpe."

"Serpe," she said licking her red lips, "that means snake, right?"

He winked at her. "For today it means detective. Let Mr. Levenshtein know I'm here, okay?"

"One minute."

Serpe watched her make her way to a door at the rear of her office and press what looked to be an up elevator button. Joe could feel he was shaking and wondered if it would be as obvious to someone standing in the same room as him. Just as the receptionist pressed the up button, a voice came over the intercom.

"Maria, let the detective come up."

Joe looked behind him and saw a tiny camera in the corner of the room just where the mural met the ceiling. Then he peered ahead of him into the receptionist's office and saw another sleek camera in the corner. Maria reached under her desk and hit a hidden button. There was a click, Joe moved to the glass door and let himself in.

"Take the elevator up to the third floor," Maria said, going back to her typing.

The elevator was the size of a double-wide coffin, but much better appointed. The walls of the little car were inlaid with angular designs of exotic woods like tiger maple and ebony. The floor was a solid piece of dark red granite. The rich facade, the mural, the opulence of the elevator did not prepare him for the starkness of Levenshtein's office.

Of course, unlike the very confused Bob Healy, who was seated outside in his car trying to figure out what was going on, Joe Serpe had no idea who Levenshtein was. He had simply heard the receptionist say his name.

All the furnishings were strictly low-end Staples merchandise. The carpeting was industrial and a drab gray. The walls were lined with family photos, and pictures of gas stations, trucks, and what looked to be a small oil terminal. Like in Ken Bergman's office at the group home, there was a bank of closed circuit monitors over the seated man's shoulder. The only thing that hinted at Levenshtein's position was the nameplate on his desk, half-buried beneath a mountain of files.

sha Levenshtein
dent and C.E.O

Even Serpe, never much for puzzles, could figure out he'd found the right man. But Levenshtein ignored Joe, continuing to work on the papers before him. Another minute went by before the man behind the desk snapped his files closed and spoke to his guest.

"What can I help you with, Detective?" He pronounced "h" in help as if it were "ch," not unlike Mr. Kazakstan from the Blue Fountain Motel.

"I'm not sure," Joe confessed. "But there are bodies piling up in my neighborhood and I think your company's got something to do with it."

This got Levenshtein's attention. "Bodies! You talk nonsense, Detective. What would my company have to do with bodies?"

Instead of concocting some half-assed story out of partial truths and convenience, Joe Serpe sat down across from the old Ukranian Jew and laid out the facts dating back to Valentine's Day. Through most of it, Levenshtein, a white-haired man in his mid sixties with work-rounded shoulders and cigarette-stained teeth, sat back in his chair and listened impassively. The man simply did not react to anything Serpe said.

Only twice, toward the very end of Joe's account, did Levenshtein give any indication that he even heard what Serpe was saying. At the mention of the Blue Fountain he fumbled slightly, reaching for a cigarette. And when Joe referred to the law firm that had represented Steve Scanlon during his purchase of Mayday Fuel Oil, Inc., the old man's lip seemed to quiver ever so briefly. But neither reaction was enough to take to the bank.

When Serpe finished, Levenshtein lit another cigarette, stood up and poured himself two fingers of vodka. He offered some to his guest, but Joe politely refused.

"Listen, Detective—"

"I'm not a detective. I used to be one, but now I don't even play one on TV."

"You have balls, Serpe. I give you that. When you come up in the world like I have, you admire balls almost more than any other quality in a person. But balls or no balls, you tell a fanciful story, no? What have you got, a license plate number and the word of a retarded girl?"

"To you, I guess, it might look that way."

"And to the cops, to the court ... Look, Serpe, it is true that we have several Navigators registered to the company and I can look that one of my old partner's sons drove maybe a little reckless on Long Island and did not report an accident. If that is the case, we will make good on damages, but beyond this, I can say nothing. Black Sea Energy has a spotless record. Check. Go check with any agency we deal with. We can speak for every drop of petroleum product we receive and pump. As for motels, whores, and bookies ... This is not the place to find them."

Serpe stood. "Thank you for your time, sir."

"As I say, I will look into this matter of the Navigator. Leave your information with the girl, Maria, as you go. Now I have work to do."

Joe thanked the old man once more and rode the slowly sinking coffin back down to the lobby. He wrote his cell phone number down for Maria and left. He had taken a gamble and lost. As the door closed behind him, Serpe knew he had to find Healy.

★ ★ ★

Levenshtein sat at his desk watching the monitors. As soon as the front door closed, he got on the intercom.

"Maria, get my son and tell him to come here immediately. Then get Sergei on the phone. Now!"

★ ★ ★

Joe didn't have to find Healy, because Healy found him.

"Are you out of your fucking mind?" was how he greeted Serpe, as a passing D train raining sparks down on the avenue. The shadows of the El rendered moot by the setting sun.

"What?" Joe shouted above the squeals and rumble.

"Are you nuts?"

"I think I must be. I blew it, Bob."

"What were you thinking?"

"I was thinking I needed to shake things up. I just got that old feeling that if we didn't do something now, it would all slip away. God, Healy, I was buzzing in there. I felt like a cop again, like a man."

"Who did you see?"

"Some old guy named Levenshtein."

"Misha Levenshtein?" Healy asked.

"I guess, yeah."

"What did he say?"

"What you would expect him to say, that his company is clean and that Black Sea leases a lot of black Navigators. He says he doesn't know anything about motels or whores or bookies."

"Bookies?"

"Yeah, bookies. It seems Scanlon was a degenerate gambler and owed half the free world money. I thought that's how they must've got their hooks into him."

"I don't know anything about bookies, but your friend Levenshtein is full of shit."

"How's that?"

"His partner in the business, some guy named Sergei Borofsky, lives out in Setauket and his kids own motels, a limo service, strip clubs, and gyms. Add all that to the trucking and the oil terminal and I'd say your hunch was right on target."

"Shit!"

"What's wrong?"

"I gotta get back to the island."

"Why the hurry?"

"Because if I am right, Levenshtein's in there calling his partner."

"Oh crap!"

"That's right, Healy. There are now people besides you and me walking around with big bull's-eyes on their backs. I can't afford to let them get rid of Scanlon and Dixie before I find out what happened to Cain. I know this is crazy, but try and get hold of Scanlon. Tell him anything you have to, but keep that prick alive."

* * *

Serpe was flying past the Flatbush Avenue exit on the Belt Parkway when he got that sick feeling in the pit of his stomach. What had he been thinking about? Had he been so intoxicated with his old sense of self that he'd completely lost sight of what he might have set in motion? Scanlon and Dixie were in danger, to be sure, but they had good reason to keep their traps shut. Levenshtein's words rang in Joe's head: "What have you got, a license plate number and the word of a retarded girl?" Donna and, by extension, Marla were in far greater danger than Scanlon and Dixie.

Serpe flipped open his cell phone, but was in a dead zone. He tried Marla's home number and her cell anyway. Neither call connected. He tried dialing 911 and got nothing. As he moved further down the Belt Parkway, he kept trying. Then, finally, passing Kennedy Airport, his phone connected to Marla's home answering machine.

"You've reached Marla Stein, Ph.D. in Clinical Psychology. I'm unavailable to answer your call at the moment. Please listen to the following menu and I will get back to you as soon as possible. If this a therapy matter, press one. For all other matters, press two."

"Marla, this is Joe. Stay calm, but call 911 immediately. Get the cops over to the group home. You and Donna are in real danger. When the uniforms get to you, ask to speak to Detective Hoskins or Detective Kramer. Do it now! I'll call back in a few minutes to check."

He tried her cell phone, again getting her voice mail, and leaving a similar, if more urgent, message. What an idiot, he'd been. She wasn't home, she was staying at her parents' house, following Joe's own instructions. Shit, what was that number? He had it written down in the apartment, but … Joe thought about calling the group home but had no clue how it would be listed, nor did he have the exact address. He dialed 911, but got the NYPD. More accurately, he was put on hold and got a recording. When the operator came on, he tried to remain as calm as possible.

"Listen carefully, operator, my name is Joseph Serpe, I'm a retired NYPD detective," he lied. "There's an emergency in Suffolk County, can you either pass on a message or patch me through to Suffolk 911?"

"Detective Serpe, did you say you are reporting an emergency in Suffolk County and are you presently in Suffolk County?"

"Let's try this again, there are two women in danger in Suffolk County. I'm currently proceeding to Suffolk County, but I won't make it there in time."

"What is the nature of the emergency?"

Good question, Serpe thought. "Kidnapping and homicide."

"Detective Serpe, do you wish to report a kidnapping and homicide?"

"Yes, for chrissakes!"

"At what address or addresses?"

Joe opened his mouth to answer, but caught sight of something parked on the shoulder, partially hidden by the stone support of the overpass.

"Never mind, operator."

He snapped his cell phone shut and swerved his rental across two lanes of traffic before bouncing up over the curb onto the grassy shoulder. When the cop came over to his window, Joe showed him his shield and screamed at him to get Suffolk 911 on the phone immediately.

* * *

Ken Bergman frequently came in on Saturdays to clear up the past week's paperwork, to review payroll, and to work on his dissertation. Then he'd shower and head out on a date or hit the clubs in Huntington. Sometimes, during the summer, he'd quit early and drive out to the Hamptons. The truth was, he came in on Saturdays because of blind hope. Marla often came into her office late on Saturday afternoons to clear up paperwork or have a few sessions with residents whose weekly work schedules sometimes interfered with their regular meetings.

So it was that Bergman sat listening to Marla's voice through the paper thin walls. It wasn't an especially pretty voice, but there was something so calm, so comforting about it that he longed to have it comfort him, to tell him everything would be okay as Marla herself rocked him in her arms. Ken did all right for himself. He had professorial good looks and had his rap down. But love had long eluded him. Yet from the first day Marla walked into his office, he was certain he would have sacrificed everything for her. He could hear Donna's nasal voice through the wall as well. Whatever she and Marla had worked on yesterday already had positive results. Donna seemed to be back to her old self.

The group home manager was so pleased, so caught up in his daydream that when the front bell rang, he simply reached back and buzzed whoever it was in. He heard heavy footfalls in the hallway outside his door and looked back at the security monitors. There was an unfamiliar man at the door holding something in his right hand. Christ, Ken thought squinting at the monitor, is that a gun? He picked up the phone, but before he could dial 911, he heard Marla scream.

Bergman burst through his office door, colliding with a larger man. The force of the impact knocked both of men to the floor, the intruder's head smacking hard into the opposite wall. An automatic pistol, likely jarred loose by the collision, lay on the floor by the big man's work boots. Bergman began to reach for it when he noticed Marla pulling Donna toward the front door.

"Not that way!" Ken screamed. "There's another one out there. Go for the back door."

"You little fuck," the big man, no longer stunned, growled at Bergman.

His opportunity to disarm the intruder gone, Bergman scrambled to his feet and ran after Marla and Donna.

"Everyone stay in their rooms! Stay in your rooms!" he screamed as his ran. He ran with his arms flailing and his legs far apart so as to keep as much of himself between the armed man and the fleeing women. As he turned the hall corner, he caught sight of Marla and Donna at the opposite end of that hall. One more turn, a few more steps, and they'd be out the backdoor.

Bang! Bang! Bang!

Bergman was laying face down on the carpet before he heard the third bullet whistle over his head. He knew he had been shot, but strangely, luckily, he thought, there was no pain. Bergman thought himself lucky until he tried to move and nothing moved except the blood filling his lungs. He waited for the shooter to come up behind him, to feel the cold muzzle against the back of his head, but did not hear his footsteps.

"Pavel," he heard someone yell as the front door clicked open. "Pavel, boy, go around the back. The back, goddammit!"

Bergman wondered if that was a Georgia or Florida accent. It's funny what a dying man thinks about. Then his bizarre final thoughts were interrupted by footsteps, but they were coming from the wrong direction and they were far too quiet to be a man's.

"Kenny, Kenny," Marla whispered to him, straining to turn him over. She cradled him in her arms, his blood covering the both of them. "Kenny," she stroked his hair. "Don't worry, everything will be all right. It'll be okay."

He died with a crooked smile on his face that Marla would never quite understand.

"Come on, bitch!"

A huge hand grabbed her by the hair and fairly lifted her out from beneath Bergman's lifeless torso.

★ ★ ★

Serpe could see the road flares ahead and that deathly sick feeling returned as he approached the two Suffolk County blue and whites blocking Union Avenue. A bored looking cop tried waving him away, but it would take considerably more than a wave to make him leave. Joe put his car in park and popped out the driver's side door. If you ever want to get a cop's attention, challenge his authority.

"Sir," the cop said in a less than friendly tone. "You'll have to move your vehicle and—"

"I'm the one who called this in."

"Yeah, right. What are you, another fucking reporter?"

In spite of his desperation and near panic, Joe did not want to risk flashing his illegal shield now unless he absolutely had to. Back in the city, they have short memories. They'd have already moved on. No one was going to hunt him down for using questionable tactics in an emergency. But a prick like Detective Hoskins would shove that shield up his ass before having him thrown in lockup. On the other hand, Serpe didn't have time to debate.

"Is Detective Hoskins on the scene?"

"Who?"

Serpe had had enough. He bolted between the two blue and whites and took off in a wild sprint. He could hear the two cops behind him, but did not look back to see. He had already done enough looking back in his lifetime.

"Freeze, motherfucker!" one cop, the one he'd spoken to, ordered.

"Stop now! Right now!" the other cop screamed.

But Joe would not stop, could not stop. His legs moved involuntarily. He did not see the road ahead of him, the whirling cherry tops, or strobes. All he could see was Marla, her slight body covered in blood, her intense brown eyes staring up at him, silently asking why me.

He was getting close now. There were blue and whites everywhere, unmarked cars, an ambulance, a crime scene van. Cops huddled in small groups, some drinking coffee. Joe's heart was pounding, his throat dry. He strained to breathe, the stitch in his side ripping him apart.

"Stop him!" one of the cops called out from behind him. "Get him down!"

But cops are not that much different than anyone else. In groups they are slower to react: looking, hesitating, waiting for the next guy to do something. Mostly, they looked confused. Some stirred, a few going for the sidearms. None committed to going after Serpe.

His legs wobbly, he fell across the crime scene tape like a runner at the finish of a marathon. Now the cops moved. His hands were cuffed behind his back.

"Hoskins! Kramer!" Serpe cried out, unable to hold down the desperation another second. "Hoskins! Kramer! I need to speak to either Detective Hoskins or Detective Kramer!"

Skilled hands moved along his body, patting him down, checking for concealed weapons, identification, etc. At least Joe had had the presence of mind to tuck Healy's Glock under the front seat of his rental before getting out to talk to the cop on the Belt Parkway. He knew the sight of his shield would be enough to get that guy's attention. That it did. Within five minutes the Suffolk County PD had been notified and Joe had a cherry top, siren blowing escort to the Nassau county line.

"Holy shit, Dom," the uniform who frisked him said. "This guy's an NYPD detective. You better see if there's a Detective Hoskins or Kramer on scene."

They pulled Serpe up to his feet and let him lean against one of the blue and whites, but didn't uncuff him. That would be the detectives' call. They got the glory, let them have the headaches. Joe was well acquainted with the attitude.

"Well, look who the fuck it is, Kramer," Hoskins said too loudly as he and his partner strolled over to Serpe. "We told you to keep your nose outta our shit, didn't we?"

"This isn't your shit, Hoskins. This has got nothing to do with gangs."

"Tell it to someone who give a rat's ass, Serpe. How do you have the balls to carry that shield with you, you piece of shit?"

"Is anyone hurt?" Joe pleaded, ignoring Hoskins.

"Not hurt, just dead."

Serpe nearly vomited. His legs so weak he needed the car to hold him up.

"Should we uncuff him?" the uniform asked, wanting to get back to his coffee.

"Fuck him!" Hoskins said, walking away. "Maybe the cuffs'll teach the asshole a lesson."

"Let him loose," Kramer said.

"Here." The uniform handed Serpe back his shield, wallet, and cell phone.

"Come on, Kramer, is Marla Stein all right?"

"We've got one dead, a male Caucasian named Bergman."

"Ken Bergman, the group home manager," Joe said, giddy with relief.

"That's him. We've got blood around by the back door and a missing woman. She's a resident, twenty years of age, Caucasian with Down's Syn—"

"Donna. Fuck, no!" The giddiness was gone. "But you haven't found her?"

"No, but there's a blood trail, stops by the sump. You know this woman?" Kramer asked.

"She was Cain Cohen's girlfriend. She might be a key witness in clearing all this shit up. That's why they came after her."

Kramer looked at Joe sideways. "What shit? Who's they? You stay put, Serpe. I'll be back in one minute. Officer, keep an eye on him."

Joe could feel the familiar buzz of his cell phone against his thigh.

"Joe?" It was Marla.

"Thank Christ, you're all—"

"Serpe?" an unfamiliar voice replaced Marla's.

"Put her back—"

"You shut your fucking mouth and listen before I cut her throat. You want then I should put her back on the phone? You have caused me so much trouble, I would enjoy to cut her throat." He was a Russian, whoever he was.

"I'm listening."

"Walk out of there, get back in your car, and start driving east on the expressway. I will call you en route. And Mr. Serpe … "

"Yeah, what?"

"Listen for the car horn." In the background, Joe heard three quick blasts from a car horn. "You heard?"

"I heard," said Joe.

"You are being closely watched, so if we even see you breathe on one of those cops, I will fuck your girlfriend in the ass and slice her tits off while I'm doing it. Understand?"

Joe could hear Marla crying. He felt like ripping the Russian's eyes out.

"Okay," he said, snapping the phone closed and sliding it into his pocket. Serpe began to ease away from the blue and white.

"Where *you* going?" the uniform asked.

"Cut myself when they cuffed me. I'm going over to the ambulance to get it looked at. Kramer can find me over there."

"Go ahead."

No one bothered Joe until he approached his car. Then the cop who had originally tried to stop him apologized.

"You just shoulda shown me your shield, man. Sorry."

"Forget it. I fucked up," Joe said.

As he drove away, he hoped Donna wasn't injured too badly, and that the Russians didn't have her too. Serpe was pretty sure she'd be safe if she headed to where he thought she might go. He was much less sure about Marla's safety. He knew the Russians had her.

The entrance to the L.I.E. was only a few blocks away and though he kept checking his mirrors, Joe could not tell how he was being followed. He thought about sliding his hand over to the center console, opening his cell phone, dialing 911, and talking loudly enough so the operator would be able to hear him. But even if he had been disposed to gamble away Marla's life, he wouldn't get the opportunity.

Something cold, metallic, inanimate pressed against Serpe's neck. Though he knew instantaneously it was the muzzle of a gun, he could not stop his body from reacting. He lost control of the car, skidding off Hawkins Avenue and into the empty parking lot of Players Auto Body. He had to stand on his brake pedal to avoid smashing into the shop's garage doors.

"Y'all always did drive like shit, Joey," said the voice from the backseat.

Serpe didn't need to see Dixie's brutish face in his rearview mirror to know it was him. Dixie was the only person on the planet who called him Joey. When Joe did look in the mirror, there was Dixie smiling that cruel crooked-tooth smile of his.

"Now get back on Hawkins and onto the L.I.E.," Dixie said, disappearing from the mirror and sitting back directly behind Joe. "You run pretty good for an old fuck. Man, them two cops was huffing and puffing the whole way after y'all. Made it easy for me to cozy on up back here."

Joe didn't say a word, the adrenaline still distorting his senses. He struggled to settle himself and pulled back onto Hawkins. A block later he turned right, then onto the L.I.E. Service Road, then quickly onto the entrance ramp. The second he pulled into the far right lane off the entrance ramp, a large SUV appeared in Serpe's rearview mirror. As it did, Joe's cell buzzed against the plastic of the center console.

"That'll be Pavel," Dixie said. "Go on, pick it up."

"Dixie is keeping you good company, yes?"

"Wonderful."

"You see me in your mirror?" Pavel asked.

"Yeah."

"I'm going to pull around you. I will call you again in one moment."

Joe waited for the SUV to pull around. As the vehicle swung out and moved along side Serpe's rental, Joe wasn't surprised to see it was a black Lincoln Navigator. He was surprised, however, when the big Lincoln did not pull past him. The Navigator's rear passenger window slid down. Joe could see Marla and the knife at her throat. She was covered in blood, her lips puffed, and her eyes swollen shut. A hand held her by the hair and shoved her head and shoulders out of the Lincoln. She screamed, panicked she would be thrown out of the moving car. Then, just as quickly, she was yanked back into the Lincoln and the window rolled up. The Navigator accelerated, falling in line in front of him.

Joe was crazed. They had beaten her, maybe to get her to tell them where Donna was, maybe they just for fun. Serpe tried not to think about what else they might have done to her.

"Don't try anything stupid, Joey. Pavel just likes to have his little bit of fun."

Serpe's cell phone buzzed.

"You fucking touch her again and I'll—"

"Shut your mouth," Pavel said. "That was to remind you to follow instructions. Now hand the cell phone to Dixie and follow closely our vehicle. I wouldn't want to have to filet your girlfriend's cunt and feed it to her."

Joe tossed the phone into the backseat. "He wants to speak to you."

Serpe thought about the Glock under his seat. He'd always been a very good shot. If he could get to it, Dixie was a dead man; one shot, two at most. He figured it would take him four shots minimum to blow out the Navigator's rear tires. At sixty plus miles per hour the thing was sure to roll over. Marla might have a chance. But the Russians were likely to see the muzzle flash when he put a pill into Dixie and were certain to see him stick the gun out his window when he went for their tires. Marla's throat would be slit before he could get a shot off. He did nothing but follow—follow and pray.

"Uh huh," he heard Dixie say before he snapped the phone shut, rolled down his window, and tossed the phone out.

After a few miles in silence, Joe decided if he was going to die, he was going to do it with some answers. Dixie was always a big mouth. For once Joe hoped it would serve some purpose.

"Where we going?" he asked casually enough.

"The Borofskys are building some kinda gym out east someplace," he said, pronouncing Borofsky like BOWrofsky. "That's all I know."

"You killed Cain, didn't you, Dixie?"

"Why don't y'all shut your mouth, Joey, and watch the road?"

"C'mon, Dixie, I'm driving to my own execution here. Who am I gonna tell?"

"Yeah, I guess I did him, though he was alive when I shoved his scrawny ass into the International's tank. I figured it'd be months till anyone even looked in there. I mean, god damn, we ain't used that truck in six months. How was I s'posed ta know the tugboat had a leak and Frank would put you on the International? That was bad luck there.

"I'll tell you one thing, though. Y'all would have been proud of your boy. Little retard put up some fight till I snapped his skinny-assed neck. Pavel taught me how do that, snap folks necks. It's kinda fun, hearin' that snap. Pavel, he was in the Russian Army in one of them special forces type units. I never met no one who likes hurting people as much as Pavel."

"Why'd you do it?"

"We caught him in the yard that night spying on us when we was doing truck transfers. I s'pose y'all figured out that's what this is all about."

"Yeah, I figured it out."

"The tard said he wasn't spying or nothing and that he had just frightened off some guy from spray painting up Frank's trucks, but we didn't believe him. Retards are born liars."

"Fuck!" Joe slammed his palms against the steering wheel. "Now I get it. The Reyes kid was still in the yard when you killed Cain. He was a witness."

"Well yeah, after he saw what we done to the tard, he ran. Stupid little wetback, all he had to do was sit tight until we was done off-loading. We wouldn't a known he was there at all."

"Unlike your buddy Pavel, most people don't get hard-ons when they witness someone being beaten to death. Running probably seemed like a good idea to him at the time."

"We had that fucking spic cornered too, but that boy climbed the fence like a monkey. We looked for him, but once he hit Union Avenue he disappeared in the dark like a cockroach. You know how them people are. Too bad for him he went and dropped the letters from his mama or we never woulda found him. Stupid ass had five hundred bucks in cash folded into them letters. Pavel told me Reyes begged for those letters to be buried with him when he stabbed him. You know what Pavel told the kid?"

"What?"

"Old Pavel told him he used the letters to wipe his ass." Dixie laughed nervously.

The car fell into silence once again. It occurred to Joe that Dixie had no idea he was just as likely to be killed tonight as anyone. He was as much a loose end as Scanlon or the blond prostitute. Then again, clear thinking had never been Dixie's strong suit.

"Y'all know this is Frank's fault, right?" Dixie broke the silence. "If he had just sold Steve the damned business the way Max and Alexi wanted, shoot, none of this would have happened. The tard, Reyes, them whores ... You should have seen Frank's face when he found out I been working for Steve and the Rooskies. He looked hurt like when a girl finds out her man been stepping out on her. But we taught him a lesson good."

"Toussant?"

"The big frog nigger cried like a baby when we had Frank do him," Dixie chuckled. "Yeah, well, y'all kinda helped us with that."

"You followed me and my friend into Brooklyn that night?"

"Didn't have to. Scanlon knew right where y'all was going. Remember, he helped set that thing up. Me and Pavel just waited. Then we followed you to that park and picked the nigger up when you let him go. Stupid nig was happy to see us, got right in the car. Pavel had some fun with him for a few days."

Serpe was confused. "But why fuck with Frank if he'd already sold out a few days before? Not just to punish him?"

"Why the fuck not? You know what it took to get him to finally sell? Steve made him a fair offer. Then they blackmailed his ass and he still wouldn't sell. Stubborn fuck, dug in his heels. You know how Frank is."

"I know," Joe said.

"Yeah well, Frank is a tough guy, but he ain't never dealt with no one like Pavel. They brought Frank to one of the Borofsky's strip clubs after it closed. They sat him in the office. It's got one of them two-way mirrors, so you can see the action on the floor without people being able to see in."

"I was a cop, Dixie. I know all about how they work."

"So this dancer comes on stage and only Pavel is sitting all alone in the audience. He gives her a hundred dollar bill and she blows him. He hands her another bill and a mask and she starts dancing for him, rubbing her pussy up against the pole and all. Only the mask ain't like a Halloween mask or nothing. It's a picture of Frank's wife's face glued on cardboard. When she was done dancing, Pavel handed her another hundred and got up on stage with her. He stood behind her, stuck a blade in her, slit her open from the pussy to her neck. Pavel said he got hard watching her try to stop her guts from falling out. So when she's twitching on the dance floor, Pavel dipped his hand inside her and writes Tina on the two-way mirror in her blood for Frank to see. He told me so much spilled out of her onto the stage that they had to close the club the next day. Frank didn't need no more motivating to sell after that. The Borofskys was going to have Frank killed in prison, but he did them a favor."

Joe was no longer interested in talking. The thought of Marla being in the hands of Dixie's sadistic friend was beginning to get to him. Suddenly, the answers to the questions which had haunted Joe Serpe for weeks no longer seemed very important. Apparently, Dixie, too, was all talked out.

It was a pretty long ride, the silence making it longer. The Lincoln's right turn signal popped on about a quarter mile from exit 68. Joe followed as the lead car made a sweeping right turn back under the L.I.E. onto William Floyd Parkway. As they proceeded north they passed the entrance to Brookhaven National Lab and continued through miles of forest on either side of the dark parkway. There seemed to be more deer crossing signs on the road than automobiles. Joe was pretty unfamiliar with this part of Long Island. They passed by places with quaint names like Whiskey Road. There was nothing quaint about tonight. People were going to die tonight—he and Marla, probably. Dixie for sure. Others too. And the further north they went, the further away from anything familiar to Joe, the less hopeful he felt.

Again, the Navigator's right turn signal popped on. Joe saw signs indicating they were headed toward Wading River, close to where New York State and the local utility had wasted billions of dollars constructing a nuclear power plant that would never produce a single watt of electricity. That's the thing about mistakes, Joe thought, it only takes a few people to make them, but everybody pays. Joe followed for a few more miles and he began to see signs for Calverton National Cemetery. They didn't make it as far as the cemetery, not yet, anyway.

The black SUV turned into an unlit strip mall along route 25A. Its driver didn't park, but dimmed his lights and continued around to the rear of the attached buildings. From what Serpe could see, this was new construction. There were no visible store signs and lines hadn't even been painted on the blacktop. There were at least two other vehicles parked in the back; Steve Scanlon's Chevy Blazer was one of them. Joe killed the ignition and waited. As he did, he noticed a backdoor open and a shaft of light cut a rectangle out of the night. Four men, one shoving Marla ahead of him, walked into building. Joe decided the time was now and attempted to reach under his seat to get at the Glock Healy had gifted him.

"Y'all looking for this?" Dixie asked, waving the Glock up so Serpe could see it in the rearview mirror. "I saw it under the seat when I laid down back here. Good thing too, 'cause I bet you'd have killed me dead by now. Wouldn't have been a fair fight when all I got is this old .38." Dixie pressed the .38 hard against Joe's neck. "Now get the fuck out of the car, Joey."

Serpe had no cards left to play and did as he was told, walking slowly toward the back door.

"Wait a second," Dixie said. "Maybe I can save your behind if y'all was to tell me where that mongoloid bitch got to. Max and Alexi and their daddies want to know that real bad."

"Go fuck yourself! Even if I told you, it wouldn't save your worthless fucking life."

Dixie drove the heel of his free hand into Serpe's left kidney. Joe went down in a heap, coughing, gasping for breath, retching.

"Pavel taught me that," Dixie bragged like a proud student. "Funny, ain't it, the way humans is wired up? Hit a man in his kidneys and it takes his breath away. Makes him sick to his stomach and turns his legs into jelly. Don't make no sense, does it? You'd be pissing blood too, but I don't s'pose y'all have to worry about that. Before we go in I guess I should thank y'all for planting that crack on the nigger. You ever watch someone get killed after smoking rock? What a rush. Now get the fuck up."

Once inside, Joe's last flicker of hope was extinguished. Marla knelt on the floor, hands cuffed behind her. She was between two steroid giants with dull, lifeless eyes and scar-tissue faces. One held a shiny .45 at his side. The other held an MP-5 with a silencer. He cradled the 9mm assault rifle like an experienced wet nurse, with the casual professionalism of a man who understood his job perfectly. Neither of these men nor their weapons particularly frightened Serpe.

The third man, however, the man who stood behind Marla flicking his thumb against the blade of a knife, was cause for concern. He was not nearly the size of the other muscle, but he had bright blue eyes, crazy, hungry eyes. This must be Pavel, Joe thought. Pavel smiled at Serpe, nodding his head to the right. Joe now understood the smile, for a few yards to his left lay sheets of plastic vapor barrier and two chainsaws. You didn't have to have a vivid imagination to figure out how things were going to play out.

Along with the muscle, the full cast of characters seemed to be there: Scanlon, Dixie, of course, Misha Levenshtein, and another gray-haired old-timer Serpe figured was Sergei Borofsky. There were also two well-kept men in their early forties in attendance. These were the sons, Joe guessed. One looked the image of Borofsky. The other was reminiscent of Levenshtein.

"Dixie, bring Mr. Serpe over by the plastic," said the elder Borofsky.

Dixie obeyed, but apparently not fast enough to suit his masters.

"Come on, Dixie. Come on! Listen to my father," Borofsky's son barked, clapping his hands. "Let's go."

Dixie did as ordered, but they were still displeased.

"No," the son said, "step away from him, we don't want his blood on you, Dixie."

"Whatever y'all say, Max."

Joe Serpe had fantasized about the moment of his death many times. Undercover detectives have good reason to think about their own mortality. So do men who transport hazardous materials for a living. How many times during the three years he worked for Frank had he looked at the million gallon storage tanks of gasoline, diesel, kerosene, and oil as he loaded the tugboat, and wondered when a single spark would blow him into orbit?

"Listen," Joe said. "If you're going to kill me, at least—"

"Shhhh!" Sergei Borofsky put his index finger to his lips, his eyes as cold as a shark's. "We're going to kill you, but not yet."

Fffft. Fffft. Fffft. Fffft. Fffft. The MP-5 whispered deadly noth-ings in Dixie's ear.

And the hulking man collapsed back onto the plastic matting, stone dead.

Serpe looked at Steve Scanlon. The retired firefighter's eyes were suddenly very frightened. Joe felt his face crinkle into a smile at Scanlon's realization.

"Pavel, you and Steve do the honors," Max Borofsky ordered in unaccented English.

Scanlon and Pavel stepped forward, slipped on latex gloves and long Tyvek aprons.

"Only one saw," Pavel barked. "You hold him when I tell you."

Meanwhile, Pavel yanked the cord on the chainsaw and it started right up. He revved its motor for effect and to get a feel for its power.

"Hold him by the hair like this." Pavel demonstrated with the flare of a seasoned practitioner.

Steve grabbed Dixie's hair, held the dead man's head up. The saw made quick work of it, tearing through the neck, spitting out shards of flesh and bone as it went. When the blade ripped through the last inch of connective tissue, Scanlon stumbled backwards, Dixie's severed head in his hand. The headless torso thumped down, blood oozing onto the plastic. Marla lurched forward, vomiting her guts up. She had company. Misha Levenshtein lost his last few meals as well.

"You were always soft, Misha," the elder Borofsky scolded. "Always the weak one. Look at our sons. Max and Alexi don't act like women. Always, you wanted the money, but never to do the dirty work. You should have been an accountant, Misha. It was the Jews like you that let the Nazis march them out of Kiev into the forests like sheep to be slaughtered."

"Enough, Uncle Sergei," Alexi Levenshtein spoke up.

"See, your son has balls," Sergei Borofsky shouted over the noise of the chainsaw.

Misha Levenshtein glowered at his partner. "That was always your problem, Sergei, mistaking stupidity for balls," he shouted back. "My son has no balls. He is greedy and foolish, as is Max. What they have they have been fed by spoon, gift-wrapped. They did not work like we worked, build like we built, Sergei. Now, because they want more, more, more and get into bed with pigs and morons, everything we have worked for will come down on our heads."

"Nothing is coming down, my old partner. After tonight … It will be as it was."

Dissecting Dixie took less than ten minutes. When Scanlon and Pavel began to wrap Dixie's remains in black plastic bags, Sergei Borofsky told them to leave it.

"Pavel," he said. "The woman."

Pavel, Dixie's blood still spattered on his face, walked slowly over to Marla. He jerked her up by the neck and pushed her face forward toward the plastic matting. With her hands tied behind her, she stumbled face first onto the concrete floor. She struggled to get up. Pavel helped her, using her hair this time to pull her to her feet. Sergei Borofsky caught the glare in Serpe's eye.

"Gentle, Pavel, gentle. You may move Mr. Serpe to try something unfortunate."

He stood Marla in front of the plastic, but to the right of where the pieces of Dixie lay. Tears streamed down her swollen, freshly bloodied face. She was shaking so that her legs could not support her and she collapsed into a pile of herself.

"Easy way or hard? It's up to you, Serpe," Max said. "You know about the blond whore they found by the airport?"

"Yeah," Joe said.

"Pavel enjoys his work, Mr. Serpe. And he especially likes an audience."

Without needing to be told, Pavel knelt down and, grabbing the handcuffs, bent back Marla's arms so that she shrieked in agony. Then he just as quickly released her.

"Do we understand one another?"

"We do," Joe said.

"Where is the girl from the group home, the retarded one, Donna?"

"First, take Marla away from there. Frightening her like this isn't necessary and it's just pissing me off."

"I could let Pavel test your will severely, so don't take me for an ass. That would be very bad for your girlfriend," Max warned. "But okay, Pavel, bring her back by Yuri and Stan."

Pavel seemed almost disappointed as he walked Marla away from Dixie's butchered carcass. All her strength and will gone, Marla sprawled out on the floor like spilled water.

"Where's the girl, Serpe?" Borofsky asked.

"Kill Scanlon first," was his answer. "Then I'll tell you."

Steve Scanlon! Everyone in the big unfinished gym seemed to have forgotten about him, but even before all heads could turn back his way, Scanlon took the first shot. And it was as if that one shot from Dixie's forgotten .38 was a signal for everything to happen at once.

The muscle with the MP-5 lurched backwards, blood spurting out of his neck to the rhythm of his heart. His finger flexed, the 9mm spraying out deadly puffs of metal as he collapsed on top of Marla. His partner took at least five bullets in a straight line across his abdomen. Both Borofskys were down, the elder leaking blood out of where his right eye used to be. Alexi Levenshtein lay twisted at his father's feet, his right leg tucked under him at an impossible angle. Scanlon's second shot caught Misha Levenshtein flush in the belly, but the old man staggered instead of going down. Then, finally, he dropped to his knees. Another second and the old man's head cracked against the unforgiving floor.

The loud *thwack, thwack, thwack* of descending rotor blades covered the noise of Pavel's 9mm. Scanlon's head seemed to explode, pieces of it flying off in all directions. Joe, still standing, somehow immune, could feel his right leg afire. He looked down at the red puddle forming around his shoes, blood pulsing out of his femoral artery. As his leg buckled, Serpe gazed across the room to Pavel. He smiled back at Joe, tossing his handgun away. A knife appeared in its place, as if by magic. The Russian slit open his left palm and made a show of licking his own blood. He waggled his red tongue at Joe. Pavel strode over to where Serpe lay, bleeding out.

"I hope you like sushi," the Russian said, wiping his bleeding palm across Joe's face.

Then he raced toward where Marla struggled to free herself from beneath the corpse.

The backdoor blew off it's hinges and helmeted men in full body armor poured in like the sea. There was a riot of noise, a chorus of guns firing at once, empty shells pinging off concrete. Joe Serpe heard only the angels singing, some of them spinning in the air above him. He looked for Vinny amongst them, but his brother was not there. Then he heard a voice calling to him as if from at the end of a long tunnel.

"Joe! Joe!"

"Vinny?" he said.

"It's me Joe, Bob Healy."

There was another voice. "He's lost a lot of blood."

Then there seemed to be a million voices. Joe could hardly hear himself think.

"Marla?" Joe asked.

"She's alive."

"Donna's in the yard," Joe said.

"What?"

"Donna's in the yard, in Cain's secret hiding spot. She's in the oil yard."

"It's okay, Joe. They'll find her. Take it easy."

Serpe felt Bob Healy take his hand. No, he was slipping something into his hand.

"What's this?" Joe asked, raising his closed fist.

"Something that never should have been taken away from you in the first place."

Serpe looked back up at the ceiling, but the dance floor was empty. The band was on break. It seemed as good a time as any to sleep.

Epilogue

FLIP A COIN

They found Donna in Cain's secret place between the cyclone fence, which mistakenly marked the rear limit of the oil yard three feet short of the actual property line, and the brick wall beyond, overgrown with ivy and the skeletons of other dead vines. Even if Frank hadn't parked the 81 Mack he used for spare parts up against the fence in the rear corner, Cain's spot would have been safe from detection. If to the rest of the world it was an insignificant, forgotten patch of dirt, to Cain it had been as important as his hose monkey shirt or the feel of Donna's hand in his. Cain had had the need as much as any man to carve out a corner of the world, put a flag in it, and proclaim it his own. This three by ten piece of dirt, rusted fence, brick, and weeds was his.

Near frozen and half-dead with a gash in her shoulder from where the bullet ripped into her, Donna remained absolutely silent until she heard Marla's voice. The cops and EMTs had tried to stop the psychologist from going with Healy back to the yard to find the Down's girl, but Marla wouldn't hear of it. She would have the rest of her life to suffer through the trauma of reliving this night. Maybe she would get over it, maybe not. She knew, however, that she would never heal if she simply abandoned Donna.

The two woman embraced when Donna crawled out through the hole Cain had cut in the fence and out from beneath the undercarriage of the 81 Mack. They rocked there together, on the soot black, packed down snow that had never fully melted away since the night of Cain's murder. Nothing remained of the makeshift memorial the people from the group home had constructed. That Cain's patch of the world had provided Donna with a safe place to hide was memorial enough.

"You look bad and your breath smells," Donna said.

Marla broke down, finally.

* * *

On the following Monday, Ken Bergman was given a traditional Jewish burial. In spite of their shock and grief, his parents could not help but wonder who the four strange men were who stepped forward and offered their respect to the dead man by each throwing a shovelful of earth on their son's coffin.

Bob and George Healy, Skip Rodriguez and Detective Schwartz never identified themselves. They all knew, of course, that Ken Bergman had been a hero. Not in some amorphous way, but in the most meaningful way possible. He had literally sacrificed himself so that others could live. Marla had described Bergman's actions to Healy as they drove to the oil yard the night of the massacre in the unfinished gym, but she pleaded with Bob to keep it quiet until after the funeral.

"Let his family have their grief, please."

On the Tuesday morning following the burial, all three New York tabloids featured headlines concerning Ken Bergman's heroics. Even the sacred *New York Times* carried the story. But with men and women being blown apart by roadside bombs in places like Najaf and Tikrit, they didn't feel one man's sacrifice for unrequited love was worth the front page.

* * *

For weeks the papers featured stories about that bloody Saturday night and the fallout from the investigations that followed. As Joe Serpe had anticipated, Black Sea Energy was the silent partner in at least two dozen small and medium-sized C.O.D. heating oil companies in New York City, Nassau and Suffolk Counties, Northern New Jersey and Connecticut. The federal investigation involved several government agencies and stretched all the way from Brighton Beach Avenue to the oil fields of Bakku. There was enough corruption and enough bad guys left alive even after that bloody night to make the feds and the local cops happy. None would remember the two ex-cops, old enemies who had come together to find justice in a world without any. Nor would they recall that it all began with a can of spray paint and a loyal retarded man who had wanted to do only the right things.

* * *

When Joe Serpe woke up, it was Healy's puss staring down at him, not Marla's.

"How long … " He tried to speak, but his throat was so dry it burned. It wasn't the only part of him that hurt. His left leg was a menu of pain. He grabbed it, panicked that it might be gone.

"Take it easy, Joe," Healy said, pushing him gently back down by the shoulder. "Let me get the nurse for you."

"Donna?" he rasped.

"They found her right where you said she would be. She was hit by a bullet, but she's okay."

"Marla?"

"She had it pretty rough, but she's been here every day. That woman's tougher than me and you put together. Even though you almost got her killed, she still loves you. I guess there's no accounting for taste."

"Guess not." He held his hand out to Healy.

"You did good, Joe," he said to Serpe, squeezing his hand. "You made it right."

After the nurse and doctors left, Healy watched Serpe sleep for a little while, then got some coffee and dinner before coming back to the hospital.

"Christ, you again!" Serpe said, still a bit groggy from the pain killers. "The bullets shattered my femur and cut my artery. They say I'm probably gonna have a limp."

"A limp's like gray hair for a man, it adds character."

"Fuck you, Healy. Get me a baseball bat and I'll give you some character."

They both had a laugh at that. Then they just sat there together in comfortable silence for about a half-hour.

"Joe, I've been meaning to tell you something for a very long time. That's why I came to the kid's funeral that day. I've been trying to tell you ever since, but the time never seemed right."

"Go ahead and say it, Healy. I pretty much owe you my life and Marla's."

"Remember what I said about your old partner Ralphy giving up two C.I.s and a cop?"

"Yeah, what about it?"

"They weren't the only ones he gave up," Healy said. "He gave you up, too."

"What do you mean he gave me up?" Serpe was agitated. "He had nothing on me to give me up for."

"Ralphy was crossing the line a long time before you ever knew, Joe. I.A.B. snagged him for doing small favors for some mob douche bag he grew up with. It was pretty harmless shit, but he could have lost his shield and his pension. I caught the case. When I asked Ralphy if he had anything to give me to save his ass, he offered you up. When my boss heard your name mentioned, he got a hard on. He wanted your legendary ass on his trophy wall."

"But I was as clean as a guy in my spot could be."

"I know that. I suppose I knew it then, but I kept pressuring Ralphy to come up with something on you or he was going down. You know all those times he asked you if you wanted to sandbag some of the blow or money before backup got there?"

"I remember."

"It was all on tape, Joe. Some of those busts were I.A.B. setups."

"But I never—"

"I know. If I had any real balls, I would have told my boss to shove the investigation up his ass. But then when Ralphy started using heavily and skimming, we had you," Healy admitted, unable to look Joe Serpe in the eye. "When you didn't report him … My boss had his trophy. I got the bump to detective first and your career was ruined."

Joe didn't say anything immediately. It took him a few minutes to digest Healy's confession. How could Ralphy, his best friend and partner, godfather to his son, have so readily thrown him to the wolves? How could Healy have continued to pursue him in spite of all the evidence that he was clean? Healy waited, but when Serpe didn't respond, he got up to leave.

"Well, Joe, I said it. I'm sorry for my part in it. Like I told you the night you were shot, nobody had the right to take your shield away and if I could undo it …

"Where you going?" Serpe said. "Sit your ass down."

Healy did, breathing a huge sigh of relief.

"I spent the last four years looking back and I'm bone tired of it. You can't undo what you did and there's only one man ever walked the earth that could raise the dead. We're stuck where we are, you and me, and I'm not going to shrink my life back down to nothing by losing anymore friends I make along the way. So consider yourself forgiven, okay?"

"Whatever you say."

"All right, now go home and get some sleep. Tomorrow, I need you in here early so we can talk business instead of bullshit."

"Business?" Healy furrowed his brow.

"Were you enjoying your retirement?"

"Christ, I hated every minute of it until three weeks ago."

"Yeah, well, with this leg, it don't look like I'll be driving an oil truck any time soon."

"There's only two things ex-cops go into with any chance of success—bars and security."

"Go home, Bob. In the morning we'll flip a coin."

★ ★ ★

Marla, her face still slightly puffy and bruised, sat in the darkest corner of the bar, nursing a light beer. In some bizarre way, she almost dreaded the doctors clearing Joe. Then she would have no more excuse to hold on just one more day. Dentists get cavities and doctors get cancer. Marla knew a Ph.D. in Clinical and School Psychology was no defense against Post Traumatic Stress. Already, her guilt over Kenny's death had prevented her from paying a *shiva* call and the nightmares had started. Even now in a near empty bar, she felt as if all her nerves were firing at once, but this was an appointment she needed to keep.

"Doc? Doc is that you?" the woman asked, hesitating before taking a seat.

"Corral." Marla brightened, leaning over and kissing her dark brown cheek.

"Hell, what happened to you, honey?"

"The night Kenny … "

"Yeah, I'm so sorry. How stupid a me. I read all 'bout that. You okay?"

"I will be."

"So what you call me for, Doc, not that I ain't glad to see you or nothin'?"

Marla slid the VHS tape across the bar. "That's yours to do with whatever you want."

Corral stared at the tape, not wanting to touch it for fear of reliving the horror Toussant had inflicted on her all over again.

"He's dead, Corral. He can't hurt you anymore. You can have a small part of your life back. It's over."

Corral began sobbing quietly. "I know you meant well, Doc. He may be dead and all, but it ain't never gonna be over for me. Some shit people take from you, there ain't no gettin' back. You take that tape and you burn it."

The group home driver stood up and ran out of the dark bar.

"What got into her?" the barman asked.

"My wishful thinking."

She tossed a five on the bar, put the tape back in her bag, and left. Outside in the parking lot, Marla sat in her locked car and wept for what felt like hours.

* * *

In early July, Marla and Joe made their way through the beautifully trimmed hedges and fresh cut grass. Joe's limp was better and he had finally switched from crutches to a cane. The sun was bright but not blinding, warm on their faces but not burning. On days like this it was easier for Marla to believe things really could be all right. Her body had healed months ago, but she had come to understand Corral's reaction that night in the bar. There are parts of your life once taken, that can never be taken back.

Cemeteries are supposed to be peaceful places, but in New York they always seem to be beneath the glide paths to airports. That was okay with Joe. Vinny had always been fascinated by planes. Now, after all these years, with Marla at his side, Joe Serpe was grateful there had been a body to bury. It was the first time he'd been to the grave since the day of the funeral. He crossed himself, uttering a prayer he thought he had long ago forgotten.

"Vinny, I'd like you to meet Marla. You'd really like her."

Marla placed flowers on the grave and gave Joe some time to be alone with his brother.

About ten minutes later, she interrupted their reunion.

"Come on, Joe, we don't want to miss your flight."

In the car, he turned to her. "What do I say to him?"

"He's your son, Joe. You'll figure it out."